He was losing it...

Each night he'd felt the tidal pull of the coast and the woman. He'd known he could unlock the sexual energy that pulsed around her. They'd been magic together. He'd had great sex before, but it had never consumed him like this. He needed to see her, to fill his head with her fragrance, to drown in her tropical gaze, to hear her sigh out his name.

He wanted to sit in her cozy kitchen again. To have her take care of him, to eat the food she'd prepared for him. He loved that blue kitchen. He shook his head sadly.

"I'm losing it, bud," he said to Mac.

Mac thumped his tail energetically.

It probably wasn't any news to his dog that Sloan was losing it. Mac knew everything. Mac had run right into Roxie's arms the first time he'd seen her. Mac didn't have any embarrassing family history to overcome. Mac had taken one look at the woman and decided that he wanted her.

A man could learn a lot from his dog.

D1525090

Praise for Maggie Toussaint

HOUSE OF LIES
National Readers' Choice Award
Best Romantic Suspense 2006

"I recommend this book to readers who love a novel that pulls at the heart strings with a side order of suspenseful action."

~Abi, The Romance Studio

"An exciting romantic suspense. Poignantly written, it touches on the emotional aspects of parental abandonment and the courage necessary to face the truth."

~Linda, myshelf.com

"The perfect blend of heart-warming romance and suspense. *HOUSE OF LIES* is a book you'll definitely want to curl up with."

~Gail Barrett, award-winning author

NO SECOND CHANCE

"*NO SECOND CHANCE* sparkles and sizzles from the boardroom to the bedroom to the barn."

~Liana Laverentz, award-winning author of THIN ICE and JAKE'S RETURN

"A fabulous contemporary romance with an intriguing social issue involving the rescue of horses."

~Harriet Klausner

"I read the whole book in one sitting. If you have a quiet evening to curl up with a good book and you enjoy suspense, horses, Cinderella stories, or all three—this book will satisfy."

~Long and Short Reviews

"A recommended read. It's been a long time since I've read a book totally in one sitting, but I just couldn't put this one down. What a totally fabulous read this was!"

~Crystal, e-Harlequin.com/review

Muddy Waters

by

Maggie Toussaint

Muddy Waters

Cover Art by *Kim Mendoza*

The Wild Rose Press
PO Box 706
Adams Basin, NY 14410-0706
Visit us at www.thewildrosepress.com

Publishing History
First Crimson Rose Edition, 2010
Print ISBN 1-60154-827-3

Published in the United States of America

Dedication

Muddy Waters is dedicated to all those
who've helped me through the muddy waters of life,
especially my husband, my family,
and my two best mud-stomping buds,
Marianna Hagan and Suzanne Forsyth.

Acknowledgements

This book would not have been possible without the vision of Laura Kelly, my editor.

Thanks also to Danny Grissette of Altamaha Outfitters for showing me the rice canals in coastal Georgia.

Realtors Vivian O'Kelley and Suzanne Forsyth were kind enough to share their real estate knowledge with me.

Writers Marilyn Trent, Keely Thrall, Diana Cosby, Polly Iyer, and Melody Scott helped with their insight and friendship.

Thanks also to my newspaper editor, Kathleen Russell, for encouraging my dual career.

Chapter 1

"How's my favorite southern realtor?"

Roxie Whitaker frowned at the slight. She wasn't just a realtor, she was a broker.

A glance at the text window of the phone yielded "Restricted" as the caller's identity. No help there. She had to wing it. "A good Tuesday morning to you as well. How may I help you today, sir?"

At his smug chuckle, her back teeth ground together. Whoever this was, he enjoyed teasing her. It wasn't any of her friends here in Mossy Bog. There was something familiar about the voice though, some element of cultured refinement that came through loud and clear.

"Rox, Rox, Rox, I hated those property prospectives you sent me. I want the place on Main Street."

Sonny Gifford. Her South Carolina customer. "I'm sorry 605 Main Street is not for sale, but I'm certain Marshview Realty can meet your property needs. Will you be down tomorrow or Thursday?"

"Can't make it, chickie. Too busy, but I'm heading your way next week."

"Great. Call me when you lock in the date."

"The way I see it," Sonny drawled into the phone. "The owner of the Main Street property should jump at my offer. I'll pay top dollar for the place, say a hundred grand?"

Sometimes people assumed that due to her relative youth, she didn't have a lick of sense. Sonny Gifford radiated that vibe. The hairs on the back of her neck ruffled. "That property isn't for sale, Mr.

Gifford, but I'll relay your interest. If the owner wants to sell, we'll move forward with a reasonable offer."

Sonny huffed a few breaths into the phone. Would he hang up on her? Tell her he was taking his business elsewhere? Roxie hovered in a breathless void of uncertainty.

"What about personal handling?" Sonny's voice roughened. "Couldn't you be extra nice to him to soften him up? Bat those pretty eyes at him and jam a contract under his nose at the same time. Old guys love private, personal attention."

Her jaw dropped. She tried to speak and no sound came out. Finally a squeak emerged. "Mr. Gifford. I'm appalled by your suggestion."

"No need to get huffy. It wasn't like I asked you to sleep with the guy to seal the deal."

"Mister. Gifford."

"It's Sonny, and I'm kidding. We wouldn't want to cross any lines here, now would we?"

"No. We would not."

Silence filled the line. She still wanted to sell a property to Sonny, but she didn't want to talk with him, think about him, or see him ever again.

"Perhaps I should speak with him," Sonny said.

"You're certainly welcome to explore that avenue."

"From the tone of your voice, you don't approve?"

A muscle twitched in her cheek. "Call me if you decide you want professional real estate assistance in Mossy Bog."

She ended the call and glanced over at her associate, Megan Fowler. "That was weird. A buyer more or less suggested I sleep with a seller to get a listing he wants."

Alarm flared in Megan's eyes. She reached for the phone. "We should report him."

"I know. But then he said he was kidding. Why

would he even joke about such a thing?"

"Your client is an idiot. I'm calling the cops."

Roxie couldn't afford to throw away a single customer. "No need. He isn't local. It's the jerk from South Carolina. If he comes here again, I'll make sure I meet with him in a public place. It isn't like he propositioned me."

"He wanted to pimp you out, which is far worse in my opinion."

****

Wednesday's Open House on Walnut Street netted a few curious neighbors but not one nibble on Naomi Thompson's adorable cottage. Roxie hoped for more success when she repeated the Open House in two weeks.

Her shoulders sagged, and her fingers tightened on Miss Daisy's steering wheel as she turned off Prospect onto her driveway that evening. A snail chewing his way through the marsh would have made more headway than she had this week.

Dusk had settled, lengthening the shadows in her yard. Once she stepped inside her house, there was dinner to fix, pies to bake for the animal rescue group, and then a quiet evening with the latest Alyssa Day book. The Atlantis theme of Day's work drew her in hook, line, and sinker.

She shouldered her purse and locked her vintage caddy. A single woman living alone couldn't be too careful, even here in friendly Mossy Bog. She took a misstep over the hose she'd forgotten to put away last night. Righting herself, she noted it was too dark back here.

Her back porch light was off.

A smidge of unease rumbled through her. Roxie peered into the deep shadows of her yard. Was there trouble afoot? The urge to run back to the safety of Miss Daisy grew from a faint whisper to a steady thrumming in her ears.

What was she doing? The crime rate in Mossy Bog was practically nonexistent. With that reassurance, her nerves steadied and logic returned.

Lights burned out all the time. She'd get a new bulb from the pantry and have it fixed in two shakes. Fortunately, she knew the traffic pattern of her ground-level porch by heart. In seconds she stood at her back door, feeling her way through her key set, searching for the key with a pointed head. Got it.

She fumbled for the knob, and the door swung open.

Fear bolted through her. No light. An open door. In one heartbeat she went from confident, assertive woman to scared out of her mind. Instinctively, she raced for the safety of her car. Locked Miss Daisy's doors. Floored the vintage Cadillac out of the driveway. Only when she reached the lighted convenience store five blocks away did she reach for the phone.

Laurie Ann Dinterman, city police officer, met her in the parking lot a few moments later. Laurie Ann pulled up next to Miss Daisy, lowered her car window. Serious brown eyes peered from beneath the rim of her police hat. "What's up?"

Roxie found it hard to steady her breathing. The lights seemed too bright. The ordinary noises of town were too loud. "Someone was in my house. They may still be in my house. I don't know. I just had to get out of there."

Laurie Ann frowned. "You all right? Did you see anyone?"

"I'm fine. Scared, but fine."

"Did you see anyone?" Laurie Ann repeated.

"No. But I didn't look either. I was so freaked out. I ran. I'm sorry I didn't pay closer attention."

"Was anything stolen?"

"I don't know. I didn't go inside. Just got out of

there and called y'all." Sirens wailed in the distance.

Laurie Ann nodded in the direction of the noise. "That's my backup from the Sheriff's department. You did the right thing to get out of there. We'll check it out for you."

Shivering, Roxie followed the police cruiser back to her place. She waited in Miss Daisy while the officers entered her house with guns drawn. Her beautiful cottage glowed in an unearthly blue wash of emergency lights. Seconds of her life ticked by, an eternity of staring at her house, her home, which had been invaded by strangers.

The world spun off center, and a heavy weight pressed on her chest. She gasped for air, realized she'd been holding her breath, and focused her thoughts on breathing.

Three cops emerged from her house. Robbie Ballard and Jink Smith waved as they hopped into their cruisers and left. Laurie Ann approached Miss Daisy.

"All clear." Laurie Ann holstered her weapon. "No one's inside your house now. You sure you locked the door this morning?"

Roxie nodded too fast. Her pulse raced in her ears. "I always lock it."

The cop took a long breath. "The kitchen was ransacked. Other than that, it may be the tidiest house I've ever been in. Come inside and tell me if anything is missing."

Heart pounding, Roxie eased inside the porch and kitchen. Laurie Ann was right. Her cookbooks had been thrown on the floor. Every drawer had been emptied, pots and pans pulled out of cabinets. She picked up her precious cookbooks and skimmed through the titles. She scanned the rest of the rubble. Nothing seemed to be missing. What was going on?

Dazed, Roxie slumped into a kitchen chair. "I

don't understand. Why did someone break in if they didn't take anything?"

Laurie Ann started to say something, stopped, then spoke. "That's why I asked if you'd locked up this morning. It could have been something simple like that. Just didn't pull the door all the way shut as you hurried off to work and a kid got in here."

"No way. Gran taught me to double check each time I lock a door. This place was locked up tight. I guarantee it. Someone must have broken in."

"The thing is—" Laurie Ann leaned forward in her chair, interlacing her fingers on the table. "There are no signs of forced entry. If you didn't leave the door unlocked, this intruder is very very good. To be honest, we've never had such a high caliber housebreaker here in Mossy Bog. There's usually a broken window or something pried open. Crime always leaves a mark. And stuff would be missing— electronics, jewelry, art, fancy clothing, collectibles, guns, liquor."

"I don't own a gun, and there's no hard liquor in this house. I don't have any of that fancy other stuff either. I don't understand."

"Someone was looking for something. But we don't know what it is. Worse, we have no evidence."

"What about fingerprints?"

"Did you touch the doorknob?"

"Yes."

Laurie Ann appeared to give the idea some thought. "Nah...seems to me this kind of housebreaker would be smarter than your average bear. We'd need to call the state boys in to process the scene." She looked at Roxie, still frowning. "If you really want us to, we can dust for prints but it's messy and my gut feeling is it won't give us anything new."

"I didn't make this up."

"No one thinks you did. We don't know what

happened. But you need to be safe and think safe. You want me to call Megan to come over and stay with you?"

Roxie rose with Laurie Ann. "No need. I'll be fine. I'm used to being by myself."

"I'll patrol extra on your street tonight and leave word with the police chief for the other shifts to do the same. You have any other trouble, you call me, okay?"

Roxie locked up after the cop left. Walking through the house, she flipped on one light after the other. She hated the thought that someone had been in here, that someone had snooped through her things. Back in the kitchen she cleaned up the floor, stuck all the dishes and flatware in the dishwasher. She tried the porch light. It came right on.

Waves of fear lapped in her head. A nameless, faceless person had pawed through her things. A ghost of a person. Heart pounding in her throat, she shrank away from the window and called her best friend. "Can you and Dave come over?"

"We'll be right there," Megan said.

Roxie's hand shook as she ended the call. Grabbing the butcher knife, she huddled on the floor to wait for her friends. Thoughts whizzed through her head like sheet lightning over the marsh.

Someone had been in her home.

Someone had opened locked doors without leaving a mark.

Someone wanted to scare her.

Someone had accomplished their goal.

****

By Friday, Roxie had her nerves under control. The break-in lingered in the back of her mind, but she wouldn't let fear dictate how she lived her life. Today she could handle the ringing of a phone or a clump of Spanish moss swaying in the breeze.

With that mindset, she initiated an online

property search. Too tacky. Too scuzzy. Too far out of town. Only one house in town was the same vintage her customer wanted, her own home on Prospect, and it wasn't for sale either.

Roxie paged resolutely through the listings. Sonny Gifford wanted an older home, but it had to be on a main road. Location, location, location. How many times had Gran drilled those words into her as she'd learned the trade?

The office phone shrilled, and fear darted into her bloodstream. With a hand to her thumping heart, she answered the call. "Marshview Realty. This is—"

Megan's anguished sob warbled through the line. "I can't do this."

Roxie leaned forward and gripped the phone tightly. The terror of Wednesday night hovered in her mind. "What's wrong?"

"There's too much to do. I can't possibly pull this off by this evening."

Wedding jitters. Nothing life threatening. "Everything was fine two hours ago. What happened?"

"These stupid tablecloths. That's what happened. These wrinkles came over on the Mayflower. The more I iron, the worse they look. I'm all hot and sweaty from ironing. Why did I let you talk me into staging my own wedding?"

"Hold up. I didn't talk you into anything. You wanted—"

"I know. I know. I made the decision to do all this." Megan sighed. "But I've got a lot of whine left. Right this minute, I'd rather be drowning in debt than working my fingers to the bone six hours before my wedding. People will be here soon, and I'll look like something the tide washed ashore."

"You're there alone? Where are your sisters? Where's your mother? They're supposed to be helping you while I man the shop."

"It's been a circus all morning. My cat stowed away in the trunk, got carsick, threw up on Mother's dress. Felicity took the cat to the vet, and Courtney is with Mother." Megan hitched in a breath. "My flowers aren't here either. Where's your brother?"

"Timmy's not there?"

"No." Muffled sobs filled her ear. "How can I get married without flowers? Brides are supposed to carry bouquets. All I've got is this iron. I'll probably kill a bridesmaid or two when I chuck this sucker over my shoulder."

"Take a deep breath. We can fix this. I'll close the office early and pick up your flowers. Keep decorating the parish hall. I'll be there as soon as I can."

"Why didn't I elope?" Her friend sniffed loudly. "People who elope don't have these issues. I've already drained three bottles of water. I'm going to swell up like a blimp, my gown won't fit, and Dave will run screaming from the church."

Roxie snorted with laughter. If Megan could crack jokes, things weren't quite at the brink of doom. But where was Timmy? Had he overslept? She hung up with Megan and dialed her brother's cell phone. It rang and rang until a recorded message announced his voice mail box was full. Had something happened to him?

Of course not. This wasn't related to her intruder. This was just par for the course. She needed Timmy and he wasn't available. How many times had this story played out in the last five years?

She'd catch up with Timmy later. Right now, she had a friend to rescue. She shut down her computer and grabbed her purse. She had keys in hand when a black SUV turned into her parking lot amid a swirl of autumn leaves. The tinted windows made it hard for her to see inside.

Through her glass storefront window, she watched as the vehicle halted under a moss-draped oak tree at the far edge of the parking lot. The driver appeared to be male, with a cell phone glued to his ear. Chances were it wasn't one of their rental clients or homebuyers. They would have pulled up to the front door and parked next to Miss Daisy, her vintage Cadillac.

Could it be a new client? A real, live client?

Quickly, she dialed the Muddy Rose. "Jeanie, I need a favor, and I have to talk fast because a potential client just pulled into my lot. Can you deliver Megan's flowers to the church?"

"I thought Timmy was on tap for that."

"He's not available. I was on my way when this car turned in. Can you manage?"

"It'll cost you."

"Name it."

"I want one of your pumpkin pies, a loaf of your raisin bread, and you have to chair the vendor committee for the spring festival. Our first meeting is coming up soon."

"Man. You're a regular barracuda today."

"One more thing."

"More?" Roxie kept one eye on the vehicle in her parking lot.

"Show the buyer my cousin Brent's house. He's got a new baby on the way."

"I'll do my best. Let's hope this buyer brought his checkbook. And, Jeanie?"

"Yeah?"

"I'm alone. If I don't call back in ten minutes on your cell, call the cops." She hadn't felt completely safe since Wednesday's break-in.

"Don't worry, I'll drive by there on my way to the church."

Roxie ended the call, popped a breath mint, and stashed her purse in a desk drawer. Glancing down, she made sure there weren't any cracker crumbs on her white blouse or khaki slacks.

The vehicle's door opened, and a large black and tan dog charged out, circled the perimeter of the sunny lot and found a tree to bless. A whistle shrilled, and the German shepherd vaulted back in the Jeep Grand Cherokee.

Her heart softened.

She'd always wanted a dog.

A dark-haired stranger in snug jeans and a muscle-hugging black polo climbed down out of the SUV. A shadow of beard lent him a dangerous air that shot her pulse through with something besides fear.

Married, no doubt.

They always were.

Think positive. He might buy waterfront acreage. The commission from a sale like that would keep her afloat for another year. She prayed with all her might that Marshview Realty was the solution to his problem.

Warm Indian summer sunshine wafted in through the front door with him, along with a fresh woodsy scent. Nice, Roxie thought. Very nice indeed.

She glanced up at him, appreciating his height. At five-seven, few men in town were taller than she was. He looked six-two, easy. His angular face wasn't handsome in the classical sense, but she found all those lines and angles interesting.

His dark brown eyes locked on her as he crossed the carpet. His sure stride made her wonder if he already had a property in mind. She loved customers who had done their real estate homework.

She beamed a welcoming smile. "Welcome to Marshview Realty. How may I help you?"

"I'm looking for Ms. Roxie Whitaker."

His voice rumbled through her in a pleasing way. He knew her name? "That's me. What can I do for you?"

He handed her a business card. Bold red letters proclaimed Team Six Security. Near her thumb was a simplistic outline of a house.

"I'm Sloan Harding. You wrote me about a property I own."

Realization dawned. Not a client. A neighbor, of sorts. She drew in a shallow breath of appraisal. And what a neighbor. Too bad he lived in Atlanta.

"Thank you for coming, Mr. Harding," she said, hiding her disappointment. "That water oak branch did serious damage to your roof. I'm so relieved you're here. Have you been by the house?"

He nodded tersely. "The yard is very well maintained."

"Oh." Roxie chewed her lip, wondering how much to tell him.

"I wasn't aware of an arrangement to care for the property," he said. "I pay the taxes, nothing more."

"Gran mowed your yard and weeded the beds," she explained. "When I inherited her house and business, I, um, took on that responsibility as well."

"Gran?"

"My grandmother, Lavinia Bolen."

"Lavinia's dead?"

Tears brimmed in her eyes. She blinked them away. "She passed away last year."

He tucked his fingers in the back pockets of his jeans and seemed to be grappling with the news. Had he been close to Gran? Gran had barely mentioned Sloan Harding to her in the ten years she'd lived in Mossy Bog.

"How much do I owe you for mowing the lawn?" he asked.

Heat flamed her cheeks. She hadn't done it for the money, but because it was the right thing to do. "You don't owe me anything." Coolly, she opened her desk drawer and extracted a page from his file. "Here's a list of local contractors you can call for estimates."

He took it and scanned the page. "Why are there plumbers and electricians on this list?"

"There may be other repairs needed. Your house has been vacant for thirteen years."

"Thank you." He frowned. "Are you always so helpful, Ms. Whitaker?"

"Call me Roxie, and I enjoy helping people."

Her phone rang.

"Excuse me." Please don't let it be another wedding emergency, she prayed as she picked up the line. Instead her brother's flat voice sounded in her ears. His problem hit her like a steamroller. She jotted down the information in a daze, then hung up the phone and sank into her chair.

"Is something wrong?"

"My brother. Timmy's in jail."

"What's the charge?"

"Drunk and disorderly conduct." Tears of frustration welled in her eyes. "Timmy and his college buddies were picked up early this morning."

Her new neighbor handed her a tissue. "I wouldn't worry. A night in jail builds character."

She stared at him, stung by his judgmental tone. "Timmy could have been hurt, or worse, he could've hurt someone. He's only nineteen years old. Where did he get the booze?"

"Really. I wouldn't sweat it if I were you." Her absentee neighbor edged toward the door. "I'm sure your brother will grow up to be a fine upstanding citizen. He's got you."

In agitation, Roxie dabbed at her tears. He was right. But she couldn't very well dance at Megan's wedding while Timmy was locked up in an Atlanta jail.

Wait a minute. Sloan Harding was from

Atlanta. "Do you know anything about the jail Timmy is in? Are the cops well-trained?"

Harding's lips quirked, and Roxie bristled. Did he think her questions were funny?

"No one has escaped from an Atlanta jail recently, if that's what you mean," he said. "You planning to bake him a cake with a file in it?"

"Of course not. Will they lock him up with hardened criminals?"

"He'll survive."

Timmy had sounded so defeated on the phone. "He told me not to come, but I should go anyway."

"You going to yell at him about drinking?"

"Definitely. I can't believe he was so stupid."

"Then don't go. Your brother knows what he's done."

If Timmy knew better, why did he keep making stupid mistakes? "He's messed up before, but he's never been in jail." She waved the man's business card at him. "Will you help me check on him? Maybe you have some connections? Someone who could give us inside information?"

For a long moment, she thought he would refuse. Then he unclipped his phone. "Where is he?"

She handed him the number she'd jotted down. Why couldn't Timmy follow the rules like everyone else? Sometimes it was hard to believe they had the same DNA. The more responsibility she took on, the more Timmy shirked.

Her unexpected visitor finished his call and turned to face her. "They'll hold your brother a few more hours, then he'll be released. I imagine he'll go home and sleep it off. You can fuss at him tomorrow."

"He's in good hands?"

"He's fine."

Relief made her lightheaded. Timmy wouldn't be in jail much longer. That was good. He'd go back to his apartment and crash. Her free-spirited brother would survive.

But he wouldn't be in Mossy Bog tonight. Which left her without an escort this evening.

Truthfully, going with Timmy wasn't much better than going stag. Everyone in town knew how many dates she'd had in the last year.

She glanced at Sloan Harding. He wasn't wearing a wedding ring. Unless she'd gotten her wires crossed, he'd been looking at her with interest, at least until Timmy had called.

She blurted the question before she talked herself out of it. "You doing anything for dinner tonight?"

"Dinner?" he asked, clearly startled.

A trickle of perspiration dampened her spine. His grimace kicked her in the gut. What had she done? Asking a perfect stranger to dinner was forward by anyone's standards.

She swallowed hard, wishing he'd turn her down and leave. It was bad enough she'd pressured him to check on her jailbird brother. The silence stretched out like a sea of ocean waves between them.

"I'm sorry. I shouldn't have put you on the spot like that. I apologize."

He narrowed his gaze. "What's going on?"

"Never mind." Her stomach clenched. She dug her keys out of her purse. Time to get going. Time to put Sloan Harding in her rearview mirror. "I shouldn't have mentioned it."

He stepped between her and the door. "I'm available for dinner tonight."

She shook her head. "I apologize. I don't know what came over me. I'm not in the habit of inviting strangers to dinner. It's just...I'm just...well, the truth is, Timmy was supposed to be my date for a wedding."

His brow furrowed. "You need me to stand in for

15

your brother?"

"You don't even know Megan or Dave. I shouldn't have said anything."

"Please, explain."

Roxie gripped her keys in both hands. "Really. It's no big deal. I feel awful for mentioning it."

"No problem. Tell me where we're going for dinner."

She gnawed on her bottom lip. "Are you sure?"

"Yes, but I don't like to go into any situation blind. What did I agree to?"

She squeezed her eyes shut, digging deep for courage. She drew in a deep breath for good measure. "My best friend, Megan Fowler, is getting married tonight. You're welcome to attend the ceremony, but coming to the dinner afterwards will be enough."

"Fine. I'll pick you up. Where are we going?"

"St. John's Episcopal Church, on Main Street. It's half a mile south of your house. The wedding is at six, and the dinner buffet is at seven-thirty. No need to pick me up because I have to be there at five. Could you meet me in the parish hall between seven and seven-thirty?"

"I'll be there."

"Thanks. I owe you big time for this."

"I owed you for the yard work anyway. Let's call it even."

Roxie's gratitude fizzled. One dinner date versus thirteen years of yard work? No way was that even.

Surprising her, he shot her a "gotcha" look, then chuckled in a way that ruffled what was left of her composure. "Don't worry. I promise to be a full-service date."

Chapter 2

Sloan drove though a tunnel of thick oaks dripping with Spanish moss. The shade they provided was nice, but the shadows soured his good mood. Worse, as he traveled the patched streets, an enormous weight bore down on his chest once again. Mossy Bog, or Muddy Bug, as he called the hellhole he'd grown up in, held no appeal for him. His late father had made sure of that.

He hadn't come back for sentimental reasons. He'd come to see Lavinia.

He could have called. Or written. But he'd let it go. Because he wanted to be somebody when he returned. Now he'd waited too late to visit Lavinia, and he had only himself to blame. It was small consolation that Lavinia's kindness and sage advice remained his constant companions.

He couldn't repay Lavinia, but he could try to make it up to her by helping her granddaughter, Roxie Whitaker.

Which was no hardship at all.

Her eyes were the color of southern seas at sunrise. They flashed and sparkled with siren-like allure. They were the most dangerous eyes he'd ever seen.

Even so, her eyes were only half the trouble. Her body had trouble written all over it. Her legs went on for miles, lending her the exact height he preferred in a woman. Just right for kissing. And more. Especially more.

His blood heated at the thought of running his fingers through her dark silky hair, of charting the feminine mysteries beneath her smooth skin. From the moment he'd laid eyes on her, he'd wanted her. It had taken every ounce of civility he possessed to ignore his primal instincts and calmly state his business.

Because he hadn't been calm. All systems had been on high alert. He'd been spatially aware of every object around him, from the baby-faced angels decorating the office to the red Miata, white Explorer, and blue Accord speeding down Main Street while he spoke with her. None of them presented a threat to him.

Roxie Whitaker, though, could do some serious damage.

Worse, he was of a mind to let her.

The attraction had come out of nowhere, blindsiding him. Why else would he go to a wedding with a perfect stranger? He didn't go to weddings of people he *knew*, for Pete's sake.

Sloan pulled up behind 605 Main Street, shoving the gear lever into park. Not a blade of grass was out of place in the yard. Shrubs bordered the two-story Victorian clapboard house in soldier-straight precision. With a coat of paint, this place could look like a real home from the curb.

By now, nature should have taken its course. The wooden house should be choked by a thicket of vegetation. Windows should have been busted out by teen-aged vandals. Rain and termites should have reduced this place to a sodden heap.

Thanks to his vigilant neighbors, nature had been thwarted.

Now he owed Lavinia…and Roxie.

Unlike his father, Sloan Harding paid his debts.

Mac stuck his head out the window, ears perked, and whined. Sloan broke free of his thoughts to pet his dog, then reached across to open the passenger door. Mac vaulted out, circling the Jeep, sniffing and exploring, tail held high.

His cell phone buzzed. Sloan glanced at the caller ID and picked up. "Harding."

"Hey, boss," Bates said. "How's the dump in the sticks?"

"It's got a tree stuck in the roof." Sloan locked the Jeep and strode toward the wood-framed house. Distaste mounted with each step. "You got anything on Gilmore yet?"

"That guy's good." Reluctant admiration rang in Bates' voice. "But not as good as me. I'll find him. Don't you worry."

Jared Gilmore had invited Team Six Security's scrutiny when he'd hacked into their computer system. His intrusion had been halted before any damage had been done, but every man at Team Six wanted answers. Why had Gilmore come after them?

His heels rang on the creaking wooden steps. "I pay you so I don't have to worry."

"I'm close, boss. I can feel it. Reg is snooping around in Charleston. The guy'd have to be a ghost to outwit the two of us. You heading back to Atlanta tomorrow?"

At a movement in his peripheral vision, Sloan whirled, every sense on alert. A frayed stub of a rope dangled from the closest oak tree. He'd spent many an hour playing on that rope. Until his father had cut it to punish him.

"Negative," Sloan said. "I'm staying here until I secure the house."

"Gotcha." Bates paused. "Walking down memory lane's a bitch. Everything seem smaller?"

It felt heavier, as if a cannon rested on his chest, but Sloan wouldn't admit that. "It is what it is."

"I can book you into that hotel out by the interstate. They've got cable TV, a swimming pool, electricity, and running water. All ya gotta do is say the word."

"Nah. I've stayed in worse places." He'd contacted City Hall and the power company this morning to get water and utilities turned back on, but they'd said it would take a few days. Even if the house was unlivable, he needed running water and electricity for his last attempt to debunk the myth of the Harding fortune.

"Suit yourself. Happy vacation."

"Find my ghost, smart ass." Sloan snapped the phone shut. The timing of Gilmore's interest, the fallen oak limb, and the letter from Roxie had been too coincidental.

Sloan Harding didn't trust coincidences.

****

Roxie glided down the long red carpet toward the altar. She was the sixth woman to walk down this aisle wearing a midnight blue strapless gown. She'd earned the maid of honor slot due to introducing Megan and Dave.

She smiled at the mayor's wife and her brood of sons. Another lucky woman. Roxie's second cousin cradled a sleeping newborn. The baby's pale blond curls sported an adorable pink bow. Gran's bridge buddies waved at her, as did every tradesman in town. With the exception of Dave's out-of-town relatives, she knew everyone here.

Behind Roxie, two flower girls waited to toss rose petals on the carpet. The circlets of sweetheart roses in their hair had been Roxie's idea. People in the front of the church strained around her to see the children.

She took her place at the front of the packed church and turned to watch for Megan. The pianist transitioned to Pachelbel's "Canon in D," and everyone stood. The little girls tossed rose petals, and Megan glided up the aisle on her father's arm. Her eyes misted at her friend's glow of love.

Bridesmaid Brenda Harris whispered in Roxie's

ear. "Who's that hunk standing in the back?"

Roxie followed Brenda's glance. The tall, dark-haired man in a black suit hadn't taken a seat on either the bride or the groom's side of the church. He stood with his arms barred across his chest, his gaze drilling straight into Roxie. Her heart skipped a beat.

Sloan Harding.

He'd come to the wedding.

The force of his attention set her pulse to racing. She should have told him he didn't need to act like he was her boyfriend. All she needed was someone to sit with her at dinner so she didn't look like a loser.

Sloan fit her needs perfectly. He was handsome and virtually a stranger. With any luck, the evening would pass uneventfully, and as a bonus she'd snag his property listing.

Roxie beamed a relieved smile at Sloan. "That's Sloan. He's my date."

****

Roxie's smile knocked Sloan back on his heels. He told himself she was an obligation, a beautiful one, at that. She was also out of his league.

She was everything he'd never been lucky enough to have. In the old days, before he'd joined the service or opened Team Six Security, no woman of Roxie's social standing would give him the time of day.

Since then he'd learned how to get any woman he wanted, but none of them stuck around very long. They wanted more than he was willing to give.

Out of habit, his gaze swept the old wooden pews and narrow stained glass windows, assessing the crowd for threats and locating the exits. Every man in the church seemed to be staring at Roxie. Men that no doubt came from good families.

If he hadn't forgotten to take the dry cleaners bag out of his Jeep before he drove down here, he wouldn't have had a suit to wear tonight. The right clothes covered a multitude of sins, but they wouldn't erase his family history.

Roxie looked like the kind of woman who never colored outside of the lines, while he crossed those lines regularly. Other than sexual attraction, they probably had nothing in common. What was he really doing here?

His question nagged at him until Roxie joined him at the back of the church after the ceremony. She smelled good enough to eat. His fingers itched to trace the contours of her creamy shoulders.

"Hi," she said.

"Hi." Smooth move, Harding. Say something else. "Nice dress."

Surprise filled her eyes, colored her cheeks. "Oh. Thanks. Ready to walk over to the parish hall for dinner?"

He gestured toward the arched doorway. "After you."

"Did you have any trouble finding the church?"

"No trouble." Her hips swayed in the form-hugging dark blue dress. A woman like Roxie should come with traffic signs. Dangerous curves ahead suited her perfectly.

A perky blond in a similar dress caught up with them, looping her arm through Roxie's. "Aren't you going to introduce me, hon?" she asked.

Roxie's cheeks turned red. "Brenda, this is Sloan Harding. Sloan, Brenda."

Brenda chattered nonstop for five minutes about the bride's bouquet, then sped ahead to catch another group.

"Loosen up, Sloan," Roxie said. "Brenda thinks you don't like her. She's a nice person."

"Sorry if I offended her. I'm not much on small talk or fancy affairs."

She patted his shoulder. "I won't let any of the

people here bite you," Roxie promised. "You're safe in my hands."

"Social gatherings aren't my specialty," he said. "I'm direct to a fault."

Amusement flickered in her tropical eyes. "You're a dateless wonder too?"

He saw no point in correcting her assumption. He scowled, and she laughed outright. Her laughter warmed him like a burst of sunshine on a cloudy day. He managed a chagrined smile.

"That's better," she said. "We'll get through this and tomorrow night I'll make you a home-cooked dinner to thank you for helping me out."

His mouth watered, but whether it was for the woman or the meal, he couldn't say. "That's not necessary, but you're on." They joined the others inside the hall, dining to soft music and the clink of silverware.

Of the two hundred people present at the reception, he didn't recognize a soul. With luck, he'd skate through the evening unnoticed. But when the town fire chief, Buford Pratt, and his mother Louise were introduced to him, Sloan noticed a predatory gleam in the old bat's eyes.

"You're that Harding boy, aren't you?" Louise clung to her walker.

His rehearsed reply stalled in his throat. He remembered something Lavinia had taught him: good manners never go out of style. "Yes ma'am, I am."

"Humph. Always said you'd never amount to anything."

"Mother!"

Louise ignored her son and gave Sloan a once over. "What are you doing with a nice girl like our Roxie?"

His fingers curled into his palm and he felt all of twelve years old again, hungry and dirty. And alone.

"Sloan owns a security company in Atlanta, Mrs. Pratt. He's a successful businessman," Roxie said smoothly.

The old biddy's eyes narrowed and settled on the empty wine glass before him. "Still sneaking around, aren't you? What some folks will do for the Almighty dollar. You got a drinking problem like your daddy?"

Roxie gasped. "Mrs. Pratt, that's uncalled for. Sloan is my guest."

The fire chief jumped in. "For God's sake, Mother. This isn't the Spanish Inquisition." He nodded at Sloan. "My apologies, Harding." He took hold of his mother's arm and led her away.

The apology caught Sloan short. This wasn't how he'd pictured his eventual homecoming.

"How rude," Roxie said once the Pratts had moved out of earshot. "I'm sorry she said those hurtful things."

Might as well get it out in the open now. "My father did have a drinking problem. He wasted his life and let me run wild as a kid. I left this town thirteen years ago to make a fresh start."

"Well, if it makes you feel any better, she's mad at me, too."

"You? How can she be mad at you?"

"I took down the Victorian wallpaper in Gran's office, hoping to attract more contemporary customers. I didn't gain new customers. Instead, Louise and her friends hate what I've done. Three of them took their business across town because of the change."

People around here apparently didn't care for fresh starts. "You like living here in Muddy Bug? I mean Bog. Mossy Bog."

She laughed at his supposed slip up. "Not everyone is rude like Louise. I have a lot of friends."

Sloan knew she was popular. Traffic past their table had been steady all evening. At least five people had said how good it was to see Roxie out enjoying herself despite recent events. He'd been a bit surprised folks had heard about her brother's incarceration when she hadn't mentioned it in his hearing, but then he'd remembered how fast news traveled in a small town.

Even so, he envied her for finding such a secure place for herself in this world. She had what he longed for- roots.

"May I have your attention please?" A man's voice sounded over the loudspeaker. "The next dance is for the wedding party only."

Sloan's mood improved. Holding Roxie in his arms would ease the sting of talking about his past. The bride and groom took the floor, followed by a smattering of applause. The two little girls in blue dresses with flowery circlets on their heads joined hands. Other couples moved toward the floor.

"This is awkward," Roxie murmured. "Do you dance?"

He danced with women, danced them right into his bed. She deserved better than that. "Dancing is a bad idea," he said. It would only attract more attention.

"We could pretend we didn't hear the announcement or we could hit the buffet for seconds," Roxie suggested, arching a conspiratorial brow.

He liked the warmth in her aqua-hued eyes. He savored her vanilla scent. Dancing with her and keeping his hands to himself would be impossible. "The buffet."

They rose together and skirted the dance floor, food the furthest thing from his mind.

"Oh no you don't," Megan called across the glittering dance floor. Strains of a haunting song about forever love filled the room. "Roxie Whitaker, come on out here and dance. I know how much you love dancing. Come on."

Roxie's face turned fire engine red. "Busted."

Sloan knew his choice had been made for him. Feigning a smile, he guided her onto the dance floor.

Folks around the room applauded when Roxie stepped into his arms. "This is so embarrassing," she murmured against his chest.

"Not a problem." Sloan danced with her in the only way he knew, up close and personal. She felt great in his arms. With her height, he didn't get a crick in his neck or back due to bending over to talk to her.

She was light on her feet and her fragrance triggered a deep, sensual hunger. The urge to kiss her thrummed through his blood. Though she felt right in his arms, he knew better than to trust his instincts when it came to females.

Kissing her would prove she was just another woman.

With that in mind, he navigated them toward an alcove, a secluded spot he'd noticed earlier when they entered the hall. With finesse, he angled her into the private space, then waited, silently urging her to look up.

When she did, he lowered his head slowly, giving her an out if she wanted it. She didn't break eye contact, didn't utter a sound in protest.

He brushed her lips with the barest of kisses. Raw current arced between them. A sexy little moan sounded deep in her chest. He went in for a second taste, nibbling, nuzzling, silently imploring her to open for him. When she did, he was lost.

****

Roxie came to her senses at the sound of a tray of dropped dishes. She jerked back as if cold water had splashed in her steaming face. "Stop. This isn't right."

"Doesn't feel wrong to me," Sloan rumbled

huskily. "Feels mighty good."

She tried to peek around his broad shoulder to see if anyone was watching them. With relief, she saw that many were helping clean up the mess from the dropped tray. "I don't know how this happened. This isn't how I conduct myself in public." Or in private.

"You sound like a woman with a lot of rules."

She'd barely spent two hours with the man, and here she was, losing all sense of decorum in his arms. She was in way over her head here. "You don't have to put on an act. I'm not that desperate."

His eyes narrowed. "You think I was acting?"

"I'm sorry," she said. "I'm out of my element here. I don't even know you."

He studied her. "You *do* have a lot of rules."

"Rules are important. They're the fabric of our society. Without them, chaos would reign."

He drew in a long, considering breath. "I bet you don't let your hair down very often."

Roxie stared. She was the friendliest person in town. Her business depended on it.

He leaned down and kissed her again, just a brief brush of the lips. "You change your mind about taking a walk on the wild side, Sunshine, you let me know. I'll take you places you've never been before."

Chapter 3

Sunlight streamed through the opening, illuminating the gaping hole in Sloan's roof and a limb as big around as a steering wheel poking through it. What else was up here?

An object tucked in the far corner of the attic caught his eye. His granddad's Army trunk. He hadn't realized it was here, hadn't thought about the trunk since he was a boy.

Any chance it held a clue to the missing Harding fortune?

He'd check it out, for sure, but first things first. He grabbed the massive limb protruding through his roof and shoved. It held fast. Sloan grabbed hold again, putting his back into it, grunting with effort.

Nothing.

He circled the stout limb and tried from the other side. Definitely stuck. If he had a chain saw, he could cut this part up, but there was more tree on top of the house than in here. From one perspective, that sorry water oak had done him a big favor. He'd expected the house to be uninhabitable and now it was well on the way to collapsing.

He rapped his knuckles against the rafters supporting the roof. They were solid. He got a funny feeling in his stomach. His grandfather had built this place with his own two hands. He'd measured the wood and hammered the nails.

Sloan had thought coming down here and seeing the house again would convince him to finally get rid of the place. But that hadn't been the reality. The house and grounds were still intact, except for the tree sticking out of his roof. Good thing he had Roxie's list of contractors. He'd need them if he decided to repair this place.

Meanwhile, going through his granddad's trunk would pass the time until dinner. Mindful of the steep pitch of the sloped roof, he ducked his head and approached the dusty trunk. Mac whined at the base of the rickety pull-down stairs.

"Just a minute, bud. I'm almost done up here." Sloan shouldered the trunk and descended the steep steps. He was breathing heavily by the time he made it downstairs. Not much furniture left in this place, but the worn-out kitchen table suited his current need. Mac followed close on his heels, his nails clicking on the bare wooden floor.

Sloan deposited the chest on the grimy kitchen linoleum just as a flurry of sneezes erupted. He hoofed it over to the back door and propped it open. Fresh air filled his lungs.

When his dog paused in the doorway, Sloan whistled him over. "You don't know what we're doing here, do you boy?" He rubbed behind Mac's ears. "Don't worry. If I find that missing money, you'll be rolling in doggie treats for the rest of your life."

He retrieved a soda out of the cooler. The utilities would be turned on Monday but even that wouldn't improve the kitchen. The rusty fridge had been on its last gasp thirteen years ago. The natural light in the kitchen wasn't the best, but dragging the old chest outside was not a good idea. Not if it held important secrets.

Sloan opened the trunk and stared at the jumble of yellowed papers. What would he find in this mess? Clues to where his granddad had hidden the Harding fortune? If there had ever been a semblance of order to these records, it was long gone. He picked up a handful of letters, cancelled checks, and statements and began reading.

****

"Hello? Anyone home?"

Roxie knocked briskly on Sloan's front door, then knocked again. Where was he? His Jeep was here so he had to be nearby. Professional interest had her scanning the wooden frame building for marketability. She could sell this house easily, even if it wasn't market ready. She'd been trying to figure out how to approach Sloan about selling it when the water oak limb fell on the house. Fate had given her the perfect opening.

And if her South Carolina customer didn't come up to scratch, two people in town had expressed interest in recent years. Thelma Whitfield wanted to move her flower shop here since it was on Main Street. A non-profit wanted to set up a small office here. With so many interested buyers, the place would sell. With two of her former clients on the zoning board, changing the zoning would be a snap.

"Sloan?" she called out again.

A growling German Shepherd appeared behind the grimy screen door, startling her into dropping her picnic hamper. The basket of homemade rolls spilled out of the top, and a dozen bite-size rolls sprayed out on the porch floor.

"Oh dear." She crouched to pick them up.

The screen door creaked open, and Sloan knelt beside her. He popped a warm roll directly into his mouth and palmed the rest. Roxie's mouth dropped open.

"Don't eat that," she said. "It's dirty."

He swallowed the roll with a mischievous grin. "Five second rule."

"That's a myth. Dirt and germs transfer on contact. You just ate dirty food."

Sloan tossed his rolls into the bread basket and offered her a hand up from the floor. "And they taste as great as they smell."

The brief physical contact jolted her nerves and pushed her voice into the squeaky range. "Wait! Don't mix those rolls with the clean ones!"

He did it anyway.

"I'm serious." She opened the picnic hamper to remove the dirty rolls, but couldn't tell the difference. "How am I going to sort them out?"

"Don't sweat the small stuff, Roxie." He collected the hamper and held the screen door for her. "Come on in."

"I have plenty of rolls. You don't have to eat the icky ones."

"I can see you've never gone hungry. No way I'm letting something that tastes this good be thrown away."

His dog sniffed Roxie's jeans as she entered the house. She bent to pet the sleek animal. "What's his name?"

"Mac."

The dog licked her hand, prompting a smile. "He's a sweetie."

"No he's not. He's one of my star employees. Mac can take down a grown man at a dead run."

"Gracious." She eyed the dog warily. "I'd better be careful not to upset him."

"Mac won't bother you now that he knows who you are."

The dog seemed friendly enough now that they were on the same side of the screen. She straightened and surveyed the interior of the house.

From the grungy walls to the scarred wooden floors, this place needed a lot of TLC. She'd previously peeked through the windows and noted the downstairs layout. A thorough cleaning and a coat of paint were long overdue.

A rough-hewn coffee table guarded a sagging brown plaid sofa in the living room. The dining room was empty. The kitchen held a small chrome table with two forgettable vinyl and chrome chairs. Handles were broken and missing from the age-darkened pine cabinets. An old-fashioned icebox and a derelict stove rounded out the room.

The kitchen counter was littered with soda bottles and a carryout container. She winced in recognition. He'd gone to Mossy Bog Carryout for lunch. Had Donna Banks flirted with him like she did everybody else?

It didn't matter. After she'd set him straight last night, they'd parted as friends, him following her home and making sure she was inside with the light on before he pulled away in his Jeep.

His company had been welcome, both at the reception and after, especially after the break-in. Secretly she'd wished he'd kiss her again, if only to distract her from her fears, but he'd been nothing but courteous at her door. A delicious shiver went through her as she wondered if he might kiss her tonight.

"Are you cold?" he asked. "I could close the windows."

Roxie flushed at being caught daydreaming. "I'm fine." She eyed the open window appreciatively. Crisp fall air helped freshen the house, which felt sad and empty. This place definitely needed a growing family or a viable business in here to dispel the melancholy mood.

"I'll need a moment to set up. Hope you're hungry." She opened her hamper, shook out a daisy-sprigged table cloth, and folded it to the right size. How many meals had Sloan eaten in this worn-out, dismal kitchen? The appliances were relics. No dishwasher. No microwave. Poor guy.

She thought about what he'd said about going hungry, then shook her head and set the table with her plates, silverware, and clean glasses. Both man and dog watched her intently. Mac's nose went up in the air when she removed the large pot from the hamper.

"Smells great." Sloan lounged beside the stained sink. "I wasn't sure if you'd changed your mind after last night."

She unwrapped the beach towel from around her pot of lowcountry boil. Her mouth watered at the rich aroma wafting from the pot. "I promised you a dinner so here I am. I keep my promises." As she added serving spoons to the cole slaw and her large pot, another thought occurred to her. "Unless you've made other plans. If so, I could get out of your hair in a jiffy."

His chuckle rumbled through the air. "Mac and I never turn down home-cooked meals, so please stay and tell me what this is all about."

Relief swept through her. "You did me a favor, and now I'm returning the favor. That's what friends do."

Sloan uncoiled and strode over to where she stood beside the table. "I forgot something earlier." Deliberately, he lifted her chin with the underside of his knuckles and leaned in for a kiss.

She couldn't move, couldn't breathe. Friends. They were friends. The light caress on her mouth made her skin tingle from head to toe and was over before she could blink.

He drew back, a smile on his rugged face. "Let's eat."

She slid into the seat across from him at the cozy table, tucking her feet under her chair. "It's plain fare. Nothing fancy."

To her satisfaction, he loaded up his plate and sampled the vegetables. "Thanks for doing this. Everything tastes great."

He munched methodically through the corn, the sausage, several new potatoes, and a double serving of rice, which she'd brought over in her rice steamer pot. She'd eaten her seafood first, wondering if she'd made a mistake in her choice of meal. She cleared her throat. "You're not allergic to shrimp are you?"

He shook his head and kept eating.

"I was wondering because you picked them out of the mix. Do you know how to peel shrimp? Should I take them off your plate?"

"Touch them and die. I'm saving the best for last."

She drew in a shallow breath. "You like shrimp?"

"Love 'em." He tore right through the pile on his plate and singled more out of the boiled concoction. "So what do you do when you're not cooking delicious food, being in weddings, or involved in real estate?"

He popped two more shrimp doused in cocktail sauce in his mouth.

"Down time? I don't have a lot of that. There's always something or someone that needs fixing or feeding. Mostly what I've been working on lately is the museum."

As soon as the words left her mouth, she wanted to kick herself to the marsh and back. The museum was a lousy topic of conversation with a Harding.

"Tell me about it."

"Oh, not much to tell," she said breezily. "How 'bout them dawgs?" Most males in this state considered the University of Georgia football team to be a step above mere mortals.

"The dawgs are the dawgs. I can talk about them anytime. I'm curious about you, Roxie. What's this about a museum? Is Mossy Bog going upscale?"

"No such luck." She toyed with a hunk of soggy onion.

"Because?"

"Never mind."

"Now you've got my curious up. What gives?"

"You're not going to let this go, are you?"

He leaned back in his chair, which creaked with the weight readjustment. The air in the kitchen, redolent with the spicy tang of Old Bay Seasoning, suddenly felt heavy. "One thing you should know about me. I have a streak of curiosity that's a mile wide. And when I get drawn into a puzzle I stay on it until I have it figured out. What's wrong with your museum?"

She could do this. Just keep things general. No harm in that. "There's a property near the linear park. It's ideally situated for a tourist attraction. We already have people coming off the interstate to see the shrimp fleet. A museum nearby, particularly a maritime museum, would be a complimentary draw for us. Folks have a wealth of nautical relics stored on their property. Stuff that belonged to family members in generations past. They'd donate it to the museum in a heartbeat."

"Sounds like a well-conceived plan. What's the holdup?"

"Everything. I can't get the idea past the committee stage. Everyone thinks it's a fine idea but no one wants to move forward. The tabby shell won't last forever. We need to get it stabilized and rebuilt. I've put in for all kinds of grants but nothing has come through. And one of Gran's friends is on City Council. She votes against the project every time."

He lifted a hand. "Wait a minute. Back up a bit. You said tabby shell. Are you talking about the old cotton warehouse on the waterfront?"

She winced inwardly at his sharpened voice. "Yes, I am." She regarded him steadily. The museum was important to her. "The Green property."

He stilled. She would not feel sorry for him. Regardless of the gossip, it was time to think of the town's future. "That place can be our salvation. It won't take much to get the museum built, but the amount is more money than my Friends of the

Museum group can raise in bake sales."

"The Green property. Couldn't you find a place with walls and a roof?"

She bristled. "It's the central property on the waterfront. Once we open the museum, we can rehab the others. Tourists love interpretive centers. All of Georgia's timber used to come downriver to Mossy Bog. We had two sawmills running on the mainland, several on the offshore islands. Ships from all over the world came here to get our lumber."

"Believe it or not, I remember the town's history. I also remember that building. The mayor and the City Council blamed my father when it burned twenty years ago."

"From what I understand, that tinder box was a fire waiting to happen. I'm sorry your dad was singled out but the whole town needs to move on. This project will make a difference here."

"Listen up, Sunshine. This town has a very long memory. Trust me on this. It may be another two hundred years before they put the burning of the Green property behind them."

"That's too long to wait. One category five hurricane passes through and those walls will crumble." She sipped her iced tea and an idea sparked. "You could help. You could donate the seed money so that we can get the matching grant money."

He recoiled. "I'm not giving this town a dime. You can play social do-gooder all you want. Take it from me, people only look out for themselves. Forget about the Green property."

"I can't do that."

"Why not?"

"It's what Gran wanted." At his pinched expression, she hurried to add, "It's what I want too. I care about this town. It is the only home I've ever known. I've seen communities all over the world.

Places that had nothing. They pulled together. Why can't we? What does this say about our society?"

He studied her for another long moment. "You were right. This isn't a good thing to talk about."

"Not my fault. You pestered it out of me."

"I often have that effect on people."

"It must be useful in your line of work."

"Very."

She recognized a dead end when she saw one. So much for a nice dinner. He'd eaten her food, but he couldn't stomach her ideas. Clearly he thought of her as a Pollyanna-like character.

Time to get this conversation back to the real estate mode. "Now that you've seen the house, what have you decided? Will you repair the damage?"

"I don't know."

Another dead end. But she wouldn't give up so easily. "What options are you considering? Maybe I can help."

"I expected this place to be in worse shape. There's no termite damage, and the timbers are sound."

She dared to hope they were on the same wavelength. "This location is ideal and the house is loaded with potential."

"Like I said, I expected to find an overgrown dump. I planned to level the house. But now I'm not sure."

Adrenaline surged. Her hand went to her heart. "Level the house? Are you serious? Why would you do that? This building is valuable. Historic, even. Do you like to throw your money away?"

He put down his fork. Dark energy filled the air. His gaze drilled into her. "My money. Are you referring to the lost Harding fortune?"

She drew back, appalled. "No one believes there was a Harding fortune."

"My father did."

How had this friendly dinner veered so far off track? He looked like he'd rather be stuck in Atlanta gridlock. But she needed his business. Best to steer this back to the realm of real estate.

"Have you evaluated the damage in the attic?" She spooned the last of shrimp and sausage onto his plate.

"Between the pitch of the roof and the weight of the tree, I couldn't make any headway. I'll make calls to contractors first thing tomorrow morning."

"Will you install a new roof?"

"I hope to get by with a patch job for now. That'll give me time to make up my mind about this place." He reached for another roll.

At last, familiar ground. She drained her iced tea. "Do you need someone locally to oversee the repair? Or will you coordinate everything from Atlanta?"

"I'll decide once I have the estimates in hand. Frankly I'm not sure this place is worth saving, even though the frame is solid."

"Of course it is. Gracious, this is your home!"

His expression hardened. "I'm keeping an open mind for now."

Roxie pushed errant bits of cole slaw together on her plate. "I could keep an eye on things for you, as your property manager. Once you decide the fate of the house, that is."

"Hire you?"

She nodded enthusiastically. "Marshview Realty handles all phases of property management: rentals, leases, sales, you name it."

"What did you have in mind?"

"How about a complimentary walk-through? I can point out upgrades that buyers look for. Over time, I've had inquiries about this place. If you put it on the market, I can match you up with three buyers today."

He watched her intently. "The house isn't for sale."

"What about renting it out? The fenced backyard would be an asset for a family with pets."

He tossed a bite of roll to the dog and stood. "I haven't thought that far ahead. But it wouldn't hurt to hear your ideas."

She rose with a nod. "Walk-through and then dessert. I hope you like strawberry cheesecake."

"Love it. Great meal, too." He patted his flat stomach. "Really hit the spot."

He loved her food. So far so good. "I like to start a walk-through at the front door. This house is the same vintage as mine, so it's got great bones. Our grandfathers must have been about the same age when they settled here."

Sloan rubbed his chin as he walked beside her through the house. "Interesting you should mention our grandparents. I read some of Granddad's personal papers today. Did you know Lavinia wrote him letters while he was overseas? He saved them."

"Wow. I assumed our families met after settling here."

"The letters were very friendly, and Lavinia's last name wasn't Bolen. It was Franklin."

She paused on the threshold. "That was her maiden name."

"How come I don't remember you when I was growing up? Why didn't our paths cross before now?"

He'd stepped too close. Her senses rioted. She dug deep for composure. "I'm five years younger than you. My parents are missionaries, did you know that?"

"I didn't. Did you grow up overseas?"

"My parents own a small place across town, but we only visited here between postings. My brother and I moved to Mossy Bog ten years back; it worked out better for all of us. I grew up helping Gran at

Marshview Realty."

"You traveled around the world with your parents and occasionally visited Lavinia while you were growing up?"

She nodded. "We tromped all over Africa, Mexico, and Alaska before Timmy and I moved in with Gran."

No point in telling him Gran had mentioned Sloan to them. That she'd predicted Sloan would one day come home and need a friend. Gran had been right about his return, but he didn't need a friend. He'd come to terms with the world.

Roxie turned her mind to real estate matters. She suggested he upgrade the electrical wiring and the plumbing, replace the windows, refinish the wood floors, install central heat and air, add a tankless water heater, and paint everything.

He listened attentively. "Suppose I change my mind about the house being for sale. What's the difference in what the house would go for if I fixed everything you suggested and if it were to go on the market as is?"

She quoted some numbers, offered to supply him with comparables.

"That's a big swing." He jammed his hands in his jeans pockets. "The roof has to be repaired. It wouldn't hurt to get estimates for everything you mentioned. I'd like to see about getting that water oak taken down too. As long as the repair cost comes in at least twenty percent under fair market price of the house, it would be a no-brainer to fix this place up."

Roxie sliced the strawberry cheesecake, her heart singing with joy. "Call the folks on that list I gave you."

"I can't stay indefinitely. I've got a meeting in Atlanta Monday morning."

Rewards came to those who took risks. If she

wanted to get in the game, she had to risk losing her seat on the bench. She ignored the tightness in her gut. "If you leave your key with me, I'll get estimates for you. It will take most of the week to obtain them anyway."

"How much?"

She handed him a dessert plate, pleased at the way his eyes lit up. "No charge for the estimates. But I'd like a percentage of the rehab costs if you hire me to be your property manager, and I'd like to list the property if you decide to sell."

Sloan ate a bite of cheesecake. The corners of his lips edged up. "Deal."

Chapter 4

On Monday morning, Beard's Plumbing and Cramer Electric beat her to Sloan's house. She popped out of Miss Daisy and waved to the elderly gentlemen. "Y'all sure got here fast."

Plumber Chuck Beard caught her in a bear hug, his round face looking ruddier than usual. "Well if it isn't Lavinia, Junior. You look more like your Gran every day, gal. You been doing all right?"

Roxie nodded, stepped away from the burly man, and turned to greet the thin electrician.

"We're glad you called." Pete Cramer spoke to her feet.

She hugged him, too. Pete Cramer's shyness often put clients off, but he was a gem. "I'm glad I have a job for y'all to bid. I have to get multiple estimates for my client, but I'm hoping he'll hire you two. You're the best."

Their heavy boots clumped up the wooden steps behind her. "This still the Harding place?" the plumber asked.

Roxie opened the screen door and turned the key in the front door lock. "It is. The owner, Sloan Harding, lives in Atlanta. Since he's getting estimates for the roof, I talked him into pricing out the rest of the needed repairs."

"That the guy you danced with at Megan's wedding?"

"Yes. He was here for the weekend." She paused in the hallway, switched on the light. The bare bulb gave off a weak glow. "The panel box is in the kitchen, Mr. Cramer. The downstairs bathroom is second door on the right and the other one is at the head of the stairs, Mr. Beard."

While the men were inspecting their work areas, Roxie wandered through the house. A ground floor bedroom window caught her eye. It didn't appear to be shut all the way.

Sloan must have missed this when he locked up, she thought, then remembered Sloan worked in security. He would have locked his place when he left at noon yesterday.

Doubt and suspicion tap danced in her thoughts. What if it wasn't Sloan? Had someone else been in here?

How would she know? Nothing had been ransacked, not like at her house. But there wasn't much furniture in here to speak of. Certainly not anything worth stealing. She jiggled the window and snugged the lock, then checked the other windows and doors.

They were locked. Even so, her unease grew as a sense of déjà vu jangled her nerves. Was it possible her burglar had been here as well?

Outside the window, the house cast a long shadow over the vehicles in the yard. Was someone out there now, watching them?

If so, what did he or she want?

She called Laurie Ann and explained the situation.

"Is anything torn up?" the city cop asked.

"Nothing. There's hardly anything to tear up."

"What about things out of place?"

Roxie checked the kitchen cabinets. "Maybe but the pots and pans were a mess to start with."

"Do you want to file an incident report?"

"I don't know if there was an incident. The window was open, that's all I know. Are there any other break-ins?"

"Just your place."

43

"Darn. Okay. Well. Thanks."

"Call me if you decide to file an incident report."

Confronting her fears head-on, Roxie waited on the front steps for the contractors. Coming from the city like she did, Laurie Ann must think she was a baby. But Roxie's nerves wouldn't settle. She glanced around, sure someone was watching her.

But no one was there.

"Gonna need new pipes and new fixtures," the plumber said, startling her when he emerged. "That stuff was junk from the get-go. The only thing Scott Harding did right was framing this house. And he was smart enough not to build this place in a hole. Your Grandpop should've taken a note from Scott on that. Your place is a flood waiting to happen, Roxie."

She didn't roll her eyes, but it was a near thing. "I haven't forgotten. One of these days we'll do something about it."

The plumber tapped his rolled estimate on his thigh. "Don't wait too long. A flood can cost you a pile of money."

"I hear you."

"Any word on that burglar that hit your place last week?"

"Nope. Laurie Ann's got a big fat nothing. It's so frustrating."

"You call me if you have any more trouble. I can be at your place in five minutes, tops."

"Thanks."

The screen door creaked open behind them. "Here's my estimate, Miss Roxie." Pete Cramer handed her a folded page. "You want me to send my son-in-law by to look at the roof?"

She handed him a business card. "Absolutely. Have him call my cell so that I can let him inside."

"Will do." The electrician glanced at his watch. "Ten-thirty. Gotta run my wife to dialysis."

As the electrician left, Mr. Beard handed her his

estimate. "Thanks," Roxie said. "I appreciate you being so responsive."

"No problem. I'd rather work for you than that Doleman woman over at BC Realty. She expects twice the work at half the price and in half the time. New people don't understand how things work."

"Yeah, but those new people have money for homes and repairs. We need them."

"If Harding fixes up the house, you running the show?"

"He said he'd hire me, but nothing is certain."

Mr. Beard ambled off, stopped, then walked over to her vintage Cadillac and stroked the hood lovingly. "Your Gran loved this old car and she loved you. She'd have my head if I didn't speak up. A man is known by the company he keeps."

"I've heard that before."

"Sloan's teenage pals came to a bad end. And his people—old man Harding was a decent sort, but the rest of that lot was sorry indeed. His dad drank himself to death. His mom and his grandmom ran off. He's not working with a full deck. You be careful around him."

"Will do."

Roxie followed Chuck Beard out of the driveway. He meant well, this friend of her grandmother's. But Gran had seen something in Sloan and encouraged him. He wasn't a drunk or a convict, and he didn't seem to be the sort to run from trouble. He was a guy who'd had a rough start.

She'd had a rough start herself.

****

"Hey, boss." Bates lounged in the doorway of Sloan's Atlanta office.

Sloan entered another number into his database. When Premium Pet Care paid their balance, Team Six Security would have a financial cushion. Nice to know they weren't still struggling to make payroll. He saved the spreadsheet and closed out the file on the secure stand-alone computer.

He glanced up at his former Army buddy. "You get anything on Gilmore?"

Bates shook his head, the overhead lighting glinting on his silver stud earring and shaved head. "The man's slippery as an eel in a mud pie. When Reg visited his office, the receptionist didn't know where the boss was. Gilmore Vacation Sports is legit. It operates as a concierge for mid-level tourists in Charleston. The budget-minded book through GVS."

"We've got nothing?"

Bates shrugged. "GVS financials look good."

"Financials can be faked. My gut says this guy is trouble. Plus he infiltrated several layers of our firewalls before we shut him out. Why the hell is he nosing around in our files?"

"Let's take him out, boss. Shoot first and ask questions later."

"We're not shooting anyone. Team Six keeps a low profile, remember?"

Bates waved a hand dismissively. "Yeah. Yeah. Low profile may be profitable but it sucks. We need action." He paced for a moment, then snapped his fingers. "I know. Let's pull the foxtrot maneuver on Gilmore. The feds would love that."

"No maneuvers. No foxtrot. It's not worth the risk. This guy is up to his neck in illegal something. We just need to find it."

"Spoilsport. All right, we'll keep working the angles. Reg has a date with the receptionist." Bates shot him a sly look. "The only other surefire ladies man we've got is you, and you weren't available."

"Get used to me being out of action. Someone's got to watch the store. None of you yahoos wanted that job either."

Bates huffed out a breath. "Paperwork sucks.

We signed up for the action. You won't catch me or any of the guys doing pansy admin stuff."

"Tell Reg his spending limit on dinner is fifty. Then tell him to report back here. How's Harris making out on the Loralou Bakery job?"

"Done. He barely finished setting up the surveillance cameras before his flight down to Captiva. I'm checking the feeds. Nothing yet, but it's only a matter of time."

"We don't work for free. Unless we find concrete proof, there's no payout on Loralou. Do that one on the side while we gear up for the rock star's new security system down in Macon."

"Gotcha." Bates hesitated. "What about Mossy Bog? That all wrapped up?"

All it took was the mention of Mossy Bog and Roxie's smiling face appeared in Sloan's mind. With effort, he banished the image. "Looks like a few more weeks there. I can manage it on the weekends though."

"Good. Cuz none of us wants to do the stuff you do."

"Grow up, Peter Pan. Adults have responsibilities."

"That's why we got you, Harding. You have CYA down pat."

With that, Bates left. Sloan stared at the stacks of files until the edges of his vision blurred. CYA—covering your ass—had been essential in the Army. Nobody wanted their butt hanging out, least of all, Sloan. He had two vulnerabilities right now, two loose ends he' couldn't tie up. One was Jared Gilmore. Everything about him screamed red alert. The other loose end was Roxie Whitaker. That kiss from the wedding reception had him ready for a green light from her.

Soon. He'd make sure it was soon.

****

47

Roxie gripped the podium in City Hall's Mildred Bagwell Room. Her ten minutes to speak were almost up. If she gauged her success by the bored expression on the city council members' faces, her project was doomed.

"The museum would bring in tourism, provide jobs, and create civic pride," she concluded. "It would be a touchstone for the coast, a unique landmark for Mossy Bog. Best of all, we'd draw traffic off the interstate. That's more tax dollars in our coffers. Please add this worthy project as a line item in your budget. We need this museum. Thank you for hearing me today."

"Young lady, I beg to differ. If museums were profitable, every town from Maine clear down to Key West would have one." Wilbur LaGrange's heavy duty suspenders strained as he leaned forward in his seat. "This isn't the right time to start a risky venture. Revenue is down. Tourism is down. The economy's all goobered up."

She gripped her note cards tighter, but her smile remained fixed. "Times are always tough. That's the beauty of the museum. It will make things better here."

"But how will we pay for it, dear?" Noreen Bagwell waved a jewel-encrusted hand. As usual, she looked like she'd stepped right off the pages of a glossy catalog. "We're barely meeting our expenses as it is. The town's water tank is pushing thirty years. You think building a museum is more important than delivering clean water to our citizens?"

"Play fair, Noreen. You've voted against replacing the water tank every year for the last ten years." Obie Greenaway's pale blue eyes sparkled behind her granny-style glasses. Her long gray braid draped over her front shoulder. She turned from Noreen to Roxie. "A museum is a great idea. We should all get on board with this and help end the cycle of poverty here in Mossy Bog. I say this idea is long overdue."

Noreen looked down her nose at Obie. "Listen to you, advocating that we spend more money in a frivolous manner. You lobbied so hard for those damned windmills on the barrier islands. After months of your nagging, we finally gave in. Those are the ugliest, noisiest things I've ever seen. I get calls about them every week. I'll tell you what you are. You're a rebel without a clue."

Air whistled in through Roxie's teeth. The sound seemed abnormally loud in the silent room. Noreen's claws were sharp all right. Would she direct her next swipe at the museum?

Rudell Strider, chair of the council, rapped his mallet on the table. The dark wood of the mallet was a near perfect match to his skin tone. "Ladies, please. Keep your remarks on topic, and be reminded that while debate is healthy it shouldn't be a personal attack." He glanced up at the videographer. "Plus, I shouldn't have to point out the obvious. This meeting is being broadcast live via local access television."

Roxie glanced around the table, anxious to take in the group's expressions. Noreen humphed. Obie beamed. Wilbur winked at Obie, and young Vance Douglas kept fooling around with his Blackberry. He probably hadn't paid a lick of attention to anything. Rudell fondled his Chairman mallet.

It didn't look good for her museum.

Rudell cleared his throat. "Now then, Miss Whitaker, your presentation time is up. Thank you for bringing this matter to the council's attention. Does anyone on the council have questions for Roxie about the museum proposal before we vote?"

She glanced around hopefully. Only Obie met her gaze directly. Her stomach sank. Sure enough, the council voted and the museum didn't make it. She walked out of the meeting in a daze.

She'd lost this battle, but she wouldn't give up on the museum.

She couldn't.

****

Roxie didn't recognize the bland white envelope in her mail. It looked like a credit card statement, but she'd paid her credit card bill last week. She tossed it in the throw-out pile, then picked it up again. Better make sure it was junk mail. She inserted the letter opener and made a neat slit across the top. The pages spilled out into her hands.

Her blood ran cold. And hot.

She owed ten thousand dollars to this credit card company. How could that be? She didn't even have an account with them. Quickly, she phoned the customer service number.

"You've made a mistake," Roxie said when a person finally came on the line. "I don't have an account with your company."

"This is a new account, ma'am. Opened two weeks ago," the friendly sounding male said. "Normally we wouldn't bill you so soon, but hitting your credit limit triggered our new policy to send a bill. Do you wish to extend your credit limit?"

"No." Roxie struggled to keep her voice from squeaking. "You don't understand. This is a billing error at your end. One of your other clients must have made these charges. I live in coastal Georgia. I would never make international charges like this."

"You are contesting the bill?"

At last. She sighed out her answer. "Yes."

"For security purposes, please answer these questions. What's your grandmother's first name?"

"It's Lavinia, but I don't see what that has to do with anything."

"It's procedure, Ms. Whitaker. Your dog's

name?"

"I don't have a dog."

"Did you say no dog?"

"Yes. I did. What is wrong with you? I didn't do this. I don't have an account with you. I would never run up a huge bill like this."

"Do you wish to cancel the card?"

"Yes. Cancel the card. And cancel the bill while you're at it."

"I can't do anything about the bill, ma'am. If you're the victim of identity theft, you should contact the police in your area. Is there anything else I can help you with today?"

The man's sugary tone sickened Roxie. "No. You've done quite enough."

Her next call was to the Mossy Bog police department. Laurie Ann Dinterman was in her kitchen in ten minutes.

"I don't know how this happened." Roxie showed Laurie Ann the bill and explained.

"Looks like somebody stole your identity all right. Your purse get stolen or misplaced recently?"

"No way. I am very careful about my purse and security."

"What about your mail? Do you have home delivery?"

About half the people of Mossy Bog had home delivery. "I have a box at the post office. You think someone stole my mail?"

"It's a possibility. Where do you stack your mail?"

"On my desk in the other room."

"Think back to the burglary, what was that, two weeks ago? Did you notice if your papers were disturbed?"

"My desk was in order. The housebreaker did this?"

"Don't have proof of anything. But we do know

someone was in your house recently. That person could have accessed your personal information in your desk."

"God. What am I going to do?"

"Sit down before you hyperventilate and let's get the incident report written up. Once we issue the police report, you can send a copy to the credit card company and that should be the end of it."

"You sure? That seems too easy."

"There's nothing easy about identity theft. You should contact your credit card company, your bank, and any other financial institution you may be involved with and tell them what happened."

Roxie nodded, a great weariness setting in. What she wouldn't do for Gran's soft shoulder right now.

"You might want to cancel your current credit card in case the thieves have that number too. The company can issue you another card."

She used her card for everything, from gas to groceries, because she didn't like to carry cash. This was going to be inconvenient.

"You keep any important documents in there?" Laurie Ann pointed toward the desk with her ink pen.

"I have records in there. Tax returns. Household appliance warranty information. That kind of stuff."

"Go through it. Make sure nothing's missing. No property deeds, stocks or bond certificates in the house?"

"Those are in the safety deposit box at the bank."

"Good girl." Laurie Ann wrote down a few more things on her pad of paper and pushed it over for Roxie to sign.

"One more thing," Laurie Ann pulled out another slip of paper, scribbled down a few words and passed it over to Roxie. "Contact these three companies to check your credit history. They'll flag any new activity in your name and tell you what's happening."

"New activity?"

"Sorry, hon. Sometimes these things take on a life of their own."

Great.

****

Sonny Gifford looked like he could buy and sell a dozen diners. His burnished gold hair framed a classic profile worthy of Michelangelo. Thick sensual lips, high cheekbones, amber speckled eyes, and golden eyebrows accented by evenly tanned skin lent him an incredibly handsome air. An open-necked blue dress shirt was tucked into sleek black trousers. Both his belt and shoes were black, inlaid with bits of silver.

Heads had turned when they'd entered Sheryl's Diner for lunch. Not many out-of-towners came in here. She'd field plenty of calls later asking about the mystery man.

"How's that burger?" she asked.

He blotted his face with a napkin. "Good. You sure that bowl of soup is enough for you? I'm happy to share my fries."

Sheryl believed in giving customers their money's worth. There were enough potatoes on his plate to feed two mounds of fire ants. Roxie shook her head. "I'm fine, thanks. Let's get back to your property requirements. Mossy Bog is a jewel in the rough. We've got all the charm and grace of Savannah with a fraction of the people. Plus, I've got some real bargains for you to look at. I'd love to show them to you today."

He appeared thoughtful, as if giving her words careful consideration. Then his features darkened. "Are they on Main Street?"

"They are very close to Main Street," she

hedged. "I'm sure you'll find them of interest."

"I'm not willing to budge on location. Did you speak to the owner of 605 Main Street? That's the property I want."

She tried to school her features, but was sure a grimace sneaked out anyway. "That property is not for sale. I have spoken with the owner. If it comes on the market, you will be the first to know. If you can afford to wait, I believe the property will become available in a few months."

"No can do. I need that place yesterday. Everyone has a price. If you can't get one from him, Sally Doleman over at BC Realty said she'd get it for me."

Roxie unclenched her back teeth. "I can assure you I have the inside track with this seller. Sally can't do anything more than I've done, and there's a good chance she'll antagonize him by asking the same questions I asked."

Surprise etched his fine golden features. "I don't want that."

"I understand you want that particular place, but I have other properties which may suit you better. Will you consider looking at them? We can view them right after lunch."

"I'm on a tight schedule today, what with my morning client meeting down in Brunswick and another client meeting in Savannah at three. What about the next time I come down?"

She let out a long breath. He would look at other places. All was not lost. Meanwhile she could continue to move Sloan along to the point of sale. "Sounds good. Shall we pencil in a date and time?"

He reached in a pocket and pulled out an electronic device. After fooling with it for a bit, he said, "I've got a fluid schedule next week. I can't commit to a date. Best guess is the middle of the week. Does that work for you?"

She wished she had a showy electronic device to consult. Her calendar was unfortunately clear. "That's fine."

"Great. That's settled." He sat back in the fifties style booth and studied her. "I have another request."

"Yes?"

"Will you go out to dinner with me next week?"

"Sorry. I'm seeing someone." That was shading the truth a bit. She wasn't dating Sloan per se, but his kiss had certainly given her plenty of new fantasy material.

His gaze swept her torso again. "Any chance you're about to break it off with him?"

As pushy as this guy was about real estate, no way would she date him. She stared him squarely in the eye. "Let's keep this on a professional level."

****

"I'm glad you came home this weekend, Timmy." Roxie lifted a bubbling casserole dish of crab au gratin out of the oven on Friday evening. "I wanted to talk to you."

Her brother carried the tumblers of sweet tea to the table and sat. His bony shoulders slouched forward, his shaggy brown hair spilled over his brow. "Yeah?"

"I wanted to drive up to Georgia Tech last weekend, but Sloan said it wasn't the right time to fuss at you, that you knew you'd messed up."

Timmy's head came up. His gaze narrowed. "Sloan? Sloan who?"

She couldn't ignore the excitement skittering through her veins. Warmth steamed up her collar. "Sloan Harding, a potential client of mine. Don't change the subject. We have to talk about what happened last weekend. What are you going to do with your life?"

"I didn't come home to get yelled at."

"No?" She tossed the salad, distributed portions into two bowls, and joined her brother at the table. "What did you expect? That I'd congratulate you on your incarceration?"

His face fell. He looked much older than his nineteen years. "I know I screwed up. The social aspect of college rocks, but studying is a drag. College is lame. I want to explore Paris at night, to ski the Alps, and to dance in an Irish pub."

"You've been lots of places already."

"Yeah, but the places I've been aren't on most people's itinerary. Mom and Dad's idea of a vacation is a shack in a third world country, indoor plumbing optional. I want to see Europe."

She counted to five before she spoke. "Stay in school. You'll have options. Europe isn't going anywhere, and it costs money to travel. Get your degree and land a traveling job. College is the key to your future."

"It doesn't feel right." He doused his salad with honey mustard dressing, leaving the cap off the dressing bottle. "Besides, one of my professors has it in for me. I can't take it anymore. I stopped going to his class."

Her fork clattered on her plate. "Stopped going? You're flunking out in your first semester?"

"I'm not going back to that class. The man doesn't know diddly about international politics. He makes mistakes in his lectures, and he expects us to regurgitate the material verbatim on the exams. He's a loser and a complete waste of my time."

Not all professors knew how to teach. "Why don't you drop that class and focus on the other ones for the rest of this semester?"

"Already dropped it." He grinned sheepishly. "What's for dessert?"

"Apple pie ala mode." She pushed back from the table to get it.

"Sit. I'll clear the table."

Her brother didn't need her to fix his problem? That was a change. Instead of being relieved, doubts crowded into her mind. What if he made more bad choices? How could she run any sort of damage control when his school was so far away?

He bused the dishes straight into the dishwasher. "Tell me about Sloan."

"There's not much to tell. He owns the house behind us, the one Gran took care of, and he's fixing it up. He was in the office last week when I found out you were in jail. That's how I ended up with advice from him on what to do."

"Wait a minute." He stopped mid-stride and shot her a sharp look. "Sloan Harding? The lost boy that was Gran's project? That Sloan?"

His suspicious tone irritated Roxie. "You know him?"

"Barely. He used to shoot hoops in the park. He came around once or twice while we were at Gran's. When I asked her about him, she said he'd lost his way. There was something in her voice whenever she spoke of him, that same something I hear in your voice. What is it with him? What does Sloan Harding have that makes women in our family want to take care of him?"

"I don't want to take care of him. Besides, he's not like that now. He's a successful Atlanta businessman, and perfectly capable of taking care of himself. I'll invite him over for dinner tomorrow so you can meet him."

"Dinner? Are you dating him?"

"We're friends, that's all."

"I want to check this guy out."

The thought of her brother interviewing Sloan gave her pause. "Timmy. Don't go all parental on me."

He grinned. "Turnabout's fair play. Mom and

Dad aren't here to look after you. It's my right as your male relative."

****

"We're almost there, Mac." Sloan rubbed his dog's head as he turned off the busy interstate to the access road that led to Mossy Bog. He'd been thinking of Roxie all week, reliving her passionate response to his kiss.

This week, he'd received pointed invitations from several women. He'd declined. That wasn't like him. But he'd rather be here with Roxie than with another woman. Her eyes were such pools of mystery.

He parked his Jeep in front of Marshview Realty. Though it was only nine o'clock on a Saturday morning, Roxie sat in her cozy, old-fashioned office, an ear glued to the phone. She was a morning person. Something they had in common.

When he opened the Jeep's door, his dog charged across him like he was hot on the trail of a drug lord. "Mac. Get back in here."

Mac had another agenda. He sat at the door to Roxie's office and barked repeatedly.

Sloan couldn't blame his dog. The same tail-wagging joy coursed through him. In her dark slacks and a cream colored top, she glowed with vitality. She had her brunette hair pulled back in a sleek ponytail and looked great. Just right, in fact. His pulse raced as she waved and walked across the carpet toward him.

The glass door opened, and Mac got the hug Sloan wanted. He tried not to feel jealous, but he wanted her arms around him, her smiling at him.

He frowned. He was spending his weekends in Mossy Bog to search for his missing inheritance. This thing with Roxie was supposed to be an adventure on the side.

Hug or handshake he wondered as she rose with

a smile on her face. She extended her hand. She smelled of fresh baked cookies and woman, two of his favorite scents. Her creamy blouse moved when she did, the buttons straining as she stepped back and held the door open for him. He quickly shoved his hands in his jean pockets to keep from drawing her into his arms.

"Come on in. I'll update you on the progress I've made."

"Let me put Mac back in the Jeep."

"It's all right if he comes in."

Genuine welcome flowed through her words, warming him. Still, he hesitated. "I don't want to cause any trouble for you."

She tugged on Mac's leather collar, urging him in. "You won't. I'm the boss here."

That surprised him. He followed his dog inside. "You're a real estate broker?"

She gestured to an ornate oval table near the storefront window. "Please. Have a seat."

He did so while Mac ran a quick perimeter check of the space. She may have charmed his dog, but Mac always got the job done. Not that Sloan expected to find any guns or bombs in Roxie's office, but he'd learned never to be caught unaware.

She selected a folder from her desk. "I should have expected that question, seeing as you don't live in Mossy Bog. Marshview Realty was Gran's business. I've worked here since I was eighteen."

She sat down across from him. "Once Gran died, I applied to the state Real Estate Commission to reissue her broker's license to me. I've completed the education and testing requirements, so, yes, I'm a bona fide broker. I'm in charge, and I know what I'm doing. Satisfied?"

"I apologize. I meant no disrespect." He reached out and covered her hand, as a friend. A spark of current flashed between them, and his blood hummed. "What have you got for me?"

She paused, then withdrew her hand from underneath his. It was the pause that had him doing a little mental jig. He was sure she'd felt it too. The attraction between them was real. All week long he'd wondered if he'd imagined it.

"I called two tree removal services to get the tree limb off your roof, and here are their written estimates. Both of them added the cost of taking down the water oak." She slid several sheets of paper toward him. "Of the three roofing companies I contacted, no one would patch the roof because of its age. So many shingles are missing already it's a miracle your entire roof doesn't leak like a sieve. Bottom line, you need a new roof and gutters."

The total was darn near twelve grand. Each contractor must have enjoyed adding zeroes to their quotes. Surely he could have a few of his guys come down here and patch things up. "And if I choose to do the work myself?"

She regarded him with cool appraisal. "I was under the impression you had a business to run in Atlanta and didn't have time to do the repairs."

Nothing like a good challenge. He could probably stretch out the repairs. Long enough to make a well-traveled path from his back door to hers. "What do you recommend?"

"Marshview Realty has a property management component for our clients. We could oversee the repairs for you, be your agent in all dealings with the contractors."

"You want to work for me?"

"I'm running a real estate business here. I'd like your listing when you put your place up for sale. Landing the property management account is my way of proving myself to you."

He tapped his fingers together. If she worked for him, he'd have reason to call her. He liked that idea.

A lot. He envisioned future business meetings in cozy settings.

"What are your rates?"

She mentioned a fee that sounded reasonable. "What time frame are we talking about here?" he asked.

"Depends. The higher estimate of the two tree limb removal companies has an earlier opening in their schedule. They can get the limb off by the end of next week. If you prefer the other company, it's a two week delay before they can get a crane in there."

"A crane?"

"That's a big limb on your roof. If it's not handled right, it could do more damage on its way down."

"So, putting a couple of my guys on the roof with ropes is a bad idea?"

"Definitely. The remaining shingles are a safety hazard to a nonprofessional. Trust me, you need a pro for this job."

It made sense to fix everything up. It made even more sense to leave it all in her capable hands. "It's a deal. Do you have papers for me to sign?"

She did. He signed her business contract and felt better than he had in days. This seduction would be a piece of cake.

"One more thing." She handed him a copy of all the paperwork. "It's been dry lately, but the Weather Channel is calling for rain early next week. It would be a good idea to put plastic sheeting up in your attic."

"I'll bet you have a plan." The corners of his lips turned up. Mac thumped his tail on the carpet. Man and dog were on the same wavelength. He could gaze into Roxie's compelling turquoise eyes for hours at a time.

She nodded. "I do. My brother is home for the weekend. We can help you install the plastic. Do you have a staple gun?"

"No." He owned a hammer and some screw drivers but they were back at his Atlanta condo. It probably would have been a good idea to bring them since he was in the home repair mode. But thoughts of Roxie had crowded tools from his thoughts when he'd left home five hours ago.

"I have one. Why don't you swing by the home repair store over in Brunswick and get two rolls of plastic sheeting and some buckets? Timmy and I will bring the staples and our staple gun after I close up here this afternoon."

"Buckets? I thought the plastic would keep the water out."

She smiled. "The buckets are your insurance policy. If you have them, there's a good chance you won't need them. But if you don't have them, you're sure to need one right in the middle of a downpour."

"Gotcha."

****

Sloan admired the way the curve-hugging denim showcased Roxie's assets. His gaze lingered on her shapely legs as she climbed the attic stairs. He'd had dreams this past week about those legs, dreams that had his libido rising.

Timmy followed him up the ladder. Her brother had her dark hair, slender frame, and her height, but the family similarity ended there. While Roxie was open and friendly, Timmy had a permanent chip on his shoulder.

The more he watched Roxie, the more Timmy glared at him. The situation would have been amusing if it hadn't bothered Roxie. She seemed genuinely agitated at her brother's hostility, so Sloan tried not to be a jerk.

It wasn't easy. There were so many ways he could yank her brother's chain. He knew the soul-searching Timmy was going through because he'd walked in those shoes once upon a time.

He understood what it was like to feel the world rushing past you while you were standing still. Roxie couldn't help her take-charge tendencies, but her unflappable self-assurance was part of her brother's problem.

"I'm hoping you and Mac will come over for dinner tonight, Sloan," Roxie said.

He'd hoped to finagle a dinner invitation out of her. That lowcountry boil she'd cooked last weekend had been delicious. "Sure. Appreciate the invite. Can I bring anything?"

"No. I have everything under control. Stuffed flounder okay with you?"

His mouth watered. "Sounds good."

After she showed them what to do, she edged toward the steps. "I'm going home to cook dinner. Will you two be all right here?"

Part of her brother's problem stemmed from her calling him a boyish name. "Tim and I will be just fine," Sloan said.

Her brother gave Sloan an odd look, then nodded in agreement. As soon as she left, Tim lit into him. "Roxie's not used to guys like you. I don't want her to get hurt."

Interesting. The pup thought he could tell Sloan what to do. "Roxie and I are friends. She's also my property manager."

"I saw the way you looked at her," Tim charged. "It's a wonder her shoes didn't catch on fire."

Time to change the subject. "So, what do you do when you're not in jail?"

"Hey, that was a one-time thing." Tim pulled the plastic taut as Sloan shot a staple into his attic rafters. "I didn't like jail, and I'm not planning to go back. And my name is Timmy."

"Tim sounds like a man on his way in the world. Timmy sounds like a boy still tied to his sister's apron strings."

Tim released the roll of plastic, and the sheeting sagged down on his head. He tore his way through it, ripping an entire panel from the sloped ceiling. "I'm not a boy, damn you. College is Roxie's idea and I hate it, even though I got a full ride. I don't want to be an old fart stuck in an office like you. I want to live. See the world."

Sloan knew what it felt like to be out of sync with the world. To feel like the only sandpiper in a flock of pelicans. Lavinia had given him an opportunity to make something of himself. He'd be remiss if he didn't pass her wisdom along to her kin.

"Have you thought about joining the Army?" He bundled the ruined plastic in his arms and set it aside.

"Heck no. Roxie would have a cow."

Roxie would not appreciate the advice he was giving her brother, but Sloan couldn't stand by and watch the boy self-destruct. He'd deal with the fallout later.

"I joined the Army when I was your age. It took me to countries I'd only dreamed of, but it's not for everyone."

Tim picked up a corner of the black plastic and smoothed it out. "You saying I'm not man enough?"

"I'm saying the Army is more structured than college. You'll have less control over what you do, but your effort counts. Doing your job makes it possible for someone else to do their job. What is it you like to do?"

Tim appeared to study the nail pattern on the underside of the sloped roof. "I like working with my hands, doing stuff like this."

"Then it wouldn't hurt to talk to an Army recruiter. There's one in Atlanta that's not too far from your school. I could give him a call if you like."

"No, thanks. If I decide on the Army, I'll do it my

way," Tim said. "And Sloan?"

"Yeah?"

"I meant what I said about my sister. Treat her right or leave her alone. She deserves the best."

"Understood."

Chapter 5

Timmy and Sloan's sudden camaraderie at dinner puzzled Roxie. Earlier, the testosterone in Sloan's attic had been thick as morning fog on the marsh.

She chewed the moist fish, half-listening to the football conversation. What had happened up in that attic? Had Timmy given Sloan the attitude he gave her these days? The thought of her slight, goofy brother taking on a tough, athletic man like Sloan was comical. A smile lifted the corners of her lips.

"Hey, where'd you go?" Sloan's brown eyes twinkled at her. "Penny for your thoughts."

"I was thinking how nicely you two were getting along. Nothing like working with tools to facilitate male bonding."

"I don't know if it was the tools or the instructions," he said. "Nothing like a woman telling a man what to do, right, Tim?"

"Hey! I made some suggestions based on my experience. You could have done it any way you saw fit. You didn't have to do it my way.

Timmy nodded solemnly. "I especially liked the part where you showed me how to use my staple gun."

Roxie gritted her teeth. The entire universe of free-thinkers hated organized people.

She carefully aligned her fork and knife on her plate and changed the subject. "Would you care for dessert? I have an apple pie in the fridge."

Timmy's face reddened. "About that pie…"

He trailed off and her stomach sank. "You

didn't."

"I did."

Roxie took a peek. Under the opaque plastic of her refrigerated pie keeper sat one lone sliver of pie. "When did this happen?" she asked.

"This morning. I needed something to wash down the cheese crackers I ate for breakfast. When I opened the fridge, the pie called my name. I left you a piece."

Mac came over and sniffed the open refrigerator. When he started licking the bowl of leftover crab au gratin, Roxie shooed him away and closed the door. "Timmy, why didn't you tell me? If I'd known, I would have baked something else for dessert."

Sloan carried his plate to the sink. "No big deal. We'd be spoiled rotten if we got dessert at every meal."

Her brother looked longingly at the refrigerator. "Does this mean I can eat the last piece too?"

"It does not. That piece is mine," she retorted hotly. "Or Sloan's, if he wants it. You had your dessert already."

"Dinner was great." Sloan nodded toward Timmy. "I saw a hoop out back. Want to play a little one on one?"

"Heck, yeah," her brother said. "Let me change out of my sandals. I'll be right back."

After Timmy sped from the room, Roxie was aware of the gleam of interest in Sloan's gaze. What was going through his head? Was her inclination toward friendliness blurring the lines of their business relationship?

She stacked dishes in her arms and carried them over to sink. Sloan followed with two empty bowls. "I can get these," she said to fill the awkward silence.

"I want to help."

She watched him out of the corner of her eye.

His quick, jerky motions suggested to her he was also on edge. Great. She made him nervous. What kind of business associates made each other nervous?

Regardless, he looked good in her kitchen. Her collection of hand-painted blue pottery interspersed with whimsical wooden cows were the perfect foil for his austere leanness. Her gaze traveled down to the gleaming vinyl floor where Mac watched her every move.

Another long second ticked by. She had to say something. "Did you and Timmy have a long talk or something?"

"Or something."

"He doesn't seem angry anymore. What did you say to him?"

Sloan held his silence for another heart-stopping moment. "We talked about his future."

She transferred the remaining stuffing into a smaller bowl, sealing it with plastic wrap. Why was he holding out on her? Why didn't he say what they'd talked about? This was her brother, for goodness sake. "And?"

"Tim needs to find his own way."

"His name is Timmy." With Gran gone, Timmy was one of the few constants in her life. Couldn't Sloan see that by changing Timmy's name he was taking her little brother away from her?

Sloan's hand covered hers. Awareness sparkled between them, jazzing her skin from tip to toe. "Give him a chance. Tim needs to figure this out for himself."

With effort Roxie focused on their conversation. "But Timmy keeps making mistakes. What if he gets hurt?"

"He'll learn. He knows you care. What he doesn't know is who he is. Allow him the space to find that out. Otherwise he'll wake up in midlife and be an extremely bitter man."

With that, she came to her senses, reclaimed her tingling hand, and glanced sharply at him. "Sounds like you're speaking from experience."

"Believe me, my childhood was nothing like Tim's."

Before she could reply, her brother poked his shaggy head in the doorway, a wide grin on his lean face. "Ready? I'm going to wipe the court with you."

"Not a chance, Tim. There's plenty of life left in this old man."

Roxie watched them play from the kitchen window as she did the dishes. Giving Timmy the personal space he needed wouldn't be easy. As it was, she wanted to be out there with them right now, helping him beat Sloan.

Sloan Harding. What were the chances he'd be in her life after their business dealings were done?

Deep within her were stirrings she'd never felt before.

Scary things, stirrings.

They tapped right into her romantic dreams of marrying Mr. Right, of starting her own family. It was rather like wading through muddy water, praying the gators were full, and hoping you didn't fall in a mud hole. There was danger in muddy water, but sometimes a girl had to take a risk. Especially when she knew her heart's desire wasn't on this side of the water.

She wanted a happily ever after. Trouble was, she had no idea what Sloan wanted.

In the past, her relationships had turned friendly and platonic after a date or two. How could she keep that from happening with Sloan?

****

The tarnished medals resting on the pock-marked kitchen table were grim reminders of his granddad's heroism. Overhead, a fluorescent light hummed as Sloan studied the U.S. Army decorations. It was a miracle any of these had survived his father's pawning fever.

Before his old man had died, he'd sold everything that wasn't nailed down. All of Sloan's grandmother's antiques. Gone. All of his granddad's rifles. Gone. All the pictures and mirrors on the walls. Gone.

And for what?

The money had been spent on booze. As a teen, Sloan had been hell-bent on getting out of Mossy Bog as soon as possible. The day he left the Bug he'd made a vow to never return.

"Anybody home?"

Mac trotted over to the back screen door and wagged his tail at his visitor. Sloan recognized the deep voice. "Come in, Tim. Door's open."

Sloan gathered up his granddad's belongings and returned them to the trunk. He needed to go through these things again later. Something about the heart-shaped medal nagged at him, something he couldn't quite put his finger on.

Tim burst into the tiny kitchen with zestful energy Sloan envied. Playing basketball with Tim yesterday had shown him how slow he'd become. At one time, he would have wiped the courts with Tim. As it was, they'd played to a draw.

"Are those Army medals?" Tim asked. "Are they yours?"

At the wonder and awe in the young man's voice, Sloan laid the medals back out on the stained table. "These were my granddad's."

"Cool. May I touch them?"

Sloan didn't want to deny Roxie's brother, but these medals were precious to him. "They're all I have left of my granddad. That and this house he built."

"I'll be careful."

Tim picked up each medal in turn. "I've never seen anything like this. These are so awesome. What did your granddad do to get all these?"

Sloan could easily fill the rest of the afternoon and most of the evening with his granddad's war stories. Tim needed the condensed version or his eyes would glaze over. "In World War II, he saved his unit even though he was injured. Granddad was a hero."

It felt good to say those words. For so long, he'd been angry with his granddad. Scott Harding's passing had changed Sloan's life. Overnight, he'd gone from having a loving caretaker to living with a vengeful drunk.

"Did you earn medals like this when you were in the Army?"

Sloan shook his head. "I fought in a different war with a much different mission. No Purple Heart, Medal of Honor, or Distinguished Service Cross for me."

"But you could have been a hero if you'd had the opportunity. Your granddad's heroism runs through your veins." Tim rubbed his thumb over the bronze eagle on the Distinguished Service Cross. "You should frame these or something."

"Someday." When he forgave his granddad for dying on him. "Are you thirsty? I have soft drinks in the cooler."

Tim shoved his hands in his jean pockets and stood stiffly. "No, thanks. I'm heading back to Georgia Tech in a few minutes. I came over to tell you I thought about what you said."

He'd said a lot of things. Sloan rose and looked Tim square in the eye. "What's this about, Tim?"

"You were right. I need to figure out who I am. College isn't doing it for me. I'm taking your advice and finding out about the Army. I'd like to earn medals like these."

Sloan swallowed roughly. The Army was great for some, a disaster for others. With any luck, Tim would sail through his hitch without facing enemy gunfire.

He'd seen the love Roxie bore for her brother. Seen it and yearned to have someone care that much about him. Roxie wouldn't want Tim in harm's way. She expected her brother to stay in college. Had he overstepped by advising Tim to do something that might endanger him?

"Why don't you finish up this semester and see how you feel about college?" he hedged. "The Army has a lot of rules and regulations. It's not for everyone."

"Hey, don't try to talk me out of it. My mind's made up. I hate college. I'm going to talk to the Army recruiter and explore my options."

"Fair enough." Sloan extended his hand, and Tim shook it with confidence. Sloan grinned. For better or worse, Roxie's little brother was on his way to manhood.

****

A yellow boat appeared in her yard Monday afternoon. Roxie hurried from Miss Daisy to see it, wonder and disbelief guiding her steps. For years she'd dreamed of owning one of these.

The kayak was made of a heavy plastic, with two seats. Clipped to the sides were two paddles. Propped in each seat were adult-sized lifejackets, one red, the other blue.

"What the—?" Roxie unclipped a double-ended paddle and held it crossways in her hands, marveling at the feel of it. She could probably paddle for miles with this thing without tiring.

The bright red lifejacket, or PFD, as the tag said, fit perfectly. With child-like joy, she climbed in the boat and air paddled. Delight crashed into logic and lost its rosy glow.

Gifts didn't magically appear. This wasn't her boat. She scanned the vicinity, looking deep into the scary shadows, sure that a camera crew would jump out and yell "surprise", but she saw no one.

If she'd been made of money, this is what she would have bought herself. But she was barely making ends meet, and thanks to her identity theft, her credit was in a shambles. No way would she have dropped over a thousand dollars on a deluxe recreational item like this.

She checked all around the kayak. No tag. No store receipt or other identifying information. No nothing.

The nearest store that sold boats like this was in Savannah, an hour's drive from here. Had it been delivered to her by mistake?

The starch went out of her afternoon at the thought. Now that the boat was here, she wanted to keep it. Glancing up, she saw the shadows had lengthened across the yard. The hair on the back of her neck stirred.

She gulped. Ever since the break-in she'd been careful not to be alone outside in the dark. Now the path to her door was drenched in shadows. Shrugging out of the lifejacket, she groped in her purse for the flashlight.

Reassuring light flicked on, but the sensation that someone was watching her didn't go away.

"Who's there?"

She angled the light around her, touching on all the hiding places. Nothing. Not even a squirrel.

This had to stop. Real estate brokers couldn't afford to be scared of the dark.

I'm not afraid. She chanted the phrase under her breath until she believed it. Methodically, she gathered her things and locked Miss Daisy. She would not let fear rule her life.

Safely inside, she called the Savannah kayak

store. "Sorry," the clerk said. "We've had no recent deliveries to Mossy Bog, and we haven't sold an Ocean Kayak in weeks."

"I don't understand," Roxie said. "How could a boat just appear in my yard?"

"Maybe you have a secret admirer or someone sent you an early Christmas present."

Sloan? Would he have sent her a boat? The idea sparkled with possibilities, but the more she thought about it, the less likely it was. She'd only known him for a week, and they'd never once talked about kayaking. In fact, she couldn't remember talking to anyone about kayaking in the last year.

How odd.

To be on the safe side, she called the city police. While she was waiting, she called her credit card company to see if it had been charged to her account. It hadn't. A knot of uncertainty formed in her stomach. What was going on here?

Laurie Ann Dinterman showed up a few minutes later with a mega-watt flood light. She whistled appreciatively at the kayak. "You got a brand new boat you didn't order?"

"Weird, I know. What should I do?"

"Nothing, I guess. If we hear of anyone missing a boat, we'll send them your way."

"Thanks. But don't look too hard for the boat's owners. I really like it, even if it reminds me of a giant banana. How could someone misplace a treasure like this?"

Laurie Ann shrugged, then snapped pictures of the items for her incident report. "I've seen a bit of everything in this job. Maybe it's cosmic payback for the break-in and identity theft. You deserve to have some fun. I'll be glad to help you break it in."

"You're on, but let's give it a week or so. Surely someone will notice they're missing a brand new boat by then."

"Deal."

****

By Wednesday noon, the bright red and blue plastic buckets in Sloan's dark attic were half-full of rain water. Good thing she'd stopped by to check on them. The forecast called for two more days of showers and with the weather out of the northeast, they'd surely get hammered. The buckets would be overflowing before Sloan returned if someone didn't empty them daily.

That someone was Roxie.

She wanted Sloan to be pleased with her property management services. Although Marshview Realty wasn't a national chain like her cross-town rival, BC Realty, her company provided a full array of real estate services.

Home sales were nice, but sporadic in Mossy Bog. People didn't move all that much, not like in the city. Property management was the way to go for security.

She lugged the first two buckets down the rickety stairs to the upstairs bathroom and dumped them in the rust-stained toilet. Her discerning eye saw that the sink faucet had a steady drip. The sagging shower curtain rod needed to be replaced, the torn shower curtain burned immediately. The loose tiles by the tub needed new grouting.

If Sloan did list this place with Marshview Realty, she'd insist on a good cleaning service and staging improvements before they made it available for viewing. The floor plan was similar to Gran's house, with big open rooms and ten-foot ceilings downstairs that lent a feeling of spaciousness unique to older homes. In the right person's hands, this place could be transformed into a beautiful living space.

How would she advertise this house? A jewel in the rough? Centrally located cozy cottage?

Commuter-friendly charmer? Adorable starter home?

Her cell phone rang. She patted the pockets of her trench coat until she found her phone and pulled it out. She had transferred her office line to her cell phone while she was running errands. "Marshview Realty," she answered.

"Roxie? Is that you?" a raspy female voice asked.

Noreen Bagwell, her adversary on City Council, was a longtime "almost" customer of Marshview Realty. "Hello, Mrs. Bagwell. What can I do for you today?

"I want to talk to you about putting Widow's Peak on the market."

Roxie groaned inwardly. Every year or two, Noreen Bagwell talked about putting her monstrosity of a house up for sale. In the past, Gran had accommodated the elderly Mrs. Bagwell. Roxie took it as a good sign Gran's friend was talking to her instead of the competition. After the museum fiasco, Noreen could be listing her place with Sally Doleman over at BC Realty. "I'd be delighted to see you. What about tomorrow or Friday?"

"Too soon. I have an opening in my schedule for the end of next week."

Roxie tried to imagine what was on her calendar and couldn't. "How does lunch next Thursday sound?"

"Heavens! I can't commit to a time right now. Too many things in flux, you know. I'll call you next week."

"You let me know the exact date and time, and I will be there. Meanwhile, I'll pull up comparables and bring them out with me."

"Comparables? Dearie, I don't bother with those. If my price doesn't suit, then it's just too bad."

Knowing Noreen, the price would be too high. Who had several million dollars to spend on a place around here? Not many locals, that was for sure. However, there was an entire universe of people on the Internet Roxie could market to. In her spare time.

Roxie pocketed her cell phone, shivering in the dampness of Sloan's shadowed attic. If she found a buyer for Noreen Bagwell's rambling architectural monstrosity, it would be headline news in the weekly paper. Ah well, she'd get to Noreen soon enough.

Right now she had Sloan's leaking roof to deal with. The tree service would be here on Friday, weather permitting, and she'd get them to secure a tarp over the hole once the limb was removed. Until then, she had to deal with Sloan and Timmy's bizarre plastic creation.

She stared at the drooping black plastic and wished she'd brought the staple gun with her. Trust them to think they'd done a good job. At least some water funneled into the buckets.

Dodging the low-hanging crossbeam by the stairs, Roxie lugged the last two buckets of water down to the bathroom, dumped the water, and returned the buckets to the attic.

What could she do to help Sloan make the house more livable? A fresh coat of paint inside and out would be a great improvement. The idea grabbed hold of her. She could help Sloan paint his house on the weekends.

She stood there listening to the steady plink plink plink of rain falling in the buckets. Was she being honest with herself? Was it Sloan's real estate she coveted or Sloan? His touch had awakened her to a whole new world.

He fascinated her. In Sloan, she saw danger, excitement, and sensuality. A pirate of the first order.

"I want him."

She clapped a hand over her mouth, surprised

by her admission. She'd devoted her entire life to helping others, living through them. Now she wanted to experience life firsthand. With Sloan.

Fancy that.

She adjusted the buckets under the plastic sheeting and headed downstairs. Living in this run-down cottage with a drunken father must have been terrible. Was that why Sloan had settled so far from Mossy Bog? To escape the memories?

She double-checked the locks and windows before she left. The window over the sink wasn't quite closed.

Her nerves skittered like oil in the hot pan of her emotions. She stilled and listened to the house. Was someone in here with her?

A shiver ripped down her spine. "Hello?"

No answer.

Fear cascaded through her head as adrenaline juiced her system. *Run like hell*, she thought, glancing around the murky room.

Heart racing, she jogged to the front door. Her hand was on the knob when reason returned. The house had been locked when she'd arrived. It was still locked. She'd been in every room. There were no creepy crawly people hiding under the bed.

She drew in a deep breath. That felt good. Sunlight bathed the foyer. She was safe.

It was only an open window.

Seven different contractors had been in here since Monday. One of them might have cracked the window.

Or it could be her intruder.

She walked through the rooms again, searching for anything that might be out of place. Nothing jumped out at her, though the spare roll of toilet tissue was on the opposite side of the bathroom cabinet. One drawer in the kitchen wasn't pushed in all the way.

Something?

Or nothing?

Laurie Ann would think she was an alarmist if that's all she had. Without any real evidence of a break-in, the cops would have nothing but her say-so. Which didn't seem to be worth much these days, with her jumping at every noise.

Resolutely, she pulled the window shut and locked it. An old Army trunk rested beside the chipped Formica table. An envelope poked out of the back side of the trunk. She raised the lid to slip the envelope back inside. A dusty sneeze caught her off guard and lifted the envelope up to reveal a man's jewelry box beside an old cigar box.

Roxie smiled. Family papers and keepsakes filled the trunk. They had to mean the world to Sloan. At least all his memories weren't bad. She reverently closed the lid.

Was Sloan searching for his roots? Or was he a true buccaneer—all alone in a hostile world? Either way, she longed to soothe his hurts.

And more.

****

Sloan tapped his thumbs against the steering wheel to the rollicking beat of "Rambling Man" by The Allman Brothers Band as he sped east. Nothing like vintage rock and roll to ease the miles between Atlanta and Mossy Bog. Thoughts of kissing Roxie had plagued him all week. No woman had interfered with his work before.

"I'm not doing this her way," he said to Mac, who lounged in the passenger seat.

His dog cocked his head in interest when Sloan spoke.

"She thinks she has me figured out, that she can tide me over with seafood and baked goods, but I'm more than an empty stomach. I want more from a woman than that."

Mac's tongue lolled to one side.

"You don't say much do you, boy?" Sloan rubbed the flat part of Mac's head and then noticed his hand was coated with dog hair. He released the loose hair outside his open window. "Don't shed in her office. We're trying to make a good impression. We're going to be so smooth she won't be able to resist us. Understood?"

He'd rescheduled his Friday afternoon appointments for next week because he couldn't wait to see her. He reached in the cup holder in the center console, picked up her business card, and sniffed the faint vanilla fragrance.

Mac caught the scent from the card. His tail wagged. Sloan ruffled the dog's head again and laughed. "You know where we're going, boy?"

She was on the phone in her cozy office when he parked next to her burnished red Cadillac DeVille. No one else was in the office. Good. He had her to himself.

Her brunette hair was pulled back in its customary ponytail with dark wisps cascading about her glowing face. The forest green shirt she wore clung to her curves and made him think of lolling his tongue like his dog.

Sloan tossed his sunglasses on the dash. Blood pounded in his ears as if he'd just run a marathon. At least he hadn't come empty-handed. He reached into the cooler in the back and withdrew the red roses he'd bought in Atlanta. After raising the windows about four inches, he shut off the engine. "Wait here," he told his dog.

Mac whined. "I get her first," Sloan said. "Stay."

Roses in hand, Sloan strode inside her office. With each step he felt lighter, happier.

"I'll call you back, Noreen." Roxie waved him forward.

He took that as a green light. "I missed you."

When he veered around her wooden desk, she backed up toward the rear wall of file cabinets.

"I wasn't expecting you until tomorrow."

He stopped when his wingtips touched her penny loafers. "I was able to leave sooner than I thought."

Her eyes widened into shimmering tropical pools. He inhaled deeply, filling his lungs with her essence. He fitted his hands to her waist and drew her close. "I've been thinking of you all week."

His forehead touched hers. He'd implode if she didn't give him a green light. "I'm dying to kiss you, Roxie Whitaker."

With a soft sigh, she mouthed his name. He moved right in, covering her rosy lips with his. A sense of rightness swept through him as he tasted her. She yielded to him, to his immense satisfaction.

He buried his hands in her thick hair, dislodging the band securing her ponytail. Her vanilla scent filled his head. As his fingers caressed the satiny skin on the nape of her neck, her soft curves pressed against him. Desire thrummed through his veins.

She wanted him.

He could practically taste her ambrosia-sweet passion. When her hands tightened on his forearms, strength surged through him. He could have easily jumped over the entire fleet of shrimp trawlers berthed at Mossy Bog's city dock in a single bound.

But he wasn't going anywhere right now.

When he stroked down her spine, she made a small humming sound and arched into him. The sound branded him with white hot need. Definitely a green light. But his timing needed work. In this glass box of an office, they had no privacy.

They definitely needed privacy.

Chapter 6

Roxie was suddenly, exquisitely, aware of nerve endings she never even knew she had. Her body trembled with need, raw and aching. Then everything went haywire as Sloan deepened the kiss.

Her arms stole around his neck, binding him to her. Heat jolted lightning fast through her, an instantaneous, disorienting combustion she craved more than air. Excitement hummed in her veins.

Oh, yes.

Her fingers threaded through his hair, glided across his broad shoulders, and down to his waist, learning the feel of his angles and planes. It wasn't enough. She needed skin. Desperately needed to touch his skin.

She tugged at his oxford dress shirt, trying to dislodge his shirt tail from his slacks, but it wasn't cooperating. Her fingers went to his belt buckle, but his hand caught hers and held it still between them.

She whimpered when he ended the kiss. Her pulse pounded in her ears. She sucked in a breath of cooler air. Then another.

Slowly she became aware of the hum of overhead fluorescent lights, the glare of the setting sun on her glass storefront, the color-coded folders on her desk. Reality jarred harshly, bringing with it a splash of common sense.

Heaven help her.

She'd nearly jumped a client at the office. So much for her professional reputation.

Sloan smiled. "Lady, you are full of surprises."

Heat shifted from her core to her face, flaming

her cheeks. Mercy. What had come over her? She couldn't quite meet his gaze. Then she decided what the heck. She leveled a look at him, intending to say something meaningful.

"Wow."

His eyes glittered with the secrets of the universe. "Did you miss me this week?"

God help her, she wanted those secrets. And she was pretty sure he knew it. "You have to ask after that kiss?"

"That was something all right." He caressed the side of her face.

"I've never lost it like that before." Confused, she backed away from him, her hair spilling across her face. She shoved it out of her way. "I need to think. We have to talk about this."

His glittering gaze followed her over to her desk where she found another ponytail holder. It shot out of her fingers across the room. Dang. She fumbled in her top drawer for another one.

"Why talk when our nonverbal communication works so well?" he asked. "I believe in keeping communication lines open on all fronts."

A nauseating chill snaked through Roxie. She hovered over a sharp precipice. "You kiss all your business associates?"

"Just the pretty ones."

He was flirting with her. After that hot kiss. Worse, he knew she had no self-control where he was concerned. She looked away and fanned her flushed face with Naomi Thompson's Open House flier.

He hadn't pushed hard for a personal relationship with her, but he'd brought her flowers today. Roses.

Her favorite color of roses.

No man had ever brought her roses before.

She scooped them up and pressed them to her

nose. They were gorgeous, and smelled like sultry sunshine languid with decadent essence. She inhaled deeply, filling her lungs with his thoughtfulness and daring to hope he might be the man of her dreams. Only she had no confidence in the realm of passion. It didn't respond to logic or schedules. Like an onrushing storm it roared in, deafening and blinding her to all else. A man who incited these strong sensations was dangerous indeed.

After that kiss, she knew a hidden truth about herself. She craved the danger Sloan Harding offered.

Whoa. Time to exercise some caution.

She met his gaze again. "These for me?"

His eyes darkened. "Like 'em?"

"They're beautiful." She stroked a velvety petal. "Thank you. I'll just...put them in water."

Gran had kept a large vase under the bathroom sink. Roxie found it, added water, stuck the roses in the gilded vase, then placed the loose arrangement on her desk.

With her gaze fixed on the flowers, she asked, "Why did you walk in here and kiss me like that?"

"Don't be afraid of me."

His comment was eerily on point. Was she so transparent? She gathered the shreds of her self-composure and faced him. "Being afraid would mean I had common sense. After that kiss, I'm not sure I have any left. Answer my question. Why did you kiss me like that?"

"I like kissing you."

As answers went, it wasn't half bad. But it didn't tell her anything new. This situation felt off-balance.

"This isn't a good idea." She circled her desk to put a physical barrier between them. "I manage your property. I don't want to jeopardize our working relationship. I need your business."

He frowned and edged closer. "That kiss had chemistry written all over it."

She managed a weak smile. "You may live in the world of chemistry, but I don't. Real estate is my world. I have obligations and responsibilities that I can't ignore. To be honest, chemistry scares the hell out of me."

"Not a problem. We'll keep it separate. You manage the business aspect. I'll manage the chemistry."

"Won't there be friction if the chemistry fizzles?"

"It might. That's a risk we both take. You'll have to trust me as I'm trusting you."

She chewed her lip. He hadn't done anything to cause her not to trust him. She'd been the one going crazy in his arms. Gran had believed in Sloan. Maybe she could too. "Okay."

He nodded and came closer. "Where are we on the property management side of things anyway?"

At last, a subject she was familiar with. "The tree people are at your house right now. The roofers are coming next week. I wondered if you might be interested in painting your house. I could help you get started this weekend."

"Good idea. Are we talking inside or out?"

"Both, but it's supposed to be wet off and on through the weekend. We could start inside if you like."

"What color did you have in mind?"

"Neutral colors work best for decorating and resale, but anything would be a vast improvement over what you've got now."

"Is there a paint store around here?"

"Still only one place for paint in Mossy Bog. Barry's Hardware. If you want a wider selection, you have to go to Brunswick."

He tucked his hand underneath her arm. "No

point in leaving town when we've got Barry's. Let's go."

Roxie held up her hand, wishing her pulse wasn't racing from his touch. "Not so fast. I have a client meeting this evening. Why don't you lay in the supplies? I'll pop over bright and early in the morning."

His face tightened. Her stomach twisted in response. Did he expect her to spend every free moment with him when he was in town? If so, he should think again. Real estate wasn't a nine-to-five job.

"You're not coming with me?"

"No need. Your choices at Barry's are white, taupe, and custard yellow. I'm partial to the yellow as you can see from these walls, but any color would work."

"I'm on my own tonight?"

"Afraid so."

She heard a thin sound she couldn't quite place. It sounded siren-like, varying in duration and pitch. "What's that noise?"

He nodded toward his black Jeep. "Mac says hello."

His dog. How could she have forgotten about Mac? Good thing she'd bought two boxes of dog biscuits this week and stashed one at the office.

"Excuse me."

Dog biscuit in hand, she went out to make amends.

****

Sleep had eluded Sloan. Nothing seemed straightforward this morning. Roxie had come over to help paint his living room as promised, but working beside her only aggravated his hunger for her.

She belonged with him.

In his bed.

Couldn't she see that?

Had she invented a client meeting to keep him off-balance? He had thought about driving around Mossy Bog until he found her red vintage caddy, but that sounded desperate. He wasn't that far gone on the lust train, but it galled him he'd misread the situation so badly.

He dabbed the roller in the paint tray and got a pleasing eyeful of her jean shorts as she bent to pick up a paint rag. She was cutting in the trim as he rolled out the walls.

He'd bought five gallons of the custard yellow paint because that was the color she preferred. She hummed along with the radio she'd brought. Top forty stuff. Not his first choice, but it beat nothing.

"Thanks again for the flowers," she said. "I put them on my kitchen table. They really brighten up the place. My whole house smells like roses."

"You're welcome." He'd hoped she would put them in her bedroom so he'd be the first and last thing on her mind. Silence weighed heavily on his shoulders. He cast about for another topic. "How did your meeting go last night?"

"Great. I listed a new property from a man who's relocating to Jacksonville. I'm thrilled to get it. You wouldn't have any interest in a three thousand square foot historic property close to the center of town, would you?"

"My business is in Atlanta. I don't need two places in Mossy Bog."

"Tell me about yourself, Sloan. What things do you like?"

"Motorcycles, women, and rock and roll."

She paused. "Oh. Should I change the radio station?"

Sloan rolled out an X on the wall and then filled the mark in with a few quick extensions of his wrist. "I like hearing you sing."

"I'm not singing. I'm humming along. There's a difference. Any chance you're into boating?"

"I didn't have many boating opportunities as a kid, and I haven't pursued it since I got out of the Army. Why do you ask?"

"The strangest thing happened this week. A bright yellow kayak appeared in my yard." She glanced at him over her shoulder. "I wondered if you sent it."

Sloan's hand jerked. He missed the paint tray with the roller, recovered, and reloaded it with paint. "It wasn't me. Do you like it?"

"I love it. I've wanted a kayak for a long time. There are so many places to paddle around here, but I never would have bought one for myself. A friend gave me a paddling magazine not too long back, and I've about worn it out, looking at it and dreaming."

"Have you taken it out?"

"Not yet. I want to, but I keep thinking the boat police will swoop in and arrest me. I don't want to get the big banana dirty if it belongs to someone else. It's got to be a mistake."

"A mistake?" His gut tightened.

"Like it was delivered to the wrong address. I called the store in Savannah that carries this brand, but they didn't know anything about it."

"I could look into it if you like."

The sharp look she sent him inspired him to explain. "Team Six Security does investigations like this."

"I don't want to trouble you. I filed a police report; that should suffice."

"It's no trouble." He very much wanted to know where the boat came from. The idea of someone else plying Roxie with expensive gifts didn't sit well with him.

After a few moments of painting, Roxie said, "I saw you brought that old trunk down from the attic.

Are we painting it as well?"

"No. I've been going through my granddad's papers. Did you know he built this house himself?"

"He did a good job. This place has great bones." They painted in silence through another pop song. "What's your favorite memory of your granddad?"

Her question took Sloan back in time. In his head, he saw his granddad sitting in this room, pocket knife in hand as he whittled away at a piece of wood. "I remember him sitting over there by the window, carving that chess set. He always said that chess set would be mine one day. I never knew he planned to leave the house to me as well."

"It must have been quite a shock when he died."

"Quite a shock," he repeated neutrally.

"What about your dad?"

His father was a closed chapter in his life, and he planned to keep it that way. "He wasn't into the social scene."

"Who is? This is Mossy Bog we're talking about."

Sloan realized he'd been staring at her again instead of painting. It was easy to look at Roxie. He could do it for hours and never tire of looking at her long, shapely legs. He would blow this if he didn't get her talking about something besides his family. "How about your parents? I don't remember them."

"Mom and Dad are two peas in a pod. They thrive on doing without. Timmy says it's a treat for them to have running water, and he's right. They live to help people."

"You help people."

"Not like my parents. They teach people how to read. They teach them life skills. They help put food on people's tables. I don't come close to that level of helping."

"Nobody said you had to. You have your own way of doing things."

"I never thought of it like that." She stopped

painting and turned to look at him. "Are you still mad at me for being busy last night?"

"Mad?" Sloan tossed his roller in the paint tray. "What makes you think I'm mad?"

"You've been scowling at me all morning."

Because she'd bustled in and started painting right away. She hadn't so much as kissed him on the cheek when she came in. Mac had gotten a warmer welcome than he did.

"You forgot to kiss me when you came in."

She straightened. "No, I didn't. You said you'd handle the personal side. Tell you the truth, I'm disappointed you didn't kiss me. Now I'm thinking these boundaries we set are too rigid. Why can't we relax and allow things to happen as they will?"

"In that case, let's see if we can't put a smile on both our faces." He reached for her.

She thrust her paint brush at him as if it were a sword. "Wait a sec. You already missed the hello-kiss opportunity. I have reservations about anything more at this point. I want to spend time with you and get to know you. Can we agree to that?"

"Sure," he grinned wickedly, taking a custard yellow stripe on the center of his shirt. Wet paint didn't bother him at all. Not when there was a sexy woman involved. "You can have all the time you want as long as I can kiss you."

Her incredible blue green eyes widened as his lips brushed against hers. He released her, noticing that she had a matching brush-shaped paint stripe on her lavender tee shirt. Whistling to himself, he walked back to his paint tray.

He picked up his paint-laden roller. "What do you hear from your brother these days?"

Her brush slapped against the trim. "Not much. Hopefully, he's bringing his grades up."

Sloan was certain Tim was spending time in the Army recruiter's office, but he wasn't going to volunteer that information. He glanced over at her when he noticed she'd stopped painting.

"What?" she asked. "What do you know? Oh God. Has he run off and joined the circus?"

"The circus? Whatever gave you that idea?"

"Timmy's adventurous. One summer he broke his arm after rigging a rope ten feet above the hammock and trying to walk across the rope. He fell, of course, right into the hammock, but his arm was at an odd angle. Mom and Dad were horrified and took down the hammock, but that wasn't the end of Timmy's adventures."

Tim sounded like the kid brother Sloan had always wanted. "What else did he do?"

"You name it, Timmy did it. One summer he took all of our shoes and threw them up in a tree. That wouldn't have been so bad except he did it right before a thunderstorm. He wanted to see it raining shoes."

The edges of his lips turned up. "And?"

"Our shoes got ruined. Mom said she didn't need more than one pair of shoes, but Dad was livid. He was barefoot at the time, so his favorite pair of shoes were in the tree."

"What did he do?"

"He gave Timmy a stern lecture, then he sent us to stay with Gran for two weeks. He said we both needed closer supervision."

Sloan rolled out a long stripe of custard yellow paint on the wall. If he'd done something like that, his father wouldn't have noticed his shoes were missing. The only thing he would have missed would have been a full liquor bottle. "Banished to Lavinia's house? That's a reward, not a punishment."

She laughed. "My dad's pretty great. I think he did it so that he wouldn't yell at Timmy. Even then, Timmy marched to his own drum. Gran let him build forts with all her living room cushions, and once, we covered a whole bedroom with fake spider webs. Gran helped us. We used every spool of thread and wove the most intricate mess ever. I don't know how she ever got that cleaned up."

"Lavinia was special," he said.

In Roxie's voice he heard her fondness for each of her family members. He'd give anything to have a family like that.

He'd just as soon forget his father ever lived. He didn't remember his mother or his grandmother. They'd both abandoned their husbands as soon as possible. His only fond family memories were of his granddad, and there weren't nearly enough good times to balance the years of misery with his father.

"Gran and Pop Pop both were special people," Roxie said. "Pop Pop taught me how to ride my bike. I'll never forget him running alongside of me, keeping my bike from tipping over. They came to see us everywhere we lived, and it was always wonderful when they visited. Gran cooked up the greatest meals, and Pop Pop always had a story or an idea for an adventure."

Sloan cocked his head in interest. "Stories? Any from his Army days?"

"Shoot yeah. He and his friend Scott did wild things when they were on leave."

Scott was his granddad's name. Did she remember that? He tested the waters. "I've been reading some old family papers. Our grandfathers served together in the Army."

Her face lit up. "That's right. I forgot about that. Did he tell you about the time they ran out of money in some bar and had to sing and wait tables until they paid their tab? Or when they missed their ride back to their unit and hitched a ride with a wagon load of pigs?"

"I'd love to hear your grandfather's version of them."

"Shoot. I can go one better than that. Pop Pop kept a journal. I have it somewhere. I'll dig it out for you to read."

"I'd appreciate that," Sloan answered neutrally, amazed he sounded so calm. That journal might contain a lead to the missing money.

"My granddad didn't keep a journal. His papers are a mess, but you're welcome to look at them if you like. You don't mind if I read your grandfather's journal?"

"I wouldn't dream of keeping it from you. There's information in there about your granddad, and I can see he means a lot to you."

If she only knew. There was no trace of the missing fortune in his grandfather's haphazard records. Not yet anyway. He approached the subject cautiously. "Did you know that my granddad managed to do something with a large sum of money?"

"He was a philanthropist?"

"Not exactly." Sloan couldn't stand to see the admiration in Roxie's eyes. His granddad wouldn't have given his money away, not even for a good cause. That wasn't granddad's style. His granddad liked to sock money away for a rainy day.

In any event, he didn't want the past tarnishing his chances with Roxie. He couldn't let her assumption about his granddad stand, and especially not when he saw it put stars in her eyes. Hardings weren't starry-eyed types who dedicated their lives to helping others. Hardings were in the game for the money.

"I'm talking about the lost Harding fortune. My dad spent years tearing through the furniture in this house, ripping up floorboards. See those marks on those boards over there? My father pried the floorboards up with a crowbar and would have torn the whole floor out if I hadn't stopped him," he said.

"He was convinced the missing money was hidden in this house, but he never found it. My granddad told my father he couldn't see his nose to spite his face. That the only treasure worth finding was in his heart."

"You mean there's a fortune hidden here somewhere? Like buried treasure? I always assumed it was a legend, like our local sea monster, Mossy Girl."

Sloan stopped painting. "Mossy Girl has gotten plenty of press through the years, even though no one in our generation has ever seen her. But the lost Harding fortune did have a point of origin. There was no money banked when my grandfather died. My father insisted granddad hid it from him, and from there the story grew.

"No one else believed my father's drunken ramblings. Granddad wasn't a rich man, and he could have had unknown expenses that burnt through his savings. But two things keep me from dismissing this outright.

"First, my father was so sure he'd been scammed. He didn't hold fast to many things, but he never wavered on this. Second, if there's any chance my grandfather hid his money, it's mine to find."

"That's why you didn't sell the house before?" Her blue green eyes regarded him expectantly. "Because you needed to come home to find the truth? To uphold your granddad's good name?"

There she went again, putting words in his mouth. He wasn't a saint. He was a Harding. "I don't need the money. My company is doing fine. I have questions about the past, that's all."

"Questions? What kind of questions?"

Why wouldn't she let the subject drop? Did she expect him to admit his father had been crazy? Or that he harbored serious doubts about his granddad's sanity? What sane man hid his estate from his heir?

And if said heir searched for the missing money, was he crazy too?

No way was he admitting all that.

"Never mind," he said firmly, rolling out a long swath of paint on the wall. "Let's talk about something else. Tell me what happened down here this week."

"Megan and Dave called. They've had a great time on their honeymoon."

Having lots of sex, no doubt, Sloan thought morosely. Dave was a lucky man. But what must it be like to commit to spending the rest of your life with one woman?

"They'll be home tomorrow. I've missed having Megan in the office," Roxie continued. "Once she returns, I'll focus on my museum project again."

To his credit, Sloan didn't wince. Thanks to his dad being unofficially blamed for the fire, the museum wasn't a pleasant discussion topic. But it was important to Roxie. He swallowed his reservations. "Didn't you have something with that this week?"

"Sure did. It was a huge disaster. The City Council turned me down. I've been thinking about it, though, and I realize that this is bigger than the city. I should appeal to the County Commissioners. Better yet, if I can get both governing bodies hooked in, along with the Board of Education, I might have enough funding to get started."

"What about other funding sources?"

"Oh, I applied for all kinds of grants. No word on any of that yet."

"What about corporate sponsorship?"

"Haven't tried that yet, but truthfully, our local businesses are generous to a fault. I wouldn't want to take money from any worthy causes they support."

"They give away money to community projects. Who's to say your project isn't as worthy as any of the others? It wouldn't hurt to send out sponsor packages to them and any wealthy citizens in the area."

Her smile brimmed from ear to ear. "That is a very good idea. Two good ideas, I mean. I'll get my Friends group right on that. Thanks."

"You're welcome."

Her sincerity zapped him in the heart. Hard. A lightning strike out of the blue wouldn't have been as startling. He liked Roxie. Enjoyed her company. Wanted to sleep with her. But that was all.

It had to be all. He was a Harding. Women didn't stick with Harding men. The truism had held for three generations now. Logic implied he'd have the same luck as his forebears.

For the first time in years, Sloan found himself wishing for a different last name.

****

The spring festival committee chair showed up at Mossy Bog Carryout in a tank top, shorts, and flip flops for the late afternoon meeting. She had a tow-headed toddler on her hip and a sturdy boy clinging to her leg.

Roxie reached for Jeanie's bulging canvas tote. "Let me get that for you," she said, grateful for the distraction from the spooky shadows under the old oak tree across the parking lot. It seemed dark shadows were her personal boogeyman ever since her house had been ransacked.

"No need. I'm balanced this way." Jeanie nodded to the group seated around the picnic table. "Hi, everyone. Once I get the kids settled, we'll get started."

Crayons came out, as did a sack of toy cars and building blocks. The toddler peeked underneath her mother's arm at the people around the picnic table

96

and then buried her face in Jeanie's chest. It was all Roxie could do to keep from reaching out to ruffle the little girl's fine hair. How innocent she was, free of thoughts of things like identity thieves, burglars, and vandals.

Donna Banks cruised out of Mossy Bog Carryout and placed drinks around the table. "If you need anything else, give me a holler," Donna said with a saucy smile. Roxie sipped her sweet tea and tried to pay attention as the meeting commenced, but her thoughts kept returning to Sloan and the kayak. Would he be able to trace the boat or learn how it ended up in her yard?

"Spring will be here before we know it," Jeanie was saying. Her eyes glowed with the fervor of a true believer. "Our Mossy Girl festival will be the biggest and best ever next year. Roxie joins us as the chair of the vendor committee. I know she can do this with one hand tied behind her back."

The committee clapped its approval. Everyone but Les Green's wisp of a daughter.

Roxie had forgotten Andrea Albert was the art association liaison for the festival committee. She drew in a breath as Andrea shot her a dirty look. Was it possible Andrea was behind her recent misfortune?

No, she hadn't signed on for this festival committee at the time of her break-in. She'd been strong-armed into it by Jeanie the day of Megan's wedding. So why the sour looks from Andrea?

"It's good to be here," she said evenly. "I look forward to working with everyone."

"We love you, Roxie," Brenda Harris said.

Hurschel Barker from the phone company grinned. "Glad to have you on board."

"Three cheers for our favorite realtor," Donna said as she sat beside Roxie.

Buford Pratt, fire chief, tipped his baseball cap

to her. "You hear anything yet about that burglar?"

"Not a thing," Roxie said. "And now I've got this mystery boat in my yard."

"You can give it me," Donna said. "There's nothing I'd like better than to float away from all my troubles."

Jeanie brought the meeting back to order by banging the table with a toy truck. "Since I have the kids with me today, we're going to do this fast. Committee reports everyone, starting with Brenda Harris."

The meeting sped by in a blur. Afterward, Roxie rose to head back to the office, but Donna Banks and Brenda Harris caught her arms and marched her inside Donna's place. They locked the door behind them and flipped the closed sign face out.

"Jeanie couldn't stay, or she'd be in here too." Excitement riddled Donna's voice. "Tell us about the new man. We want juicy details."

"There's not much to tell."

"Give it up, my friend," Brenda said. "We know there's more than that. My uncle said he tried to warn you off, but you were seeing the Harding boy anyway. How bad is he? Inquiring minds want to know."

Brenda's uncle was Chuck Beard, the jolly plumber. Roxie wasn't thinking jolly thoughts about him right now.

Donna shivered dramatically. "Sloan came in on Saturday for carry out, and I practically drooled over him. I was wearing that clingy white shirt, the one with the lace edging, and he didn't even notice. Please tell me he isn't gay."

"He isn't gay."

Brenda chortled and rubbed her hands together. "Did you sleep with him yet? Do those big brown eyes glaze over with passion?"

"I'm not dating him. Well, maybe just a little."

"Can I have him?" Donna said. "I've got a real itch for a bad boy like Sloan Harding."

"He's not mine to give away. But I like him. He seems nice."

"I'm dying here," Brenda said. "You're dating the hottest guy to hit town in ten years, and that's all you've got? Come on, the guy is a legend like his dad."

Her cheeks stung. "Sloan's nothing like his father."

"They say his father got kicked out of every bar south of Savannah." Donna reached behind the counter, snagged three muffins, and tossed one to Roxie and Brenda. "Parents locked up their daughters so Edward Harding couldn't have his way with them. The old man was a naughty charmer; my money says Sloan is too."

Words clogged Roxie's throat. But she didn't let them out. Instead she bit into her muffin. Poppy seed. She tried not to choke on it.

"At least tell me this," Brenda jumped in. "Is he a good kisser?"

Boy was he. But she didn't kiss and tell.

Brenda punched Roxie's shoulder. "He is! I can tell by your expression. You minx, you. How'd you land such a hottie?"

Roxie rubbed her shoulder. "I sent him a note saying his roof had a tree in it."

"Dang. Who knew home repair could be so exciting? I thought I'd meet hunks galore in the hospital. That's why I became a nurse, to surf mankind. Only the pickings have been slim to none here lately. I caught the wrong career wave. When's he coming back?"

"He's here on the weekends. His business is in Atlanta."

"Uh oh. That's no good," Brenda said. "We'll never get the museum going if you pick up and move to Atlanta."

"I'm not going anywhere. That museum and our Friends group are important to me."

"Andrea Albert nearly sucked her cheeks the rest of the way in when she saw you'd joined the festival committee," Brenda said. "I thought her eyes would pop out of her head."

The muffin in her stomach solidified. She didn't hate anyone, but it seemed like Andrea hated her. "All I did was visit her dad in the nursing home. From her reaction, you'd think I'd stolen the family fortune. Les is the sweetest guy, and he's so lonely. His brain is sharp as a tack. I can't stop going over there on Thursdays just because Andrea doesn't like it—or me. It would break his heart."

Donna patted Roxie's back. "Never mind about her, girlfriend, we've got your back. Any word on your identity theft?"

"Laurie Ann's working on it, but no, nothing yet."

Chapter 7

Since the first time she'd realized her identity had been stolen, Roxie dreaded opening her mail, but it had to be done. Today, as she sat in Miss Daisy outside the post office, three fat envelopes were from stores she'd never heard of. She'd already received five other hefty credit card statements.

Not good.

At the rap on her passenger window, she started guiltily. She unlocked the door and city police officer Laurie Ann Dinterman slid into the seat, her police hat and a sheet of paper in her hand.

"Saw you sitting here and thought you could use some moral support," the cop said. "You doing all right?"

"I'd be fine if these darned bills stopped coming."

Laurie Ann handed her the piece of paper. "Here's your incident report from the identity theft. Mail or fax a copy of this report to those five places."

Roxie dropped the fresh batch of bills on Laurie Ann's lap. "Soon to be eight places. This is a nightmare. Even though I cancelled my card and got a new one, I worry it will be declined when I use it."

Laurie Ann copied the contact info from the bills and handed them back. "You've done everything right. No more new cards or loans can be made using your identity without your approval. Your credit record will clear in time. The only problem is if you need to borrow a big chunk of money in the interim. You planning to remodel your kitchen or replace Miss Daisy anytime soon?"

"I wish. Can't afford it."

"Smart woman. Folks get into trouble with credit purchases thinking they need things."

"Someone sure is enjoying themselves spending money I don't have. Can't you catch this thief?"

"Working on it."

"How about the person who ransacked my kitchen? Any word?"

"Dead end, unfortunately."

****

Friday afternoon found Roxie willing the clock to tick faster. Sloan would arrive at six. The thought of seeing him again sent her pulse into the stratosphere. But no matter how hard she wished, time continued its logical progression, one agonizing second at a time.

She reached for the ultimate time-killer, her McClintoch folder. Abram McClintoch wanted to sell his property. He'd lived there for forty years. However, it was titled in his late grandfather's name, and it had been inherited by Abram's twelve children. Some had died, and their share fell to their children, who had scattered across the country.

What a mess. Unless she tracked the missing relatives, the sale wouldn't go through and the buyer would walk. She chewed on the end of an ink pen and tried to come up with a fresh investigative approach.

"What time are you knocking off?" Megan asked.

Roxie jumped as adrenaline whooshed into her veins and she half-rose to bolt. Then she realized she was safe in her office. Megan had been so quiet she'd forgotten she wasn't alone. "I'm meeting with Mr. Harding at six."

"Roxie? You all right?"

"I'm fine."

"You nearly blasted into orbit when I spoke just now. What's got you on edge?"

Roxie pulled her shoulders down from her ears.

"You mean aside from the break-in at my house, my identity theft, the surprise kayak that I can't afford, my brother being out of touch, and roadblocks in the museum project?"

"Yeah. Aside from all that."

"That's my complete list of troubles. Thank goodness Miss Daisy isn't acting up."

"Wait a minute. You said *Mr.* Harding." Megan's eyebrows arched into her tanned forehead. "I thought you two were on a first-name basis after my wedding."

Her face heated. "It's complicated."

"It always is." Her friend chuckled. "Tell me about him."

She rolled her pen between her fingers. What could she tell her friend without sounding like a hopeless romantic?

"Come on," Megan prodded. "It can't be that bad. I saw the way he looked at you."

"You did?" Roxie's chair squeaked as she leaned forward. Megan understood men. Perhaps she could decode Sloan's behavior. "What did you see?"

"He couldn't keep his eyes off of you. Then he danced with you when I wouldn't let you sneak out. He's quite a gentleman, isn't he?"

He didn't kiss like a gentleman, but he hadn't pushed her into bed either. "Sort of."

Her friend laughed deep and low. "Come on, Rox. Does he make your heart flutter?"

"He does, and I hardly know which end is up."

"That's how it should be, my friend." A dreamy look filled Megan's eyes. "Is he going to be The Guy?"

As if on cue the front door opened, and Dave breezed in, eyes on his new bride. "Hi, honey. Ready to go home?"

Megan melted into his arms. Embarrassed by their public display of affection, Roxie studied the orange and gold maple leaves littering her parking

103

lot. She could easily imagine herself running into Sloan's arms to kiss him like that. But was that love? Or was it merely physical attraction?

The newlyweds disentangled. Megan dashed back to her desk to gather her purse and sweater from her desk drawer.

Dave watched his wife's flurried movements, then turned to Roxie. A masculine smile of bemusement filled his handsome face. "Hey, Roxie. What's up?"

"She has a love life, Dave," Megan piped in. "She was starting to tell me about it."

"Really? Is it that Sloan Harding from our wedding?"

"You remembered his name? I thought you were busy on your wedding day."

"Of course I remember his name. Is he treating you right? If not, I'll set him straight."

Irritation coursed through her, a riptide of unrest. She didn't want anyone hovering over her shoulder while she figured out this thing between her and Sloan. "We're business associates."

Dave's blue eyes twinkled. "*Business* makes the world go around. Don't you ever forget that."

"I'm not talking about that kind of business," she almost snapped. She ignored the heat in her cheeks and closed the McClintoch folder. She wouldn't get any more work on that done today. Her concentration was shot.

"Well, you should." Megan laced her fingers through Dave's. "Nothing wrong with that kind of business."

"I want his property listing," she explained patiently. "Putting up a Marshview Realty for sale sign on his Main Street address would do wonders for our visibility."

Dave smiled. "Loosen up, Rox. Customers will come your way. Meanwhile, have some fun. You're only young once, you know."

"Don't I know it." She pasted a cheery smile on her face and waved goodbye to her friends. "Enjoy your evening."

As they left her in the silence of her office, she could hear her biological clock ticking. Roxie wanted children. Lots of children. But for that, she needed Mr. Right. Would she have any good eggs left by the time he showed up?

One man she'd dated had called her an uptight workaholic. She was focused. Big difference. Being focused didn't mean she was dull, did it? Did her work ethic scare guys off?

Could her singleness be her own fault?

The questions rattled around in her head. To quiet them, she stuffed file folders for her Saturday morning meeting with Noreen Bagwell in her Marshview Realty tote bag. She was reviewing the list of expenses submitted by Sloan's roofing contractor when the phone rang.

"Can you meet me at the house in a few minutes?" Sloan asked.

The low rumble of his familiar voice sent a thrilling shiver clear down to her toes. She curled into the phone. "Depends. Did you bring your dog?"

"Of course I brought Mac. He really missed you this week."

Roxie's insides warmed. Was Sloan talking about his dog, or himself? "I'll bring him a special treat."

"He'll be waiting with bated breath."

****

Sloan directed the mattress mover to the second floor master bedroom. Only after he'd hauled the old particle board dresser out of the room was the guy able to assemble the king-sized bed frame.

While the mattress guy carried the empty cartons to his truck, Sloan made up the bed with brand new sheets. He had big plans for tonight.

When Mac barked excitedly at the front door, he smiled. Roxie had arrived. His dog had it bad for the tall brunette. He understood exactly where Mac was coming from. He wanted to jump on her and lick her all over himself.

He descended the bare wooden stairs at a fast clip. Through the glass panel side lights framing the door, he saw Roxie talking to the mattress guy. When the wind gusted, her shoulder length hair blew across her face, and she smoothed it to the side.

He didn't like how close the man stood to Roxie. Was he looking down her shirt? Sloan's mouth twisted into a scowl. He let Mac out and followed, flexing his fingers.

Roxie turned, smiled, and knelt down to hug his dog. Mac licked her hands and face in delight. Sloan kept his gaze on her face as he approached.

Dogs were straightforward. If they needed food or attention, they let you know. They didn't play games. Was Roxie playing him to get his business?

"Hey, you." Her voice washed through him like great scotch. Smooth and with a strong kick. He pulled her to her feet and into his arms for a kiss. "My turn," he said.

He meant for the kiss to be brief, to let Roxie know he'd missed her this week, but as soon as he touched her his good intentions vanished.

She tasted like peppermint ice cream, and she felt as welcome as a dryer-warmed blanket on a cold night. Anchoring his hands in her hair, he savored her vanilla fragrance.

It felt so right having Roxie in his arms. As if he'd finally come home. He clung to that foreign sense of homecoming.

His dog barked and Sloan ended the kiss. Later, he promised himself. They had the whole night to explore each other.

"Sign this," the mattress guy grunted.

Sloan scribbled on the form.

"You take care, Miss Roxie," the mattress guy said.

"I will," Roxie said. "Tell your mom I asked after her. I'll stop by to visit her next week."

With that, mattress guy hopped in his truck and drove away. Sloan found Roxie studying him in a way that made him want to loosen his shirt collar.

"You bought a bed?" Roxie asked with a shy smile.

"Yep."

He loved watching her face. Her wonderful blue-green eyes flared with excitement. Was she thinking about sharing a bed with him?

"I thought you planned to sell the house," she said, meeting him look for look.

"Whether I sell the house or not, my back won't take too many more nights on my musty old bed."

"Oh." She paused. "You mean buying a bed has nothing to do with a big seduction scene?"

Her smile had grown bolder, not so shy now. Was she teasing him?

"I seem to remember you promising me a special treat," Sloan teased back, running his fingers down her slender arms.

She chuckled. "No, that was Mac." She reached into her pocket and withdrew the dog treat. Mac barked excitedly, gulped it down whole, and wagged his tail.

"You're spoiling him," he said. "This dog chases bad guys, not treats. Besides, I'm jealous." His voice deepened. "I want a special treat too."

"We'll see." She flashed him a too bright smile and reached into her car for a tote bag. "I have invoices from the roofer for you to review. I had other contractors here this week as well, so there are plenty of estimates for you to consider."

Her change of subject from personal to business didn't fool him. She was nervous about their relationship. Nervous wasn't bad. He could work with nervous.

"You hungry?"

"Starved."

So was he. For her. He linked his fingers through hers. "Let me tell you what I've planned for dinner."

"Seems like we're always hungry when we're together."

"Lady, you don't know the half of it."

****

Candlelight flickered at the exclusive seaside restaurant. In all the years Roxie had lived in Mossy Bog, she'd never once been to Vandella's. The evening was Cinderella perfect. Sloan had looked great at the wedding in his black suit, but she couldn't get over how his charcoal brown suit highlighted the smoky mysteries in his eyes. A girl could get lost in those eyes for hours. Not to mention the expensive material flattered his broad shoulders and narrow waist to perfection. Her mouth watered.

Unfortunately, his athletic physique had the same effect on the buxom waitress. Said waitress kept hovering at their table. Roxie fumed silently every time he gave the woman his attention.

Her wine glass sat untouched. She'd sucked down four glasses of water and hit the ladies room twice.

Nerves.

It had to be nerves.

If she'd quit obsessing over where she'd be sleeping tonight, she'd be fine.

While she enjoyed her devilled crab, she searched for a neutral conversation topic. "The police never heard from anyone missing a boat. I'm still reluctant to call that kayak mine."

Sloan nodded. "My luck wasn't much better. We found no kayak orders in the southeast over the last month that went missing. The only thing that looked halfway like a match was a sporting goods dealer up in Richmond who pro-dealed one for his wife. They apparently split up soon after he brought home the boat."

"I can see why. These boats are expensive. Even at a dealer discount, he probably used money they'd agreed to spend otherwise. Trust is so important in a marriage."

Heat flamed Roxie's cheeks as she realized what she'd just said. What had possessed her to bring marriage up? She didn't know those people. Well, in for a penny, in for a pound.

"My parents felt quite strongly that a couple's financial decisions should be made jointly."

"I see the wisdom in that," he agreed as the coffee and dessert arrived. Caffeine and sugar. Just what she needed. "Try this." Sloan spoon-fed her a bite of the chocolate mousse.

"Delicious."

His eyes gleamed in the intimate setting, as if he were mentally undressing her. She remembered how perfectly his hands had molded to her curves, how her body had come alive under his sure touch. She gripped her linen napkin tightly.

At a light tap on her shoulder, Roxie turned. She saw the diamonds first, the white-haired matron in flowing burgundy crepe second. She groaned inwardly. Noreen Bagwell.

"Hello, Noreen."

Diamonds accented Noreen's hands, wrists, neck, and ears. "Roxie, dear child, who is this handsome fellow? He looks good enough to eat."

Sloan rose and extended his hand. "Sloan Harding, ma'am."

Noreen faltered, then reached forward and

shook his hand. "Harding, you say? Any relation to Edward Harding?"

Sloan seemed to draw into himself. "My father."

"I went to school with Edward. Poor man never lived up to his potential."

Roxie knew Sloan didn't like talking about his father. "I'm looking forward to our breakfast meeting tomorrow, Noreen. I'll see you at eight at the diner."

Noreen's lady friends waved her over and thankfully she left, but the mood at Roxie's table had gone from seduction to brooding silence. "What's wrong?" she asked when they were alone and Sloan was seated again.

"I thought you were spending the day with me tomorrow," he said. "We have a lot of painting to do."

"I am, but I also have a business to run. Saturday morning is when Noreen wanted to meet. If I sell her place, Widow's Peak, I won't have to worry about my finances for a very long time."

"What's the big deal about that property?"

"Noreen is the big deal. She has ties to many community groups, and she's very outspoken. If she is pleased with my work, I'll be set for life."

"Mac will be disappointed. Why don't you spend the night to make it up to us?"

His bald proposition shocked her. She glanced away to the darkness of the curtained window. A thick knot formed in her stomach. Why did he have to bring up sleeping arrangements right now? Why couldn't he let things progress naturally?

"Never mind." His expression hardened. "I see the hesitation on your face."

Roxie stiffened. "I resent that. Do you think you can buy me with a fancy meal? Do you think I'm easy?"

Sloan winced. "I'm sorry. I...don't know what came over me." He looked lost, like he didn't deal with this situation often, if at all. The idea fueled her resentment.

"I thought I knew you, that we were friends."

"We *are* friends." He caught her hand and held it. "Please, I made a mistake. I'm sorry."

"Why should I even believe a word you say?"

"Roxie, I didn't lie to you. I haven't lied to you about anything."

"Then tell me the truth now. What do you want from me?"

"I care about you. There's something between us, something that takes my breath away. I sensed you pulling back and I….well, I freaked."

She snorted, then covered her nose. "Men don't freak over me, Sloan."

"This one does. You're beautiful and sexy and I enjoy your company."

The tightness in her chest eased. "I enjoy your company too, but I'm old-fashioned about dating. I don't jump into bed with every man who takes me to dinner."

"You have rules."

"Sure do."

His thumb played over the back of her hand, sending her senses into hyperawareness as he shot her a roguish smile.

"Understood."

Soft music filled the dining room and as other diners moved toward the small dance floor in one corner of the room, Sloan invited her to dance. As they stood, he held out his hand to her and she willingly followed, but with reservations. Though she loved being in his arms and dancing, she wasn't sure of her feelings for Sloan.

Her rules were justified. She didn't blithely hop into bed with men. Didn't do friends with benefits. Was that he expected after dinner? A sexy tussle? She didn't do tussles either. And she had serious doubts about sexy.

This sucked.

She wanted him.

He wanted her.

Why couldn't she trust that it would work out? Her stomach burned, riling up her undigested crab cake even as the answer came to her. It was something Gran used to say all the time.

Trust had to be earned.

Unexpectedly, the hair on the nape of her neck bristled. She opened her eyes, scanning the room. There. The man with the military bearing at the bar. He'd turned away right as she glanced his way.

Was it her imagination or was he watching her?

Chapter 8

Midnight found Sloan pacing around the chipped Formica table in his kitchen circling back to the sink. Tonight's romantic dinner had been perfect. He'd nailed the place. Romantic atmosphere. Delicious food. Roxie had been full of smiles just for him. Everything had proceeded nicely until Noreen Bagwell stopped by their table.

Something had flickered between the women once Noreen mentioned his father. His hands fisted at his sides. His deadbeat father wasn't a secret, but he was tired of being tarred with the same brush. It seemed like everywhere he turned in this town he ran into his father's memory.

He stared out the window over the sink. Nothing but night outside. Not a light in sight. The unrelenting darkness out there matched the emptiness he felt inside.

At dinner, he'd sensed his time had run out. Like a drowning man, he'd yanked the lifeline of Roxie's friendship until it snapped in his hands. Stupid. Not at all his style. He'd spent years perfecting his seduction technique. But when things fouled up this time, instead of cutting his losses, he'd dug a deeper hole for himself.

He wanted her. Wanted her so much that he'd been careless with his feelings. He knew better than to let emotions get involved. Only, this time it mattered. This time he didn't want to be anyone's boy toy. This time, this woman, they mattered.

He opened the new fridge he'd just bought and pulled out a root beer. His dog stared at him with reproach in his eyes. "I screwed up, okay?" He sipped the cool beverage. "I tipped my hand too soon. She panicked, so we're alone tonight. My bad."

Mac rested his head on his paws with a long-suffering sigh. Sloan knew just how he felt. He scanned the tiny kitchen, his attention coming to rest on his granddad's Army trunk. Might as well entertain himself with the past. He sat down and opened the battered green trunk. Last time he'd sorted through the stack of papers on the left. He reached for a handful of papers from the center.

Hours later, he held three canceled checks for five thousand dollars each made out to Matthew Bolen. Lavinia's husband. Roxie's grandfather. Curiosity sliced through him, along with suspicion.

What were the checks for? The other canceled checks in the trunk had been issued to cover routine expenses. These checks made out on the first of three successive months didn't follow that pattern. They lent credence to another theory and established another pattern. Further, this money trail had no known outcome.

Fifteen thousand dollars. Twenty years ago, that was a small windfall. What had Roxie's grandfather done with the money? His pulse raced in his ears. Was this a lead to the lost Harding fortune?

Had his father seen these checks? Was that why he'd been so certain he'd been cheated out of his inheritance? The idea tantalized Sloan. By all accounts, his father had been unhinged. Had the old man been onto something all along?

To know that he had to dig beneath the surface. Was he willing to risk even more ridicule and disdain? Not that anyone's opinion in Mossy Bog amounted for much in his book. Except Roxie's.

She mattered.

What a mess.

What happened to his inheritance? Had his

granddad gambled the money away? Had he been blackmailed? What could possibly explain the missing money?

Had Roxie's family benefitted from Sloan's inheritance all these years? Was his granddad's money the seed capitol for Lavinia's real estate business?

He shifted uneasily in his chair. Was this the underlying reason for Roxie's caution in their personal relationship?

Was she afraid the truth would come out?

That she'd have to give the money back?

****

Roxie unfastened the last button on her coral blazer and sat down in the bench seat across from Noreen. Sheryl's Diner was hopping at eight in the morning. White-headed seniors dotted the fifties-style booths and burly men with hearty appetites lined the bar stools at the counter. The cozy aromas of bacon and fresh perked coffee filled the air. "Morning."

"Don't you look pretty as a picture," Noreen cooed. "How's my favorite realtor this morning?"

For five years, Noreen had dangled Widow's Peak as a potential listing. Gran had done everything short of buying the property herself, but Noreen never signed a contract. Would this year be any different?

"Doing good." Roxie opened her silverware roll and placed her paper napkin in her lap.

"What about all that hoo-rah over at your place? The burglar and the boat and the credit card mess?"

"I've stopped the bleeding on the credit card mess. Laurie Ann's got no idea who my burglar was or where the kayak came from. Fortunately, the burglar hasn't returned."

"What will you do with the boat?"

"Use it, I guess. I can't believe no one is missing

a kayak."

The waitress appeared, and Roxie ordered coffee and toast. Noreen got a steak and mushroom omelet, a fruit platter, and a side serving of pumpkin pancakes.

"You're looking good, Noreen," Roxie stated, anxious to shift the conversation away from her troubles. Noreen's dashing camel colored ankle boots, crisp tweed slacks with matching brown pullover, and gleaming amber pendant could have been plucked from a glossy catalog.

"No point in looking shabby. Men pay attention when you look good. Learned that lesson a long time ago."

"You looking for a man?"

"Honey, I'm always looking for a good man. Trouble is, they're darned hard to find. Too many of that other kind."

Roxie dumped sugar and milk into her steaming coffee and took a cautious sip. Fortification was essential when dealing with a formidable opponent. "What other kind?"

"The kind that does you wrong." Noreen's diamonds flashed as she waggled a finger at Roxie. "You better watch that Harding boy."

Her hand jerked. Coffee sloshed over the top of her hand. Wincing, she quickly dabbed it dry. "Sloan? What about him?"

"As a kid, he stayed one step ahead of the law. If there was trouble in Mossy Bog, you could bet your bottom dollar that Harding boy was involved."

Roxie's hackles rose. "I don't remember any major crime sprees."

"Your grandmother, bless her heart, did everything she could for that boy, and he still had a bent for mischief. He ran wild, that's what, and his crowd ended up in jail, every last one of them."

The waitress appeared with a tray of food.

Roxie's toast plate was dwarfed by the multiple platters of food for Noreen.

"Sloan's turned his life around." Roxie slathered her toast with orange marmalade and took a bite. "He has a security business in Atlanta."

The older woman snorted. "Hiring that Harding boy for a security job is like asking a shark to patrol the fish pond. Mark my words, nothing good can come from that family. His father was a complete wastrel."

Unwanted fascination flared. "Last night you said you knew his father."

Noreen's pale blue eyes glistened with excitement. She pointed a forkful of omelet at Roxie. "Edward Harding ended up wrapped around a bottle. He had everything, a good job, a pretty wife, a golf club membership, a brilliant future over at the college, but he threw it away chasing after foolish things."

"Like what?"

"Like women half his age, like backroom gambling with the boys over at the Green Door, like taking for granted the good times would never end. When life turned on him, Edward imploded. He gave up."

"Why does that bother you so much?"

"Edward had potential. He was the smartest kid in our class, but he never applied himself. He put forth the minimum effort and slid by. That boy of his wasn't much better."

Roxie placed her toast crust on the empty white plate. Blood rushed in her ears. "What are you saying?"

"You should be very careful."

The hair on the back of her neck sprang to attention. This conversation had strayed too far into the personal for her comfort. And—for God's sake— was the man in the corner having coffee the same

117

man she'd seen last night at the restaurant? This was getting bizarre.

Time to get refocused. She removed a sheaf of papers from her tote bag and placed them on the marble-like tabletop.

"Let's talk contracts, Noreen," she said firmly. "Have you settled on an asking price?"

"I want two million." Noreen studied her. "Lavinia always told me that was too high."

Was this a test? Would Noreen be unreasonable about the list price? "It is. In this down market, you're more likely to get one million."

"That won't do. Not at all. I'm counting on you to do better than that."

"I want your business, but even if your place went on the market today, it could take years to find the right buyer. Especially if it's way overpriced."

Noreen's fork paused on the way to her mouth. "Years, you say?"

Roxie nodded.

"I assumed folks would stand in line to own Widow's Peak." Her watery gaze sharpened. "It would make a nice bed and breakfast if you get that museum of yours going."

Irritation simmered in Roxie's blood. "That project was vetoed by City Council. I'm sure you remember."

"Details. You're a fighter, like Lavinia. You'll find a way to fund that museum and when you do you'll have my vote."

"You're no longer opposed to the museum?"

"I'm not opposed to the museum, just paying for it with my taxes. It would be a lovely addition to Mossy Bog."

"I see." Roxie rubbed her throbbing temples. Dealing with Noreen after a restless night taxed her patience. She desperately wanted to believe the woman, but this could be another game she was running.

Was it too much to ask for the woman to sign a property contract and leave the museum out of it?

"I thought you might." Noreen shoveled in the last of her pumpkin pancakes. "Time is running out for me, I'm afraid. I can't afford to wait years to cash out of Widow's Peak. Something has come up, you see—"

Alarm replaced Roxie's irritation. "What's wrong, Noreen?"

The older woman shook her head. "I can't say, dear. Not even my bridge group knows yet. I'm willing to sign that listing contract with you right now."

Roxie blinked at this strange turn of events. "You are?"

"Yes."

"Okay," she said slowly, not trusting her good fortune. She dug through her briefcase until she found a blank contract. Her hands shook. Her commission as the listing agent would be a huge chunk of cash. She started filling in the particulars. "What's your real asking price?"

"How about a bonus to sweeten the pot? Everything I clear over a million dollars I'll donate to your Friends of the Museum group."

Roxie's excitement dimmed. Clearing a million would be hard, if the place sold at all. Still, it was better than nothing. "That's more than generous of you, Noreen. Thank you."

"What do you say to a million five? That would give us negotiating room."

Dollar signs danced in Roxie's head. If she listed and sold the property and took home a bonus for the museum, she'd be sitting pretty. "A million five it is." She completed the form and passed the document across the table.

While the woman reviewed it, Roxie thought of

ways to attract a big ticket buyer. Definitely Internet ads. She could contact people off the richest people in America list. This was so cool. She couldn't wait to tell Sloan her good news.

"There's an itty bitty catch to my offer."

Roxie toned down her mental happy dancing. "What?"

"Youngsters like you are the future of this town. I've seen how you care about this place, and I'm impressed. Therefore, I've taken it upon myself to protect you."

"Oh?" She picked up her coffee cup, saw that it was empty, and put it down.

"Lavinia would be appalled if she knew what was going on."

"I don't understand."

"I realize I have no right to say anything. Your private life is just that." Noreen blotted her face with a napkin. Roxie braced for the rest of it. Whatever it was, it wouldn't be good.

"I'm no fool," the woman continued. "Selling my place will secure your financial future. If you do as I ask, your Friends group could gain a boatload of money. Here's the bottom line. I asked around. Sloan Harding goes through women like water, same as his father. My condition for the bonus is that you stop seeing him socially."

The noise from the diner faded. Roxie's heart pounded in her ears like a kettle drum. "Excuse me?"

Noreen signed her name in large script. "You don't have to tell me your answer. I'll know by your actions." With that, Noreen swept out of the restaurant, sticking Roxie with the check.

That was one part of the morning she'd expected. The rest boggled her mind. But she held a signed contract in her hands. That was a fact.

Her stomach knotted as she digested Noreen's pointed remarks. She had worked so hard to get where she was today. It hadn't been easy selling real estate and going to school. Passing the broker's test had been as hard as any collegiate exam.

Harder.

But she had garnered the credentials to succeed in Gran's business. Given Noreen's ridiculous demand, dating Sloan could cost her thousands of dollars.

She stared into her empty coffee cup as people bustled in and out of the busy diner. The coffee-drinking man from the corner left too. Grimly, she ranked her objectives. Securing the future of Marshview Realty was her priority.

She wouldn't let a spate of hormones jeopardize her business or the museum.

Would she?

The waitress paused beside the booth. "More coffee, hon?"

"No thanks. I'm all done."

****

Sloan rose with the Saturday sun. He ate a peanut butter sandwich for breakfast, then drained the rest of the milk from the carton. From the kitchen window, he watched Mac romp in the backyard. His gaze lingered on the back gate that separated his property from Roxie's. Suddenly the proximity of her place took on sinister connotations.

From Prospect Street, her modest two-story house appeared unassuming. But then, her roof didn't leak, her plumbing worked, her electrical connections were up to code, and her appliances were modern.

As he was finding out, house repairs weren't cheap. No telling how much money had been sunk into her place over the years. A fortune, most likely. If they'd paid in cash, it would be untraceable.

Had her family stolen from his?

The question swirled through his mind. Not

even a lukewarm shower cleared his head.

He stared at the painting supplies neatly stacked on his coffee table. Frustration gnawed at his gut. Painting was too tame for his mood. He needed action. He grabbed his shiny new sledge hammer and started bashing in the kitchen cabinets.

Wood splintered and crunched as he made his way from the ancient stove toward the new refrigerator. With each heft and crash of the heavy tool, his satisfaction grew.

The sooner he got this house fixed up, the sooner he could shed his ties to the past. Pots and pans clattered to the floor as another cabinet fell victim to his blows. Plastic cups and tin foil pie pans spilled across the weathered linoleum. He didn't care about any of it. There was nothing in this house worth keeping, with the exception of his new bed and refrigerator.

Outside, Mac woofed a welcome.

Sloan turned, sledge hammer in hand. Roxie stood at his back door. From the wary expression in her tropical eyes, she wouldn't be jumping into his bed this morning either.

His rising spirits plummeted.

What had the Bagwell woman said to her this morning?

He risked a wry smile as he opened the door. "Watch your step. I got an early start."

She skirted past him, picking her way through the rubble on the floor. "I see that. I thought you were keeping the repairs simple and cosmetic."

"Changed my mind this morning."

Her thick hair was snugged back in a ponytail, her long legs encased in body skimming jeans. There were no buttons open on her prim white blouse. Something intangible had changed between them. His gut tightened.

"We need to talk," she said.

His grip on the sledge hammer tightened. Every conversation where he'd been dumped had started like this one.

"I don't want to hurt your feelings," she began.

"But?"

"But, I don't think this is a good idea."

"Define this."

"This." Her hand gestured between them. "Us."

He'd been right.

She was dumping him.

A cold wind swept through him. Not trusting himself to speak, he pressed his lips together and waited for her to say the words.

When she didn't say anything else, hope flickered in the back of his mind. He hurried to fill in the silence. "I'm sorry about last night. I made a mistake by pushing too hard. I want to spend time with you, Roxie. We have something good going on here. Please give us another chance."

Her hands clenched together. "This isn't a decision I've made lightly. All my life I've searched for a place to belong. Mossy Bog is my home. I've put down roots here—"

"I'm not asking you to give that up."

"Let me finish. Last night, I saw a different side of you, one I'd refused to acknowledge before. Being here is painful for you. Once you conclude your business with the house, you'll head back to Atlanta. Right?"

"Maybe."

"Even if we got along famously, geography would be a problem."

"I can make it work."

"Why should you have to? Truth is I don't want to go to Atlanta. You don't want to stay here."

"You're calling it quits because we live in different cities? That's a challenge, I'll grant you that much, but it isn't a deal breaker."

"It is to me."

"Let's think about this."

"Nope. My mind is made up. This is for the best."

He took a step forward. "Not for me. This isn't better for me."

Her palm shot out. "Stop." She cleared her throat. "I don't think you need a property manager, not if you take charge of the rehab work yourself, but if you still want one, I'd like to suggest my associate, Megan. She is very organized and will do a good job for you."

She didn't want to work with him either. Old fears and uncertainties swam into his consciousness. A small voice chanted in his mind, *You're no good, Harding.* "We have a contract," he grimly reminded her.

"One that I'm willing to let you out of without billing you for any of my time to date," she countered.

She didn't want anything to do with him.

What was the point of tying her to him with a business contract if he couldn't have her?

She'd had him dancing to her tune for three weeks. He'd almost forgotten his true goals. Find the money and unload the house. He didn't need permanent ties to Mossy Bog. About time he came to his senses.

"You're right." He lowered the sledge hammer to the floor. "Looks like I don't need a property manager."

Silence yawned across the abyss between them.

A great heaviness settled on his shoulders. He felt so weary he could barely hold his head up, but his eyes drank her in.

Strands of dark hair trailed down her neck from her ponytail. Those incredible blue-green eyes of hers, watery now, but so much a part of her that he'd never forget her.

Or how she'd melted against him.

She placed his house key on the table, squared her shoulders, and took a deep breath. "Good-bye, Sloan."

Mutely, he watched her go.

He felt like the sun had gone behind a dark cloud. He wanted to crawl back in bed, but he wouldn't give in to the emptiness he felt. Mac prowled around the demolition debris on the kitchen floor, sniffing purposefully, as if that would bring her back.

"Sorry, bud." Sloan couldn't explain what had happened to his dog. Hell. He couldn't explain it to himself.

He'd gotten dumped before he'd even slept with her. That was a first.

To hell with her.

To hell with a property manager.

He'd show everyone in this lousy town what he was made of. He'd be his own property manager. Sell his own house, too.

Why share his profits with anyone? Mossy Bog had turned its back on him long ago. Nothing had changed. Roxie was right.

Mossy Bog wasn't his home.

He didn't belong here.

Chapter 9

Sonny Gifford's personality occupied a lot of space in Miss Daisy. Worse, he seemed at ease in the luxury car, an ease she'd never quite mastered. Roxie had kept gran's Cadillac because customers expected to have spacious accommodations, but she'd rather be driving a gas-friendly hybrid.

If her business took off, she'd upgrade her transportation. Until then she was stuck in the cavernous Miss Daisy. Thank goodness she'd also inherited gran's mechanic. Elmer Lowe was a dinosaur, but he knew his way around Miss Daisy like no one else.

"The old hotel has possibilities for your business." She pointed out the empty two-story brick structure and pulled into a parking slot on Seaside Drive. "It's in the heart of Mossy Bog and stands out from the other buildings on the block. Plus, it has ample living space on the second floor."

Sonny wrinkled his nose. "Looks too pretentious for what I have in mind. Let's keep going."

At Birding Square, she showed him the colonnade-fronted Colonial which he hated and a lovely shotgun cottage which had just been remodeled. "Our premiere craftsman, James Arden, did the work on this cottage," she said proudly. "He installed period crown molding and a claw-footed bath tub."

The investment counselor dismissed the property with a flick of his hand. "Not interested. Too far off the beaten path."

"Okay, we'll move right along then. I have more

prospects to show you."

They were two blocks off Main Street, not five miles out of town. What was with this guy? The way his eyes darted and the almost sneer of his lips didn't add up. On the surface, Sonny Gifford was a lanky blonde businessman with expansion on his mind. But Roxie's gut instincts were a little off kilter lately. Jumping at every shadow, imagining she was being followed, now suspecting clients of ulterior motives. What had gotten into her?

It didn't matter. She didn't like him and she didn't have to like him. There were plenty of clients she didn't like. And that was okay. She only had to like their money.

"This town is so quaint," he said. "There must be quite a few legends associated with it."

She drove on, making a series of turns. "We do. Our Chamber of Commerce revived the legend of our sea monster, Mossy Girl. She's reputed to be kin to Nessie, the Loch Ness monster. Like Nessie, she's often seen on misty mornings or at twilight."

"Mossy Girl. I like that. I could use the story on my website once I relocate here. Any other legends I should know about?"

"Blackbeard Island is off the coast here. Edward Teach's treasure was never found. Every year or two someone gets interested in searching for that again."

"Ah yes. Buried treasure. That might work even better to entice investment clients. Mossy Bog has a rich natural history. And other legends around here, say pertaining to the land or homes?"

She was used to selling the town as well as the property, but his insistence on this line of questioning made her uneasy. "We have our share of ghost stories, if that's what you mean."

"Ghosts, eh? Give me a second here. Ghosts. Hmm. No, I don't think that's a good investment image. People might think their money would vanish into thin air."

She stopped on River Street at the tabby coated shell of a single story building. The exterior limestone had darkened with age, but the thick walls of sand, lime, and oyster shell were still as strong as when they'd been shaped a century ago. "This property is dirt cheap, but as you can see, it needs extensive work inside and a new roof. It's been on the market for awhile, and the owner is willing to deal."

Sonny studied the building, then tugged at his cufflinks. "It has potential. What's the price?"

Finally. A nibble. Roxie drew in a deep breath and quoted a figure. "Would you like to walk the property?"

"No need. I've got the gist of it for now."

She eased down the block, stopping at the larger tabby shell. "I'm working with a group to establish a nautical museum here."

Sonny perked up. "Oh? Where are you in the process?"

"The community is receptive to the idea. We've drawn up plans. But funding is still a challenge. We've yet to figure out how to pay for it."

"You've pursued grants and loans?"

"Sure. We're keeping our fingers crossed. I mentioned the museum because the other property will increase in value and cost as the museum moves forward."

"So noted. What else is on your list this morning?"

She scooted a few streets over to the three-bedroom ranch on Third Street, drove past the waterfront contemporary on Octavia Drive, and even pitched him the abandoned convenience store a block off of Main.

His response never wavered. "Not interested." Defeated, she turned down Prospect Street to head back to the office. "I like that one with the yellow kayak in the yard," he said.

Her house. Roxie blushed. "It *is* the same vintage as the other property you like, but that house isn't for sale."

"Everything's for sale. What would the owner say to $400,000?"

She'd say holy cow. But she'd never sell her house. Not in a million years. It was her home. "I'll pass your offer along, but don't get your hopes up. That house has belonged to the same family since it was built."

"What about the Victorian on Main Street? Any chance the owner is ready to part with it yet?"

Sloan's house. Her heart sunk. "I've spoken with the owner about your interest. He was very clear. His house is not on the market. But, it may become available later."

"Circle by there again, if you would."

"Of course." Roxie kept her polite real estate mask in place. Thank goodness it was a Tuesday and Sloan would be in Atlanta. There were several pickups on his lawn, two men standing on the roof.

"That house is perfect," Sonny said. "The architecture is elegant yet understated, the grounds are manicured, and it doesn't feel slick or glossy. It says Old South. Plus the location is exactly where I want. Any chance we could walk through?"

"No, it's private property. Mr. Gifford, there are two vacant lots on Main Street that are this size. You could build this same house and be ready to go in six months."

"I want 605 Main Street." His voice sharpened. "If you can't make it happen, I'll call Sally at BC Realty."

Roxie pulled into the office lot beside his sedan, her face in perma-freeze mode, her head pounding. "Call as many realtors as you like. It won't make any difference. That property is not for sale."

****

"What's bugging you?" Megan asked. "You've been down in the dumps for over a week. Did you have a fight with your Mr. Harding?"

Roxie looked up from the search she was running for a new buyer. Was she that transparent? Saying goodbye to Sloan had been awful. Even though she'd amputated him from her life, she secretly craved the comfort she'd felt in his arms. It felt as if he should still be there, still eating her up with those hungry eyes.

She'd done the right thing. Securing her financial future was her top priority. She wouldn't let her relative youth or a bad economy tank the family firm. She'd promised Gran to keep it going, and she would.

"I'm no longer seeing Mr. Harding," she admitted.

"What about your contract with him?"

"We parted ways."

Megan's brown eyes brimmed with speculation. "You want to talk about it?"

She shook her head. "Things didn't work out between us. That's all."

Her friend drummed her fingers on her desk. "Um hmm. Why don't I believe you? Could it be that you've spent most of the week staring out the window, watching leaves fall from the maple tree?"

"So?"

"I'm not buying your story one hundred percent, but I'm giving you the benefit of the doubt because you're my boss. Anything else bugging you?"

Everything was bugging her, from the annoying tag in her shirt collar down to her absent-minded brother. "I haven't heard from Timmy in weeks. He should have checked in by now. Why won't he return my calls?"

Her friend walked over to the coffee pot. "If you're so worried about him, why don't you zip up to Atlanta and check on him?"

Atlanta was where Sloan lived.

Her heart lurched. Though it was a big city, her luck would be that she'd run into him. She wasn't ready to see him yet. She might never be ready to see him again, not without her heart breaking in two.

"Could you think of anything worse than having your big sister drop by your college apartment to check up on you?" Roxie shuddered. "I should accept that no news is good news, but Timmy has always been a mix of free-spirited and needy. I can't imagine him going so long without calling home."

Megan carried her coffee back to her desk. "Let me get this straight. You're worried because he's settled in at college and doesn't need his big sister to watch over him?"

"No. That's not it. I'm worried there's something he's not telling me, that he's deliberately avoiding me until it's too late for me to help him." Was that why that man had been watching her? Was Timmy in trouble with the law?

"You are worrying yourself to a frazzle." Megan chuckled. "You need to get out of this office and have some fun."

As soon as Megan said fun, Sloan's face popped into Roxie's head. He knew how to have fun. He was probably knee deep in some intriguing security problem, running his house rehab from his swanky Atlanta address, and dating a different beautiful woman every night of the week.

The thought of him with someone else nauseated her.

His rehab was in full swing. She awoke each morning to the whir of saws and the clatter of hammers. She wouldn't go over there, wouldn't give him the satisfaction of knowing she had regrets.

Regrets. That sounded so benign. Regret didn't begin to cover the heaviness in her heart, the darkness in her days, the angst in her dreams.

Worse, she'd let someone else influence her judgment. She'd been swayed by the money Noreen had dangled in front of her. Never before had she sold herself. The thought left a bitter taste in her mouth and an ache in her heart.

She'd traded one dream for another and in the process lost something she valued more.

Her self-respect.

****

"I expect that entire section to be redone, at your expense." Sloan couldn't believe the roofing contractor had done such shoddy work. There was a half-inch gap between the plywood sections covering the hole in his roof. He could have installed a new roof in the time it had taken the roofer to get this far.

When his cell phone rang, he walked outside to take the call in privacy. His second-in-command, Jeff Bates, briefed him on the events of the week. Though it was only Wednesday morning, they were falling apart without him there at the office. "Damn it Bates, you're supposed to be handling this. Send a second team over to Castle Technology if things are so backed up. How hard can it be to fingerprint a firm of computer geeks? Are the background checks for that new drug store completed yet?"

"We're working on it, boss."

Sloan pinched the bridge of his nose. Yelling at Bates wasn't productive. The man was rock solid. Work was getting done, that was good. He wasn't running the company into bankruptcy by playing hooky with this rehab project. "Everything in place for the peanut company's dog and pony show?"

"The caterer is lined up. Terence is tweaking

your slide show presentation, glitzing up the graphics and animation. The office is clean. All that's left is to get you back up here in time for the nine o'clock show Friday morning."

"I'll be there."

"Great."

"What about Gilmore? Did Reg have any luck searching his records?"

"He's putting together his report, but here are the basics. Jared Gilmore was born in Albany, Georgia, the son of Vera Chapman and Alfonso Gilmore. His father took off before he was born, died of a drug overdose in Tallahassee a few years later. His waitress mother married Walter Cummings, a not-so-clever con who served time in Reidsville. The mother died of cancer while his step-dad was in prison. Gilmore dropped out of high school and became a gopher for a high roller. He branched out on his own eight years ago, building a reputation as an ambulance chaser for a shyster in Charleston."

"What does any of that have to do with Team Six Security?"

"I don't know, boss. None of our clients match up on a cross-check. You sure his interest isn't personal?"

"I've never met the man." Even as he said it, a tentative connection forged in his thoughts. His father had served time in Reidsville. What were the odds the two men would have run into each other in prison? And what would that have to do with Gilmore?

"We didn't check Gilmore's phone records. Reg could do that in between Castle Technology and the drug store dealio."

"Do it." Sloan ended the call and noticed the electrician exiting the freshly painted white house. He followed the man out to the driveway. In the last week and a half he'd found that contractors took a lot of breaks. If he didn't watch out, they'd bill him for all that down time. "Where are you going?"

"Lunch."

The electrician's curt tone fueled Sloan's simmering frustration. "It's ten-thirty in the morning. If you walk off the job now, I'm going to fire you."

"Suit yourself." The electrician shrugged. "I've got more work than I can handle."

Sloan ground his back teeth together. "You're fired."

Minutes later the cluster of pickup trucks on his lawn vanished. His house, which had been a beehive of activity, resembled a ghost town. These contractors didn't know what hard work was. None of them would've lasted an hour over in Iraq. Sissies, all of them.

Earlier, the plumber had walked off the job after a day and a half of muttering. The other three plumbers in the phone book had no availability. Which meant no new hot water heater and cold showers.

He'd just fired the electrician. Who the hell went to lunch so early? It wasn't like the guy had started before dawn and was starving. He'd reported to the job at nine a.m.

The roofer and his helper departed with the electrician. Good riddance. They hadn't been setting the world on fire either. So much for that cream-of-the-crop contractor list from Roxie.

How did anyone make a living doing this? Keeping track of varied work schedules and additional contractor expenses was an unending nightmare. It would be easier to do the work himself.

With that thought, Sloan put Mac in the fenced backyard and picked up a screw driver he'd found in the kitchen rubble. How hard could it be to connect a few wires?

****

The barking wouldn't stop.

Roxie held her pounding temples and peered out into the damp night. She hadn't slept well in ten days, and this incessant noise was pure torment.

Had someone left their dog out overnight? Where was the noise coming from?

When she walked out her front door, the noise receded. Next she tried her back porch, and the sound increased. She squinted into the murky drizzle.

Mac? It couldn't be. This was Wednesday. Sloan was in Atlanta.

Her head ached with the constant barking. Mac wouldn't bark like that anyway. He was too well trained. Still, the phone calls she'd planned to make this evening to track down more missing McClintoch heirs would have to wait.

She reached for her hooded khaki trench coat and lantern-style flashlight. The dismal weather suited her mood. She felt gray inside, like the drizzle falling in the cool night air.

She'd felt crappy for days. Ever since she'd decided against seeing Sloan. Ever since she'd told him she didn't want to see him again.

Instead, she'd focused on her work with tunnel vision. The Ashburn property had closed. Another Open House had netted a contract Naomi Thompson had accepted for her cottage.

She'd even attended the Garden Club meeting last night to chat up the museum. The ladies had lauded her idea, so it had been worthwhile. And as a bonus, she now knew how to force her Christmas cactus to bloom, and that it was time to take her potted geraniums in for the winter.

She clicked on the flashlight while she locked her door behind her. The darkness bothered her but that couldn't be helped. A dog was in trouble.

Following the sound of the barking, she crossed her soggy backyard, skirting a puddle near the heirloom azaleas. The dampness had her shivering in her sneakers. When would the rain stop? The ground couldn't absorb much more water.

The barking grew louder the further she walked from her house. At least the animal wasn't trapped on her property. When she found it, she'd befriend it with Mac's dog biscuits in her pocket.

She opened the wooden gate into Sloan's backyard. Funny, the noise seemed to be coming from his dark house. The grounds were clear. That was odd. Where was the equipment that went along with a big rehab job? All she saw was a construction dumpster sitting at the end of a newly paved driveway.

Suddenly, a large animal bounded out of the dark toward her. Fear rooted her feet to the ground, trapped a scream in her throat. A wet nose burrowed into her side, very near the pocket of dog biscuits. Her flashlight beam revealed a very familiar German Shepherd, whose tail wagged a mile a minute.

"Mac?"

The dog licked her hand. It *was* Mac.

Where was Sloan?

She rubbed the dog's head and pulled a treat from her pocket. The odor of wet dog filled her nostrils. Mac gulped down the treat without chewing it, then raced toward the house and back to Roxie. Her stomach clenched.

Something was wrong.

Sloan would never ignore his dog. Hadn't he told her Mac was one of his best security employees?

She glanced at the dark house again. Her misgivings increased with each second. Why was Mac alone out here in the rain? Should she call Laurie Ann?

No. There had to be a logical explanation for the dog being outside. More than likely it wasn't a police matter.

Summoning her courage, she climbed the concrete steps to the back door and knocked.

The dog cried beside her. She called Sloan's name and knocked louder.

No answer.

Icy fear twisted around her heart. Holding her breath, she tried the knob. It turned easily in her hand.

Exhaling cautiously, she leaned inside. A chill thickened her blood at the absolute silence in the pitch-black gutted kitchen. Had the intruder returned? "Sloan?"

Mac barreled past her. She followed the dog, her heart thumping madly. "Sloan?" she called again. Her flashlight beam illuminated the light switch near the back door. She flipped it on. Nothing happened.

Her heart skipped a beat. No electricity. Figured. She used the beam of her light to trace the wet paw prints up the staircase.

In the second floor hallway, Mac barked at the base of the fold-down attic stairs. Roxie mounted the creaking stairs and shone her light into the rafters. Sheer black fright swept through her. This was so creepy. It was as if Sloan had vanished in thin air. "Sloan?"

The rain was much louder up here. The air felt cooler, damper. She shivered uncontrollably at the steady plink plink of water dripping through the roof into a bucket. "Sloan? Where are you?"

As soon as her head cleared the stairwell, she beamed her light over the floor. Her heart raced out of control. Sloan lay on his back not four feet away, an overturned water pail by his head. She hurried over and knelt at his side.

As a child of missionaries, she knew first aid basics. With trembling fingers, she monitored Sloan's vital signs.

Airway—clear. Pulse—good. Skin—warm.

He was alive.

Relief swept through her as she checked his pupils.

Dilated, but responsive to light.

She noticed a slight abrasion in his hairline above his left eye. Skimming the area with her fingertips, she discovered a golf ball sized lump on his head.

What had happened? It looked like he'd been emptying rain buckets because of the storm, but he'd beaned his head on the low hanging rafter by the stairs. How long had he been out?

An hour? More? Should she call nine-one-one?

Sloan moaned.

The dog barked from the base of the stairs.

Warmth flooded her veins, melting the shards of ice that had settled there. She said a silent prayer of thanksgiving that she wasn't too late.

"It's all right, Mac. I found him," she called. The dog hushed at the sound of her voice.

Sloan opened his eyes and tried to sit up. "Roxie?"

"Don't move," she cautioned, laying a hand across his chest. His heart thumped a steady rhythm under her fingers. Sympathy tangled with concern. "You've had an accident. Where does it hurt?"

His hand covered hers. All the emotion she'd been battling since they'd parted ways shot to the surface. The deluge of feelings stole her breath, but she couldn't give in to them now. Sloan needed her to think for both of them.

"My head hurts like a son of a gun," he said.

"I found a lump in your hairline. Looks like you hit your head on a rafter. Can you move your arms and legs?"

He sat up. "Everything seems to be in good working order. It's just my head that's giving me fits."

"Stay put. Are you woozy? Seeing stars?"

He glanced at her, his dark brown gaze sweeping over her in a very familiar way. Her blood heated. "I'm surprised to see you," he said.

Not nearly as surprised as she was to find him passed out cold in his attic. That was a sight she wouldn't soon forget. "Mac has been barking like a dog possessed trying to get someone's attention for over an hour," she said. "I thought some poor animal was hurt, so I went looking for him. Mac led me here."

"Where is he?"

"At the base of the stairs. He's very anxious to see you."

"He hates those stairs."

"I hate them, too. What happened to your electricity?"

"I fired the electrician today, and the roofer quit too. I tried to finish the wiring job, but I short-circuited the whole house."

She stared. The electrician she'd recommended was the most reliable, most easy-going contractor in the lowcountry. "You fired Mr. Cramer?"

He gingerly ran his fingers along his jaw. "We didn't see eye to eye. I fired him. I'll hire another electrician."

"Don't waste your time." She shot him a critical glance. How could she be upset with him when she was so happy to see him again? "If you fired Mr. Cramer, not a soul in this county will work for you."

"Hell. It's not my fault. The man wanted to take his lunch at ten-thirty in the morning. This job will never get finished at that rate. I had to take a stand."

She wanted to shake some sense into him. "I'll bet you didn't ask him why either."

"Wouldn't matter. There's nothing that would make me change my mind. He took advantage of me."

Roxie lost it. "You moron. He always takes his wife in for dialysis on Wednesdays at lunch time."

Sloan flinched. "Why didn't he say so?"

The startled expression on his face pleased her. Mr. Successful Atlanta Businessman didn't know everything. About time he learned the world didn't revolve around him. "Because everyone knows about his wife. He's related to half the town. Your roofing contractor is his son-in-law."

"My ex-roofing contractor. He walked off the job when I fired Cramer."

"Sounds like you need a property manager."

"Had one. She quit on me."

He struggled to his feet, swaying wildly. She grabbed him around the waist and stabilized him. Did he think he was invincible? "Hold on. You can't go down the stairs weaving like that. I'll call the fire department to carry you down."

"Hell no. I can get down the stairs." He clutched a cross beam for support. "I don't need a house full of people laughing at me for beaning my head."

"Wait a minute." She righted the overturned bucket underneath the biggest leak in the ceiling. Trying to catch that single stream of water was probably a wasted effort when rain sprinkled around them in the attic.

She scrambled to the stairs first. "Follow me. If you lose your balance, I'll catch you."

"Bad plan," he grumbled. "If I lose my balance, I'll flatten both you and Mac."

"It's the only plan we've got. Come on. People get concussions from hitting their heads like you did. You should be checked out at the hospital."

"No doctors." He eased down the ladder.

"You can't out-stubborn me, Sloan Harding. If you won't get medical attention, then you will come home with me."

"I'll be fine here by myself."

She gripped his waist again and steered him toward the back door, stopping to help him into his jacket which was slung over the chair. "Do you want me to yell at you again? Your head is probably pounding something fierce. I would have taken a dog in out of this storm. I'm not leaving an injured man alone in a house with no electricity."

To her surprise, he gave in. She forced her confused emotions into order. She had to be strong enough for both of them.

Mac dogged her heels all the way home. She heaved a sigh of relief when they crossed her threshold. "I'm putting you in Timmy's room. Can you make another flight of stairs?"

"Nice place," Sloan said as she steered him toward Timmy's double bed.

She turned down the bedding and helped him remove his damp jacket. Mac sniffed the perimeter of the room, then lay down on the rug.

"Can I get you anything to drink or eat?"

"I want to sleep."

"Not happening. I need to periodically check your pupils to make sure they are responsive to light. Why don't you get out of those wet clothes?"

He grinned and tugged off his shirt. "I thought you'd never ask."

"I'll be back in a few minutes." She left the room while he peeled off his clothes. Even injured, his charm was potent. Her thoughts weren't Florence Nightingale pure to start with.

She returned with a damp washcloth. "How about a cold cloth for your head?"

He patted the covers beside him. "How about if

my nurse lays down next to me?"

He couldn't be hurt too bad if he was flirting with her. "Are you cold?" She unfolded the white blanket at the foot of the bed and arranged it over the bedding covering him.

He caught her hand and pulled her across the bed, down to his chest. "Please. Stop moving. It hurts my head to keep following you around."

"I'll leave, then."

Sloan didn't release her hand. "How are you going to check my pupils out from out there?"

"With a long stick?" she improvised, wishing her pulse would settle.

He swore under his breath and brought his other arm up to reach for her, the cold compress sliding onto the pillow. "I'm not road kill. I've never jumped a woman in my life."

She eased into his bare arms, grateful for the layers of bedding separating them. He didn't feel very cold. He radiated heat like the barrier island sand dunes in July.

His arms tightened around her as they lay on the bed together, him under the covers and her on top. "Thank you for taking good care of me."

His nearness sent her senses spinning. "Just being neighborly," she said.

He sighed, and she guessed he'd closed his eyes. "Things are different in the city. I don't even know who my neighbors are. You're the best neighbor I've ever had."

Her insides jangled with excitement. She had no doubts about who her neighbor was. Just how she felt about him.

She thought he'd fallen asleep when he turned his head and asked, "Roxie?"

His masculine scent filled her lungs with wanting. This wasn't a good idea. She was far too vulnerable where he was concerned.

Turning her face up to his, she answered him. "Yes?"

His fingers stroked the side of her face. His gaze was as electric as his caress. "I want to kiss you."

"You do?" Her spirits soared. She'd dreamed of his kisses. "We shouldn't. I mean, you're hurt."

The corners of his lips twitched. "I don't mind playing the patient if you're my doctor."

"I'm not a doctor. I'm not even a nurse."

His lips hovered over hers for a second, then brushed lightly against hers, leaving her yearning for more. Her arms tightened around his neck as she lost herself in his surprisingly gentle kiss. A delicious sensation rippled through her. As his kiss deepened, she hungered for completion.

"This isn't a good idea," she murmured. His lips nuzzled the pulsing hollow of her throat. Feverish chills raced down her spine.

"I can't think of anything I'd rather be doing." He kissed the buttons of her blouse open. His warm breath inflamed her with reckless abandon.

Need bubbled through her. She wanted him. She'd known it from the moment she'd first laid eyes on him. Staying in his bed invited disaster.

It was also the most thrilling thing she'd ever done.

Chapter 10

With only the faint light from the hallway to guide her, Roxie stroked Sloan's strong back. She craved the sensation of his skin next to hers. Hope fluttered as delicate as butterfly wings.

Speech wasn't possible as his stubble-roughened face and tantalizing lips explored her neck and collarbone with delicious kisses. Instinctively, she arched toward him.

She splayed her fingers across his broad shoulders. "If this is a dream, don't wake me."

He caressed her breast and skimmed down her length, his warm hand coming to rest lightly on her thigh. "You're the dream. You feel so good. Like quicksilver in my hands."

He sought her core. She hummed with need. "You have nice hands. Don't. Stop."

Years of pent-up desire emboldened her. His touch felt wonderful, but he was taking his sweet time. She wasn't in the mood for slow. She pushed the covers down past his waist. He groaned as her fingers closed around him. The sound ruffled her senses. Then caution flitted into her head. "Am I hurting you? Is this too much?"

He inhaled shakily, his dark pirate eyes eating her up, his hands making short work of her clothing. "I'm fine, or I will be in a few minutes. I've wanted to do this from the first moment I saw you."

"Same here." Want and desire and need swirled through her bloodstream. She laughed, low and throaty, and was astonished at the sultry sound. She pulled him down for another head-spinning kiss.

A sense of urgency drove her.

She wanted more. So much more.

Her legs clenched around him, bringing him intimately close. She shivered under his dark perusal. Inside her, a tempest roared. "Now," she said. "Do it now."

His teeth flashed in the near darkness. "As you wish."

Her nails dug into his shoulders. "Oh yeah. That's it."

Like a wave runner riding high on a massive wall of water, she soared through the heights of passion. Sensations blurred into one powerful surge rumbling toward a distant shore. Taste, sight, hearing, and smell faded until touch reigned supreme.

Him touching her.

Her touching him.

She teetered on a cresting wave, flying high, and thrilled at the heady freedom. With Sloan. Together they spiraled through the surge of raw energy, creating a universe of two. Her heart roared in her ears, and she let go, calling his name aloud.

In this moment, this time and place, he was exquisitely hers.

She drifted in a mellow haze, warm, secure, sated.

Sight was the first sense to return. She smiled at Sloan sprawled out on her chest. Their mingled scents perfumed the air, a unique elixir of love. Breath eased into her lungs, sound buzzed in her ears. And love. It danced around her on fairy wings, twirling and gliding, delighting her heart.

All those years she'd missed out on this wonderfully contented feeling.

She'd finally found the right man.

****

"Are you all right?" he asked, rising up on his

elbows.

"All right?" Roxie had discovered a new universe, learned a potent new body language, and experienced sensations out of this world. She was gloriously spent, and she couldn't move a muscle if she tried. "Yes."

It felt like she'd swallowed the sun and brilliant rays illuminated her from within. She felt better than all right. Gloriously right. Fabulously right. "I'm fine."

"You're thinking." He stroked the side of her flushed face.

She trembled. Her entire nervous system was locked in hyperdrive. What would it be like to do this frequently? Could she stand the excitement? Would making love with Sloan ever seem dull and routine?

"I can't help it," she said. "I've never felt like this before. I need to understand what happened."

"You seduced me."

His smug attitude sliced through her bubble of happiness. "I did not. I was caring for a hurt neighbor, and you made a pass at me."

"You see it your way, I'll see it mine."

Her joy faded. Insecurity whispered in her ear. This wonderful act of love had no special meaning to him? Was she just another toss in the hay? She should have known better. She pushed against his broad chest. "Get off me."

His arms cradled her protectively. "Not so fast. What's wrong?"

"You have to ask?"

He stared at her for a long moment, then rolled to his back, bringing her with him so that she remained intimately pressed to his side. "I'm an idiot. I forgot to use the condom in my wallet."

"You *are* an idiot if you think that's the only problem. I never would have let things go this far if I wasn't protected. I've taken the pill for years to regulate my cycles. Unless," she paused as a sudden chill swept through her. "Unless you're—"

"Hell no. I've always used protection before. Always. No exceptions. What about you?"

"The same." Not that there had been that many times for her. Once actually, and it had been a huge mistake. But there had been a condom. If she harbored any diseases, they were news to her.

After a moment, he turned on his side, facing her. "That was awesome."

"Me, too. I mean, it was awesome for me, too." She blushed, glad for the relative darkness of the Timmy's bedroom. Heat emanated from Sloan's body, cloaking her in his warmth. Awesome, he'd said. Awesome was better than good. Awesome was in a class by itself.

Now what?

Why didn't he say something?

"How's your head? Does it still ache?"

He kissed her again, slowly, languorously, until she felt an ache of her own. "Sweetheart, it's not my head that's aching," he whispered in her hair.

She cuddled closer, thrilled that she had this effect on him. "Dang. Who knew that getting hit on the head would have this side effect? I should have clobbered you weeks ago."

"Come here, you." He rolled her across the rumpled bed in slow circles, laughing and nuzzling her neck.

****

Sloan awoke out of a deep slumber. Golden sunbeams radiated through the window, filling the room with warmth and cheer. The pillow under his head smelled fresh and felt wondrously soft.

He gazed at his unfamiliar surroundings. Baseball pennants lined the baby blue walls. A poster of Henry Aaron grinned down at him from the closed door. Baseball caps and foam tomahawks lined the bookshelves. Timmy's room. Roxie's house.

He sat up slowly. His head still throbbed, but it wasn't as bad as it had been last night.

Last night.

Roxie had slept with him. She'd gone up in flames, just like he knew she would. Where was she?

Now that he'd had her, he wanted another helping, and he wasn't a man to deny his appetite.

He shrugged into his still damp jeans. And where was his dog? His stomach grumbled. Food. He was hungry. With any luck, he'd find food, his dog and his woman in the same place.

He slung his shirt over his bare shoulder and went to find them. Mac intercepted him at the kitchen door. He paused to ruffle the dog's head and straightened. Roxie sat at the table in the cozy blue kitchen, watching him. Though her hair was snugged back in a ponytail, he remembered the rich feel of it in his hands. A shirt that reminded him of the color of pumpkins accented her breasts. Tan slacks hugged her hips.

Working clothes. Was she thinking to sneak out on him? A dark emotion seized him by the throat. No way was she giving him the brush-off again. Not after what they'd shared.

He wouldn't let her pretend last night didn't happen. He prowled toward her and leaned in for a proprietary kiss.

She kissed him back but not as wholeheartedly as last night. What was going on?

"Roxie?"

She met his gaze briefly, then averted her eyes. "Morning, Sloan. I made breakfast. You hungry?"

"I'm hungry for a lot of things." His eyes followed her as she bustled around the cozy kitchen. A plate of bacon and scrambled eggs emerged from the microwave. The toaster popped.

He let it go for the moment and sat at her table,

the same table where her grandmother used to feed him, and he ate the meal she'd prepared. "Thanks," he said as he wolfed everything down.

"Slow down. You eat like Mac."

Testy this morning, wasn't she? He'd have her in a good mood again soon enough. He spread strawberry preserves on his toast. "How long have you been up?"

"Long enough to run over to your house, feed your dog, grab your stuff, and bring it back here."

Sloan smiled slowly. He hadn't expected her to be so straightforward about the practicalities of their affair. "You want me to move in with you?"

"Not exactly." Her heated gaze met his firmly. "I need you to move out of your place. Mr. Cramer and his son-in-law said they'd finish the job, but only if you weren't there."

"Oh." She saw him as a bumbling idiot who couldn't manage his subcontractors. His good mood tanked.

"I hope you don't mind that I took the initiative." She loaded his dishes in the dishwasher. "I assume your plan is still to fix up the house."

"Sure." He wanted the repairs finished, but he wanted to sleep with Roxie more. With this arrangement he got the best of both worlds.

She propped a hip against the counter and cleared her throat. "I have a buyer that keeps calling about your house. If you're going to sell it anyway, it might be to our mutual advantage to get the repairs completed as soon as possible."

Suspicion clouded his head, twisted his gut. "You trying to get rid of me?"

"No. You're welcome to stay here as long as you like. It's serendipity that you have an interested buyer, and you plan on selling at some point in the not-so-distant future. Why not take advantage of this opportunity?"

Still no mention of their lovemaking. Her evasion worried him. Obviously she wasn't wowed by his technique. Was he losing his touch? That bump on his head must have affected his performance.

He felt fine now. He could have her shivering in his arms, five minutes tops.

But maybe he was missing the big picture. Maybe he'd have a better chance of holding onto her if he kept his pants zipped. It wasn't a strategy he'd considered before.

"I appreciate your initiative with the house," he said. "I should have trusted my gut instinct and held you to our original contract. You've got the job again, if you want it."

Emotions flashed across her face. She seemed to be on the verge of a smile but then her features tightened as if she were about to spit nails.

"Is this about last night?" she asked.

He replayed his words in his head. Getting laid had cleared his head. But judging by the grim set of her lips, he was dead in the water if he mentioned sex.

"This is about me thinking I didn't need a property manager. I have a profound respect for your expertise. You are very good at what you do."

She drew in a long breath. "Thank you. I had to make sure that was the case. I wouldn't want anyone to think I sleep with clients to get their business."

The thought of her sleeping with any other clients was unacceptable. He jammed his hands in his pockets. "You know better than that, Roxie. So, what's the deal with my house? How long until it's ready?"

"A month, tops, but you could move back in next week. You'll have hot water and electricity by then." She paused. "About the buyer. He's crazy about your place."

More likely he was crazy about Roxie. Sloan didn't want to sell the house now. He especially didn't want another guy becoming her back door neighbor.

"No deal," he said. "My house is not for sale."

"This guy has money. He offered me $400,000 for this house, and it isn't even the house he wants. He wants yours."

"Not interested."

She nodded. "I told him as much. But he's very insistent. Says he'll take his business over to Sally at BC Realty."

"I'd hate for you to lose a client because of me, but I've decided to keep the house after all. I plan to spend a lot more time in Mossy Bog."

"You do?"

He edged closer, intent on kissing Roxie. "I do. Because of you. I want to spend time with you. I know we have the geography thing against us, but we'll make it work." His arms snugged her close. Greedily, he inhaled her scent.

"How's your head this morning?"

"In need of your attention."

Feather light, her fingers skimmed the knot in his hairline. "Still there but better than last night."

"Nothing could be better than last night." He kissed her lightly, taking his time about it. "Except maybe this morning."

She pulled back. "I was hoping to interest you in trying out that kayak with me this morning. I've got a client meeting this afternoon."

"Call me crazy but you may be overdressed for paddling in the marsh."

"That's because I just called my morning client and moved our appointment to the afternoon. I was covering all my bases."

"You sure hit a home run with me. What about dinner tonight?"

"On Thursdays I eat with Les Green out at the nursing home. He owns the property where I want to put the museum. I started visiting him months ago to find out more about the property. He's so lonely. I don't want to let him down."

"It's Thursday? Damn. I'm due back in Atlanta today. Big client presentation first thing tomorrow. I'm the closer."

"I'll bet you are."

"Talk about lousy timing." He kissed her again. "I've got something else on Monday," he said, then frowned, thinking. "I'll drive back here Friday afternoon, then back to Atlanta late Sunday evening. That would give us the whole weekend together."

"Sorry. No can do. I'm committed to helping out at the Fall Festival this weekend. If you want to join me, I'm working in the shrimp frying booth."

"I'd do just about anything for your cooking, but I'm not sure I could keep my hands to myself that long. The people of Mossy Bog might object to a naked cook."

"Naked cooking would get us both arrested. That's no good."

"Good point. Plus there'd be all that hot grease from the deep fryer. What if we kayak this morning and I come back Monday night for the naked part? Does that work for you?"

"Perfect."

****

Sloan dipped the paddle into the shallow water of the man-made canal. The kayak glided across the smooth surface like a dream. The vaulted tree branches lent the historic canal a cathedral-like feeling.

He drank in the sight of the thick ferns and shrubs lining the banks. It wasn't a stretch to assume he and Roxie were the only people for miles and miles.

Just the two of them.

He liked the sound of that.

"We need to do this again," he said. "Soon."

She turned and smiled at him. "Definitely."

"Put kayaking on our schedule for Tuesday. I never knew this was out here."

"I came out two years ago when we had an outfitter's business in town. The river guide brought us here and gave me the map we've been using. I love how peaceful it feels out here. I'm glad you like it too."

"I can't recall ever feeling so mellow." Contentment hummed in his bones. Was it the woman, the sex, or the natural surroundings? Whatever it was, he wanted more. "I've been avoiding Mossy Bog for years, but right now this is exactly where I want to be."

"You don't fantasize about driving a speedboat or a Jet Ski through here?"

He shook his head. "Wouldn't be the same. This sounds corny, but I feel connected. Like I belong here. I've never had that sense of rightness in any place I've lived. I don't remember feeling this way when I was growing up here. I couldn't wait to leave this place."

Though the water they traversed was less than three feet deep, the ever present mud obscured the water's clarity. Roxie rested her paddle across her lap and glanced at him over her shoulder. "I understand. When I traveled with my parents, I felt so off-balance. I would start to feel the rhythms of a place, and we'd be off to a new town. Living with Gran in Mossy Bog saved me. I missed my parents, but I found myself."

He considered her words, testing them, trying them on for size. "Sounds like Lavinia was home, not the town."

"That could be. But it's more than that. Not

153

having to move every six to twelve months gave me the chance to be me. Gran provided the stability I craved, but this place by the sea, it healed my heart. Gran's gone now, and I could pick up stakes and move anywhere in the world, but why would I? This is my home."

Her truth resonated deep within him.

Muddy waters. He wasn't just crossing them, he lived in them. Gators trolled beneath the murky surface, waiting for him to display weakness.

His everyday life was far from this place, this woman. But he could adapt. A glance at his watch confirmed what he knew. As much as he wanted this idyllic moment to never end, both of them had places to be.

"I hate to mention this, because I would be happy to stay here all day, but we need to head back."

Roxie sighed. "I wish it was Monday already."

They paddled steadily through the lush setting, a gentle breeze stirring the tree leaves and airy swags of Spanish moss overhead.

Suddenly Roxie stopped paddling, glancing around.

"What?" he asked.

"Do you feel it?" she whispered. "I'm sure someone's out here watching us."

Adrenaline shot through him. He hurled forward in his seat, giving her a hard shove. "Get down!"

A split second later, a gunshot rang out. A bullet thwacked into the trees about head high. "Stay down," Sloan ordered, reaching for the pistol strapped to his ankle.

"Hey! There are people over here!" Roxie yelled. "Stop shooting."

"Roxie," he hissed. "Stay down!"

Sloan cursed himself for letting his guard down.

He quickly appraised the wooded canal. No shooter visible on the banks, but they didn't have to be close with a rifle. His mission crystallized.

Protect Roxie.

Neutralize the shooter.

She glanced over her shoulder at his handgun, disbelief marring her face. "You've brought a gun? Here? Are you nuts?"

Heart hammering, he beached the craft on the soft bank and tugged her out, tucking her behind a cypress tree. "I'm going to sweep the area. Don't move."

The roar of an outboard motor reached his ears. Gun in hand, Sloan ran through the tidal forest, leaping fallen trees, sinking into the muck that passed for soil.

His mind raced with possibilities as he saw a small aluminum craft speed away. Was this a random act? Or had someone meant to harm them? The person in the speedboat wore a green jacket with the hood pulled up.

Sloan noted a high point where the ferns were crushed. He stood there and sited back to the rice canal. A portion of creek they had just paddled was visible. His chest tightened. Someone had stood here and waited to ambush them.

Fear grabbed his heart and wouldn't let go. He hurried back to Roxie and hustled her into the kayak.

"What? What did you find out?" Her voice trembled. "Did you see the hunters?"

"No hunters. Just a boat heading down river. One person. This was deliberate."

Roxie's paddle stilled. "Deliberate? Not hunters?"

"Looks that way. We're calling the cops soon as we hit town." He studied her. "Thanks for the early warning. Ever thought about a career in security?"

She shuddered. "No. I hate guns."

****

"I've got your description of the boat." Laurie Ann Dinterman's pen tapped the narrow notepad on her knee. She rocked slowly in Lavinia's padded rocking chair. "But without the hull identification number, we're out of luck. There are hundreds of boats this size in the county. And a small john boat like that wouldn't need the public boat ramp. The person could run it right up into a nearby tidal slip and hunker down."

Though the danger was past, Sloan's heart still raced. It had been close. Too damned close. No time for recriminations now. Calling upon his military training, he suppressed his frustration and anger.

The scene replayed in his head. "Sorry, I didn't notice any hull numbers," Sloan said. "I focused on the shooter. It was a single assailant, male I believe, about medium height and build. The gun was a rifle. And the person was a bad shot. From where he was standing he had us dead on. Or he did until Roxie sensed someone watching us."

Roxie's mouth dropped. "He did?"

"If he wasn't a bad shot, then he meant to miss," Sloan said to the cop. "Either possibility will keep me awake tonight. How many men can you put on this case?"

"There's two of us per shift, and the police chief is out of commission with a busted hip. Trouble is we have nothing solid to go on. I'll canvas the docks and ask about the boater with a green jacket, but our local hardware store sells that jacket. Hell, I've got a jacket like that in my car."

Sloan's jaw tightened. "What about the boat angle?"

"Again, I can call the Coast Guard, but without something more to go on, we'd be wasting taxpayer dollars by patrolling the old rice canals. If this shooter is after you two, they won't be in the river unless you're in the river."

Roxie huddled into the sofa. "You're saying we shouldn't kayak again?"

Laurie Ann pocketed her notepad and rose. She set her police hat on her head, pulling the brim down to just above her eyes. "Don't put yourself in any tight spots until we catch this guy. Listen to your gut. You feel like something's wrong, you let me know."

Sloan stood and shook the cop's hand. "I'm scheduled to return to Atlanta this afternoon. If the person is after me, and I hope they are, Roxie should be fine."

"You got enemies, Mr. Harding?" the cop asked.

He shrugged. "I run a security and investigation business. Some folks are unhappy with our findings."

"Be careful." Laurie Ann turned to Roxie. "And, while we're exploring possibilities, do you think this is related to your other troubles?"

Sloan felt like a trapdoor had opened in his stomach. "What other troubles?"

Laurie Ann enumerated them on her fingers. "The break-in. The identity theft. The banana-colored boat."

"Whoa. Back up." Sloan took Roxie's cold hands in his. "What break-in?"

"It happened before we met." Roxie regarded him steadily. "Someone entered my house and trashed my kitchen. We think this burglar stole my identity."

"Why am I just hearing about this now?"

"We took care of it." Roxie shrugged. "There was no need to tell you."

Sloan was very aware of the women watching him. Did they expect fireworks? It hurt that Roxie hadn't confided in him, but he couldn't dwell on that now. They had to move forward or they'd never identify the shooter.

"I sense a pattern here." He eased back down on the sofa beside Roxie. "Someone is trying to get your attention."

She shivered. "They've got it."

He regarded her steadily. "Who'd you piss off?"

Alarm flared in her eyes. "Nobody. I'm in real estate, not high tech espionage. Why would anyone care about what I do at Marshview Realty?"

Sloan enfolded her in his arms. "*That* is a very interesting question."

****

A few hours later, dog and man stared at Roxie as they lounged in her kitchen. She stirred the lumpy muffin mix and tried to find the solace cooking usually brought her. Under pressure from Sloan and Laurie Ann, she'd canceled her appointment today with Roger Cleary.

But she wouldn't cancel her entire weekend.

No way.

"Keep Mac here with you," Sloan said from the doorway.

"I appreciate the offer, but no thanks. I'm not risking your dog getting shot."

"This is insane. I want you to be safe. Promise me you'll keep the doors locked."

Ever since Sloan's wild dash through the woods, Roxie had been aware of the brooding tension in him. Sloan was born to be a protector.

He was also very confident of his authority.

He would take over this area of her life if she let him. A girl had to draw the line. "Cut me some slack, Sloan. I'm a single female. I don't leave personal security to chance."

"Take my gun. I'll show you how to use it."

She poured the thick batter into the wells of a cupcake pan, her nerves refusing to settle. Sure she'd been scared, but she'd helped to save them. "Forget it. I don't like guns. And I didn't know you carried a gun. What's with that, by the way? Did you think our sea monster would attack? Shooting Mossy Girl would not endear you to the locals."

"I carry a gun because I'm in security."

"Guns kill people."

"People kill people." He frowned. "When were you going to tell me about the break-in?"

"When were you going to tell me about the gun?"

"Touché. Now when were you going to tell me?" She turned to face him.

"I wasn't. It didn't seem relevant."

"Didn't seem relevant? My gut says it isn't finished. Someone is after you, Roxie."

She had to distract him or he would never leave. She wouldn't let him jeopardize his career for her. She wasn't paralyzed by fear. She'd been living with it for weeks. She could take care of herself. Sloan had to be deflected.

Going for humor, she waggled her eyebrows. "Someone caught me."

He rose. "This is serious. The danger is escalating. I'm cancelling my trip to Atlanta. Bates can give the damn presentation to the peanut people."

She shoved the pan in the oven and stalked over to him. "You said you were the closer. I don't want your work to suffer because of something that happened down here. I'll be fine. I won't go out in the kayak, and Laurie Ann will circle my house like a hammerhead shark." She gestured toward the door. "Go forth and win new clients."

"I don't like it."

"I'm not your responsibility. I can take care of myself."

"Luck was with us today, but you can't count on luck to hold. We have to figure out what this is all about."

"We'll do that, just not today. I'm a big girl, and I've been looking after myself for a long time. I'm flattered by your protectiveness, Sloan, but you're crowding me. I'm not a helpless female who needs a big strong man to protect her."

"You saying I'm big and strong?"

As he neared, her lips tugged into a smile. "Definitely."

Her toes curled at his kiss. She wrapped her arms around his neck, savoring his nearness, his strength.

"You could come with me," he said. "Mossy Bog would survive without you for one weekend."

"Give it a rest, Harding. I've got this."

He kissed her again, a thorough remember-me kind of kiss. "I'll be counting the minutes until I'm back here with you."

The dreaminess in her eyes cleared. "Wait. In all the excitement, I almost forgot. I have something for you." She smiled tremulously and handed him a bound book. "I found it in Pop Pop's papers. He talks about your granddad in here. Maybe it will be helpful in your search."

"Thanks." He accepted the small leather-bound book. The corners were bent like a well used billfold. It pleased him she'd remembered his interest in the journal. "Don't forget me."

****

Roxie drove to Marshview Realty with a police escort. *Overkill,* she thought, but she'd agreed to it before Sloan left.

Being shot at had been horrible, but Sloan and Laurie Ann were worrying enough for the whole town.

Sloan.

She sighed with a smile. He was everything she'd ever dreamed of in a man. Sexy. Dashing.

Tender. Protective. Resourceful.

And he cared for her. He wouldn't go platonic on her. It wasn't his way. His name bubbled through her giddy thoughts, filling her with joy.

The sun had never shone brighter, the autumn leaves had never been so fragrant. Maybe it had to do with being shot at, but she suspected Sloan was at least half the reason she felt so alive today.

So what if she'd messed up her signing bonus with Noreen? It wasn't like that had been written in stone anyway. She'd find a way to get the museum funded or die trying. You couldn't put a price on love.

Love. She floated into the office, stored her leather purse in a desk drawer, and retrieved her messages. After returning the Ashburns' call about their pending closing and touching base with Mrs. Centineo about her scheduled walk-through, she noticed Megan was staring at her. "What?"

"You know what." Megan waggled a finger. "Something happened last night. My guess is that you and Mr. Harding are once again on a first name basis."

"You're right." Roxie brimmed with energy, and she bounced across the office to hug her friend. "So much has happened since yesterday, I barely know where to start."

"Easy. Start with the good stuff."

Roxie blushed. "I can't talk about that, but it was *good*. I thought my Mr. Right would never show up."

"You've got it bad. Please tell me he's just as smitten. How'd you make the transition from bite-his-head-off mad to happy dancing in the briar patch?"

Roxie quickly explained about the accident. "I was worried about him. There I was tucking him in Timmy's bed, planning to stay awake all night to watch over him, and he made a pass at me. I thought about the times in my life I've said no to things I wanted to do. The plain truth is I didn't want to say no to him. I said yes."

"I can see that."

Roxie stopped. Why wasn't her friend excited for her? "But?"

"But, and I hope you don't hate me for saying anything, but in this specific area I know what I'm talking about. He's not a beginner-date kind of guy. You entered the game at the expert level." Megan smiled thinly. "I don't want you to get hurt."

"I appreciate your concern, but I can't imagine going my whole life and never feeling like this."

"Tell me this. Has he called yet?"

"Of course not. It's only been half an hour since he left. It's too soon to expect him to call...isn't it?"

Megan shrugged. "You know this guy. I don't. All I'm saying is that any guy who was ever crazy about me, Dave included, wanted to spend every waking moment with me. I think it's odd that everything could be so wonderful and then you both go your separate ways. When will you see him again?"

Some of the shimmer leaked out of Roxie's happiness. Then she remembered how hard she'd worked to convince him to leave. "Monday. He has meetings over the next few days. But Megan, I didn't tell you all the news. When we went kayaking today, someone took a shot at us."

"A shot? With a gun?"

"A rifle. According to Sloan, the shooter was a male of medium build wearing a green jacket like Barry's Hardware sells."

"Get out! Where you scared?"

Roxie nodded. "But Sloan took matters in hand and brought us safely home. He was amazing."

"Sounds like it. Dave and I will keep an eye on you 'til he returns. You should move in with us."

"Thanks, but there's really no need. I've got new door locks and police circling my house every hour. Laurie Ann's calling me in between, too. I'm safe as I can be. I'd rather talk about phone calls."

"Ah...phone calls. Right. The dating gospel according to Megan says that Sloan should call you every night he's away. If he's really got it bad, he will call you in between as well."

Roxie sat down at her desk and studied her to-do list. "We're adults. I don't need to check up on him when he's out of sight, and he shouldn't feel that way either."

"Don't kid yourself. Humans are jealous creatures. We're all emotional and not entirely rational either. Mark my words, something is wrong if he doesn't call."

She considered Megan's words. If Sloan wasn't crazy about her, how would she handle that? How could she work with a guy who didn't return her feelings? What came first, the romance or the job?

The phone rang and Megan answered it. Roxie heard her friend field the inquiry, but her mind was miles away, in a black Jeep with a large German Shepherd.

Sloan would be back in four days. If he didn't call her, then she'd call him. The gospel according to Megan might need to be re-written. Right?

****

Sloan watched the seconds tick by on his Rolex. Where the hell was Bates? He'd trusted Jeff to run a tight ship while he was gone, and it seemed his trust had been misplaced.

The Edinger account wasn't closed out, and there were no new proposals on his desk. When he'd left, there'd been three physical security jobs needing estimates. What was going on?

"Sorry I'm late, boss."

Sloan gestured toward a chair and Jeff sat.

"What's the status on the Edinger account?"

"I need to talk to you about that. I thought something was off about that job all along. I did some digging around. Our background checks were part of a setup to frame an employee for stealing from the company."

"You have proof?"

"You mean like surveillance photos and computer transactions linking the supposed bad egg to the crime but all the while incriminating Troy Edinger?"

"Yeah. You got that?"

Jeff grinned. "Sure do."

"Did we get paid yet?"

"The final payment cleared the bank yesterday."

Sloan rubbed his chin. "Damn, Jeff. You're good. The bad guy will go to jail, and we still get paid. It doesn't get any better than that."

"You thought I'd screwed up, didn't you? I knew you'd check the files when you came in. I bet you almost blew a gasket when you saw I still had the account open."

"I'm not an admin machine, but I am on edge. Someone took a shot at me and Roxie."

"You back with her?" At Sloan's nod, Bates continued. "You want us to take this guy out?"

"Couldn't ID the shooter. Local LEOs are keeping Roxie under close surveillance for now. The only saving grace is the guy's a lousy shot."

"That's a helluva note. You want me to do tomorrow's presentation so you can drive back down there?"

Sloan shook his head. "She'll have a fit if I turn around and drive back down there. But I can't stop worrying about her."

Bates grinned. "Feisty is she? No wonder you're after her."

"When I'm with her..."

"Yeah?"

"Never mind."

Bates tapped Sloan on the shoulder, hard. "Give it up."

"I feel different. Like I'm somebody."

"Hell, you always was somebody. 'Bout time you realized it. Is she hot?"

Sloan couldn't wipe the goofy grin off his face. "Yeah. She's hot."

He'd had his fingers on the phone to call her twice since he'd left her. He wanted to hear her voice again and that worried him. A lot.

What sort of hold did she have over him? He hadn't expected to see her in his house, hadn't expected her to make love to him. He hadn't expected to lose control and forget to use a condom.

That had never happened before. Was that what made him want to be with her so much? The fact that she was the first woman that he'd ever been skin to skin with like that? He'd thought having sex with her would get her out of his system, but if anything, it had made the craving worse. He really wanted to talk to her.

Talk to her.

But he couldn't go against everything that he knew. He couldn't go changing his personal rules. There had to be some semblance of order in his world.

He'd see her on Monday. That would be soon enough.

He gazed at the black phone on the corner of his desk. Calling her right now would be crazy. He'd be opening himself up to all kinds of trouble. She'd expect him to call all the time, he'd forget, and there'd be hell to pay.

He called anyway. "Hey, Sunshine. Miss me?"

"You know I do. How was the traffic?"

"Steady. Any word from the cops about the

165

shooter?"

"Nothing to report. A cruiser goes by every hour or so and Laurie Ann has personally called me on the half hours in between. I'm okay."

"Good. Stay alert. I don't want anything to happen to you."

"Back atcha."

****

Roxie covered her mouth with her hand. When she'd gone to visit Les Green for their regular Thursday night dinner that evening, she'd been shocked to learn of his hospitalization. She'd had to see him for herself. He looked so frail lying there in the hospital bed, almost a caricature of himself.

"How long's he been like this?" she asked from the doorway.

Her fellow bridesmaid and nurse, Brenda Harris, tugged her away from Les's room. They strolled down the tiled corridor under the hum of fluorescent lights. "A few days. His temperature spiked, then he went into a coma."

Roxie hugged her middle. "I had no idea. You should have called me."

"Can't do that. Patient confidentiality."

"Has his daughter come to visit?"

"Haven't seen her."

"I guess I shouldn't be surprised. Andrea didn't visit much when he was healthy. Will he get better?"

"That's up to him. He has a DNR."

Roxie knew what a do not resuscitate order was. "Poor thing."

"I'll take good care of him. For however many days or hours he has left."

Moisture blurred her vision. She hated to think of Les dying, but at least death would end his suffering. "You better. He's one of the good guys."

"And what's this about you and Sloan being shot at? Why didn't you tell me the cops are riding circles around your house?"

"I figured word would get out soon enough. Besides, Laurie Ann and Sloan are both driving me nuts about safety."

"They should be. I'm walking you to your car."

"No need. I've got a police escort waiting for me out there."

"Yes, there is a need. I'll help you look for bad guys on the way."

Roxie sighed as her friend took her arm. "If only we knew what they looked like."

****

"Hey you."

Roxie smiled all the way to her toes. She set aside the file she'd been working on at home and leaned back in the comfy pillows. "Hey."

"How'd the presentation go?"

"Signed 'em."

"You are a closer."

"My team is good. Makes a difference. How'd dinner with the old guy go?"

"It didn't. He's in the hospital."

"I'm sorry."

"He wasn't in the best of health to start with. Chances are he won't pull through. What a waste. He's such a nice guy."

"Anything I can do?"

Roxie sighed. "No. There's nothing I can do either. I like to fix things, but you've already seen the full extent of my nursing abilities. And you want to know something else?"

"What?"

"I feel guilty saying this, because I do care about Les Green, but if he dies my museum project dies. His daughter inherits his estate, and she hates me. Andrea Albert wouldn't sell that old warehouse to me if I had millions to toss at her."

"Want me to adjust her attitude?"

"Heavens, no." She paused. "You wouldn't. Would you?"

"I would if you wanted me to."

"I shouldn't have brought it up. I wouldn't have said anything if she hadn't accused me of trying to hustle my way into Les Green's life as his next wife."

"You like this guy?"

"Not like that. We're friends. We played gin rummy and talked about his days at the mill. I planned to buy the property from him, but I don't have enough money pulled together yet. We have ten grand in our Friends of the Museum account, but that's not nearly enough."

"You seem to know everyone down there. Have you considered getting a fixer-upper instead and having people donate their skills?"

"Of course I've considered it. But the old cotton warehouse is the place the museum has to go. I know it good as I know my own name." She huffed out a breath. "I'm sorry. I get excited about the museum."

"How about me? Do you get excited about me?"

"I do." Heat rose to her cheeks as she realized she'd given the traditional wedding response. "I mean, of course, I enjoy your company."

"What about my body? Enjoy that too?"

She shrieked. "You're trying to embarrass me, aren't you? Isn't phone sex against federal law or something?"

"Don't know about that, but it pales beside the real thing. I wish I was there with you."

"Me too."

"And for the record, your nursing skills are top notch. I've never been treated so nicely. I plan to bring all my concussions to you."

****

By Saturday evening, Sloan couldn't stop pacing in his condo. He'd already been for a late night walk

168

with Mac. He'd picked up his clothes from the cleaners and paid his monthly bills. His packed suitcase waited by the front door.

He'd reviewed the last two weeks worth of time sheet logs, okayed the payroll amounts, and agreed to hire another employee because of the increased volume of physical security jobs. He'd organized a mental outline of what he wanted to say to his team at Monday's staff meeting.

But no matter what he did, Roxie's smiling face stayed in his mind. She had gotten under his skin all right. He had a million things he wanted to talk to her about and that worried him.

His usual MO was to half-listen to the women he dated prattle on and on. They didn't expect him to respond. They needed someone to listen to them, and they valued his contribution in the bedroom. He understood that behavior.

What he didn't understand was why he needed to pick up the phone and call Roxie. Friday night they'd talked about his dog and her favorite desserts. Tonight she'd talked about cooking shrimp for the fall festival, he'd told her about his Army buddies. Each night it had been harder to hang up. Each night he'd felt the tidal pull of the coast and the woman.

He'd known he could unlock the sexual energy that pulsed around her. They'd been magic together. He'd had great sex before, but it had never consumed him like this. He needed to see her, to fill his head with her fragrance, to drown in her tropical gaze, to hear her sigh out his name.

He wanted to sit in her cozy kitchen again. To have her take care of him, to eat the food she'd prepared for him. He loved that blue kitchen. He shook his head sadly.

"I'm losing it, bud," he said to Mac.

Mac thumped his tail energetically.

It probably wasn't any news to his dog that Sloan was losing it. Mac knew everything. Mac had run right into Roxie's arms the first time he'd seen her. Mac didn't have any embarrassing family history to overcome. Mac had taken one look at the woman and decided that he wanted her.

A man could learn a lot from his dog.

Chapter 11

Bates leaned in on the sweating guy. "We've got you cold, Turk. There's nowhere you can run we won't find you."

"I didn't do nuttin' to you guys." Turk glanced first at Bates, then over at Sloan sitting in the shadows of the Team Six Security conference room. "I swear on a stack of Bibles."

Sloan tapped the edges of his fingertips together, waiting for the guy to trip himself up. His kind always did. Especially at three in the morning.

Bates opened the folder he held and tossed out photos of seniors. Each one spun down like individual playing cards. "You fleeced fifteen old ladies, dickhead. You and Jared Gilmore."

Turk scrunched up his jowly face, slitting his wide-spaced eyes. "So?"

Satisfaction unfurled in Sloan. Turk was looking for an angle. There wasn't one. Sloan and Bates had done this before. Lesser men than Turk had cracked under the pressure of the truth.

"We take offense to your con. Robbing little old ladies." Bates pounded his fist on the table. The pictures jumped and so did Turk. "You should be ashamed of yourself."

Turk shrunk back in his seat, his fear tainting the air. Sweat dripped down his cheeks, collected on his shirt collar. "We didn't steal from anyone that couldn't afford it. Gil made sure of that."

"He fooled you. We know for a fact three of these ladies buy cat food now. Cat food. They're eating cat food because of a slimeball like you."

Turk glanced at the door, sucking air through his teeth. Bates stood between him and the only exit. Bates was not a small man. "Gil selected the m-m-marks. That wasn't me."

"You got their credit card numbers with the fake car repair scam, and he did the rest?"

"I'm just a cog in a wheel."

Sloan leaned forward out of the shadows. "Tell us about Gilmore. What did he do with the money?"

"How the hell should I know? We're business associates, not friends. We don't hang out together, if you get my drift." Turk swallowed nervously. "Crap. You guys are gonna ruin this for me, aren't ya? You're gonna take him down, and I'm gonna be out of a good job."

"Count on it," Sloan said. "Tell me what you know about good old Gil, and we might not tell the cops where you are."

"Gil's moving up in the world. He's got a line on a high roller place, but he can't swing it yet. Besides the old lady scam, he's running a few others to get a stake together. He keeps bragging about buried treasure. Some fool is sitting on a cool million and doesn't know it."

Air stalled in Sloan's lungs. He forced the question out. "Where?"

"Some podunk place on the coast. South of Savannah."

Sloan's gut twisted. This *was* personal. Gilmore was coming after his inheritance. How the hell did he know about it? The prison connection? And where the hell was it?

"You got fifteen minutes to get out of town," Sloan said. "Don't go home. The cops are already there."

Turk looked like he didn't believe his good fortune, then he bolted for the door.

Bates shook his head as the door slammed open.

"Will he make it, boss?"

"Not a chance," Sloan said. "He's addicted to easy money. The cops will have him in two days."

"Nice to have you back."

"Good to be back." Sloan stood and stretched. "Thanks for finding this guy. Now I know what Gilmore wants. Hidden money. My alleged inheritance."

"You holding out on us, boss?" There was a teasing quality in Bates' voice.

Sloan was not amused. Anger colored his words. "Gilmore is on a fool's errand. My father chased the same empty dream until he drank himself to death. Trust me, there's no treasure in the Mossy Bog house. My granddad used to say the only treasure is the one that's in your heart. He was right. Chasing foolish dreams will wreck your life."

"A million dollars, though. That'd be worth looking for."

"My dad *thought* it was a million dollars, but that was wishful thinking. My grandfather lived in a nice house, collected retirement from the Army, and worked for the furniture store. No way he had a million dollars saved up. On the other hand, my father lived like he had a million dollars but it was all a sham." He rubbed his dry eyes. "An empty illusion."

"Too bad. You could retire on a million dollars."

Sloan snorted. "A million dollars doesn't go far these days. Besides, I've got a good job. Team Six Security is better than any pie-in-the-sky pipe dream." He yawned again. "I'm bushed. See you Monday morning at the staff meeting."

****

Sloan woke up late on Sunday. He'd dreamed of Roxie again. Of how she looked beneath him, her dark hair spilled out on the pillow, his name on her lips.

173

Tomorrow. He'd see her tomorrow and they would take up where they'd left off. He smiled. Tomorrow couldn't come soon enough.

The journal. When he did see her, she'd be sure to ask about that journal. Better take a look at it.

He grabbed a bowl of cereal, tucked the journal under his arm, and headed to his den.

With Mac at his feet, he settled into his leather recliner and began reading. After a few paragraphs, he got the hang of the sprawling handwriting. Matthew Bolen's journal entries began after his tour of duty during the Korean Conflict.

Sloan's granddad, Scott Harding, was mentioned as the best man at Lavinia and Matt's wedding. He wondered if both men had pursued Lavinia as he read a few more pages. The next mention of Scott Harding was at the baptism of Lavinia and Matt's only child, Roxie's mother Valerie.

His granddad wasn't mentioned again until both men were building houses for their brides in Mossy Bog. Poor sod, Sloan thought. Putting all that effort into the house and his grandmother had left anyway. Once she'd given birth to Edward, she'd filed for divorce and left town.

He skimmed through the bulk of the entries about bird watching, gardening, and the weather until he reached an entry where Matt was worried about his good friend Scott. The words jumped off the page at Sloan.

Scott had a rough time bringing up Edward alone. The two aren't close and Valerie tells me Edward drinks to excess. I should've said something to Scott, but I let it ride. Then a woman from Edward's college town claimed he'd gotten her pregnant. Scott forced Edward to marry her, saying he would disinherit Edward if he didn't honor his obligation. Now the woman's abandoned them.

Scott took the boy in, of course. Is history

repeating itself? Will Scott do a better job raising Sloan than he did with Edward?

Sloan stared at the yellowed paper. He'd known of his mother's desertion, but he'd never known his father hadn't wanted her. After his stint in the Army, Sloan had tracked his mother down. Inez Harding lived in a Mississippi trailer park with her common-law husband. He'd been shocked to learn he had six half-brothers and sisters.

He'd seen nothing of himself in the slovenly woman, and he didn't want her to have any claim on him. She'd abandoned him all those years ago. He didn't need her now. He'd left without introducing himself.

He flipped through more journal pages until he saw his granddad's name again. He traced the words with his fingertip.

Scott asked me for help with his finances. I don't care for deception, but I owe Scott for saving my life in Korea. If he wants to protect his savings from Edward, who can blame him? Edward would run through Scott's nest egg in short order, and then where would Scott's grandson be? Lavinia has tried to mother Sloan, but I fear her gentling influence hasn't been enough as the boy has a rebellious nature.

Am I helping Scott hide his entire net worth from one wastrel in hopes of saving it for another? Will his grandson ever be the man Scott wants him to be?

Sloan stared at the journal. Hell. He'd been a screw-up back then, but he'd had lousy parenting. Lavinia had made it clear that he was always welcome in her kitchen, that he could count on her for a meal and a kind word. He'd frequently taken her up on her offer.

He didn't pay attention to his father before his granddad died because his granddad had raised him. His granddad had been a rock. Once the rock was gone, his father came to live with him. His drunken, enraged father who obsessed over the missing savings.

From the journal entry, it appeared his father's searching had been warranted. His granddad had accumulated savings. His friend had helped him conceal it.

No wonder his father had been so relentless, so driven. Nothing in the house had been safe from him. He'd ripped up floors and slashed open mattresses and the sofa. They'd thrown out the ruined bedding, but for years afterward, stuffing came out of the couch every time they sat on it.

What did Matt Bolen do with granddad's money? Had he taken the secret to his grave?

Or had something else happened? Had Roxie's grandfather helped himself to the money after Scott died? Had he bought his wife a real estate business with Sloan's inheritance?

Thoughts tumbled through his mind. Team Six Security was solid. He didn't need the missing money. But it *was* his inheritance and his granddad had meant for him to find it. If Roxie's family had stolen it...

He shoved his fingers through his hair, grimacing as he passed over the lump on his head.

Hell.

Roxie.

What was he going to do about her?

How could he see her if her family had stolen his money? His poker face wasn't *that* good.

Oh. Man. What was he going to do?

How the hell could he sort this mess out? He couldn't pretend nothing was wrong. Not when he was crazy with wanting her.

Best not to go back until he had a plan.

****

He didn't call. Roxie checked the phone for a dial

tone again. It was nearly eleven at night, and he hadn't called. She'd sat here on the sofa waiting for his call until she was stiff.

Did he forget?

How could he forget?

He'd sounded so attentive each evening when he'd called. Now with him not calling, she wondered if something had happened. Had the other calls been a lie?

Her stomach twisted, sending a wave of dizziness through her. She steadied her balance with a few centering breaths, but deep inside, cold winds howled through her heart.

She paced to the kitchen. How could she fix this? All her life she'd fixed other people's problems but she'd never once had to fix her own life. She'd been so careful of her feelings.

Sloan had come along at a vulnerable time, and she'd let herself be wowed. This mess was her fault all right. She'd allowed herself to believe in the fantasy of her own happily ever after.

He hadn't made any promises about forever. The only promise he'd made was to return tomorrow. But would he?

What if something had happened to him? If he'd been in a car accident in Atlanta, no one knew to contact her. He could be lying in a hospital bed in a coma or worse, on a cold slab at the morgue.

She had to call him. She pulled his business card out of her purse and punched in his cell number. He answered on the second ring.

The sound of his voice brought a giddy wave of relief. He was all right. No coma. No slab at the morgue. Remembering his advice about not fussing at Timmy when he'd been jailed for his mistake, she tried for casual banter.

"Hey, you. Remember me?"

A long pause followed. Roxie hunched over the

kitchen counter and held her breath. How many women phoned him and didn't give him their names?

If he called her by another woman's name, she would die. "It's Roxie. Roxie Whitaker."

"Believe it or not, I recognize your voice."

His voice made her skin tingle. She shivered excitedly. He was okay. He sounded more than okay. Now she had to explain her need to hear his voice. Would he think she was too clingy and demanding? Too bad.

"I expected you would call me tonight."

"Is something wrong?"

His voice sounded different now. Like he was annoyed with her. Had she crossed a line when she'd called him? Did he hate assertive women?

"Nothing's wrong. I wanted to make plans for dinner tomorrow. The weather looks good for a picnic on my back porch. How does that sound?"

If only he were here so that she could see his face. She could tell so much more about a person from his body language.

The silence lengthened. Dread chilled her veins.

"A picnic sounds great, but I can't make it," he said. "Something's come up."

Disappointment lanced her fragile dreams.

A new, grim reality surfaced.

It had been all about the sex.

She'd been dumped.

Her hand covered her mouth to keep from gasping her distress. She squeezed her eyes tight to keep the tears in.

"Oh?" He wasn't coming back to Mossy Bog anytime soon. The precious feeling of being cherished leaked out of her heart, leaving her empty and bereft. She wanted to hang up immediately, but she had property management business to convey. "All right, then. Mr. Cramer and his son-in-law worked on the house on Friday and Saturday.

They'll finish up on Monday morning."

"Good."

"The plumber came back. All the pipes need to be replaced."

He sighed. "If it needs to be done, do it."

Tears welled in her eyes. She needed to hang up before her voice betrayed her. Another thought popped in her head. "Did you look through my grandfather's journal?"

"Yes."

"Did you find anything helpful?"

"Depends."

"Depends? How so?"

"I don't want to do this over the phone, Roxie. Give me a few days to break free, and I'll come down there. We'll talk then."

He *was* dumping her. Anguish roared through her. She didn't want to be left dangling on the romantic vine until he had time to vet her replacement. If this was it, she needed a clean break.

"You can't leave me hanging like this." Her voice rose with each syllable. "It sounds like you don't want to see me again, and I want to know why. Is there someone else? Was it the journal? What?"

He swore. "This isn't a good idea."

"It wasn't a good idea for me to go to bed with you either, but I did it anyway. Tell me the bad news, and stop stringing me along."

"This subject is hard for me to talk about." His voice roughened. "It's a family thing. My father and granddad. Their actions haunt me. Looking for hidden money wrecked my father's life. I don't want to become as consumed with the search as he was, but the journal confirms money was hidden."

She drew in a sharp breath. He'd nearly given her a heart attack over money that had been missing for nearly twenty years? "You wanted confirmation, right? Why is that bad news?"

"Because your grandfather helped my granddad hide the damned money, that's why. The money's not in that house. Your grandfather knew what happened to the money. More than likely he knew where granddad hid it. That leads me to only one conclusion."

Though she heard dangerous undercurrents in his voice, she pressed ahead. "Which is?"

"Damn it Roxie, I don't want to do this over the phone."

"Well, I do. What's so horrible?"

"I think Matt Bolen took the money."

Denial swept through Roxie like a raging fire in a Georgia pine forest. This was outrageous. Her grandfather had been a bank officer for heaven's sake. "He did not. My grandfather was an honorable man."

"According to his journal, he had access to the money. The money's not there anymore."

Roxie blinked back hot tears. "Pop Pop was not a thief."

"Don't shoot the messenger. I'm telling you what the journal implied."

Anger vibrated through her entire body. "My grandfather was the nicest, most generous man I've ever known."

"You're upset."

"No shit, Sherlock."

"That's why I didn't want to do this over the phone. I wanted to think this over."

Fury almost choked her. "And do what? Check out my bank account? Let me save you the trouble. All the money I have in the world is tied up in Marshview Realty. There's no cache of secret funds anywhere. Thanks to my identity theft, my credit rating is shot. My parents are missionaries. Don't you know what that means?"

"They give all their money away?"

"No," she snarled into the phone, breathless with rage. "It means they are broke. They never *had* any money."

"Look. Why don't we give this a few days and then see where we are?"

"You think I'll calm down in a few days? That you can sashay back into town and warm my sheets? Forget it. I don't sleep with men who call my relatives crooks."

Sloan swore. "You're still my property manager, Roxie. I'm holding you to that contract."

"Take your business over to BC Realty. You'd be doing us both a favor."

So what if it wasn't professional to hang up on him?

It sure felt good.

****

Afternoon sunlight filtered into Mr. Fogle's study in structured shafts, illuminating legions of dust bunnies reproducing freely on the baseboards. Roxie sneezed.

"I will be happy to take your listing, Mr. Fogle," she said. "But this place needs work. A thorough cleaning would make a big difference, and you need to thin out your furnishings so the rooms appear spacious."

Mr. Fogle petted the small furry creature in his ample lap. Roxie thought it was a cat, but it was hard to tell under that wad of matted fur. "I couldn't possibly part with anything. Mother collected every item in this house. Getting rid of something would be a slap in her face."

Clara Fogle had been dead for ten years. "At a minimum you should replace the windows. The seals are gone. The one in this room is the only window that's okay. Is it newer than the others?"

"Sure is. A hooligan threw a brick through my window thirteen years ago. I replaced the glass myself."

Roxie sipped her glass of water. How was she going to unload this place at the inflated price he wanted? If he dropped the asking price thirty thousand dollars, she had a fighting chance.

"The police never found out who broke my window, but I knew who did it," he said. "I hear he's come back to town. Went to a wedding with you."

Her guard went up, and her stomach tensed. She set her glass crisply down on the dusty glass-topped coffee table. "Sloan Harding? He broke your window?"

"I'm certain of it. He failed algebra, and he wanted revenge."

"Sloan was your student?" The sugary sweet song about the world being a small place shrilled through her head.

"You seeing him?"

Roxie worked to unclench her jaw. "We have...had a professional relationship. He's renovating the property he owns on Main Street. I was his property manager." Still was. She might have hung up on him, but he hadn't taken his business elsewhere and she never defaulted on a contract.

"He's a wild one. Never thought he'd amount to anything. The two hoodlums he ran with are doing time up in the state pen. I'd be careful of him if I were you."

Great. Another warning about Sloan. "I don't discuss my clients, Mr. Fogle. That would be unprofessional."

"You were always good at following directions. I remember you got an A in my class."

Mr. Fogle had been a crotchety, bow-tied bachelor even then, but he'd had strict classroom rules which she'd religiously followed. She'd needed good grades for a scholarship, and his class was a ticket she'd had to punch.

"Thank you for remembering me, Mr. Fogle, but let's get back to staging this house. Will your furniture fit in your new place over at the retirement center?"

His grey eyes clouded with tears. "I can't bear to part with a thing."

Roxie wouldn't blow this deal over a few sticks of furniture. "Some folks place extra pieces with relatives. That way, everything stays in the family. Do you have family nearby?"

He looked thoughtful. "My cousin Lula's daughter has been after my furniture for years. But Mother said that branch of the family couldn't be trusted."

Her smile didn't dim. "How about a lease? You'd own the furniture and your cousins could maintain it. What do you say to that idea?"

He tipped his head to one side, considering. Then he nodded. "I like your style, young lady. No wonder Lavinia was pleased as punch with you. You're definitely a chip off the old block."

"You were friends with my grandmother?"

Mr. Fogle adjusted his red bow tie. "We were in the same class in high school. I couldn't believe it when Matt Bolen stole her out from under my nose."

This appointment kept getting weirder and weirder. "You were in love with Gran?"

"She was a wonderful woman. Matt Bolen may have won her heart, but she was *my* bridge partner for thirty years."

Amazing how people's lives interconnected in a small town. Could he help her prove her grandfather's innocence in the alleged theft of Sloan's missing inheritance? She seized the idea. "About my grandfather, someone recently said the most outrageous thing to me. They suggested he may have come across a large amount of money that

183

wasn't his and he kept it."

Mr. Fogle snorted. "Not likely. Matt Bolen was as straight as the day was long. I can do the math as well as anyone else. If he'd had extra money, he would have spent it on Lavinia. There were no fancy cars, no exotic vacations, no second homes. Matt didn't steal anything. You send that rumor-monger over to me and I'll straighten him out for you."

Her spirits brightened. "Thanks. I thought the same thing, but it's nice to hear it from someone else."

"The only unusual thing Matt Bolen ever said to me was the time he asked me about gemstones. He asked me if I thought they were a good investment."

Spots swam before her eyes. "Gemstones?"

"Mother lost her shirt in a diamond mine once. I told Matt mining stocks were too risky. I advised him to invest in blue chip stocks."

Her grandfather hadn't had a stock portfolio. He'd spent all the money he made in his lifetime. Gran had opened Marshview Realty with his life insurance after he died. Roxie had seen the policy. Gran had said the business was a poor substitute for a good man.

"Oh, well. Thank you, Mr. Fogle. It's nice to hear you had such a high opinion of my grandfather."

His leathery face crinkled into a fond smile. "Matt was a good man, and I wouldn't be doing my duty as a friend of the family if I didn't tell you to steer clear of that Harding boy. He's nothing but bad news."

Her first instinct was to defend Sloan. But she couldn't do that now. "I appreciate your concern, but I can take care of myself."

Mr. Fogle slapped his generous thigh and laughed. "You sounded just like Lavinia there. I love independent women. You'll help me then? You'll get this place spruced up and get me the money I need to buy into Cunningham Woods?"

"I'll do my best."

****

Roxie thought it strange that attorney Chad Powers had invited her to his office for the reading of Les Green's will two days after his death. With effort she pulled herself together and drove over there, glancing in the rear view mirror in irritation. How was she going to attract clients with an ever-present police escort? Then again, without it, she'd end up shot or worse.

She entered Chad's office and apologized for being late. She spotted Les Green's daughter, Andrea Albert, sitting on the edge of her seat, her knuckles white around her black patent leather purse strap. Her thin face pinched in disapproval when Roxie entered. Trevor Nagle, the other attorney in town, rose and shook Roxie's hand. On most nights Trevor could be found at the all-you-can-eat buffet; consequently his shape resembled a very large egg.

Chad came over to her and hugged her. "I heard about all your troubles. You doing all right now?"

The police cruiser was parked directly outside the window. Anyone with a lick of sense would know that having someone take a shot at you and having a police car shadow your every move were nerve wracking.

"Sure," she said. "I'm fine."

"Because I can bring Old Blue over and sit on your porch until we catch this fool."

Old Blue was Chad's favorite shotgun. "I'm fine. Laurie Ann has everything under control."

"She'd better or she'll answer to me." He waved her toward a seat. Once they were all seated, Chad began reading the will.

Why am I even here? Roxie wondered as the familiar words washed over her. She'd heard them when Gran's will was read last year. Gran. Gran would know what to do about a shooter and this constant sense of being followed and watched. She'd also know what to do about Sloan.

The words "Friends of the Museum" slipped through Roxie's fugue. She blinked, tried to replay the words in her head, and failed. "Excuse me. Would you repeat that part?"

Chad nodded. "I, Les Green, being of sound mind and body do hereby bequeath my property on the waterfront, also known as 103 River Street, to Friends of the Museum with the understanding that a nautical museum be established on this site."

Roxie's breath stalled. Les had given her a chance. With a little luck and a few grants, her Friends group would succeed. Her dream for Mossy Bog, Gran's dream, would become a reality.

"That's not fair!" Red flags dotted Andrea's sunken cheeks. "That property is mine. I'm daddy's only family. I put up with his crap for years."

"I'm sorry, Andrea," Chad said. "This wasn't my doing. Your father wrote this will."

"He messed up. He hasn't been himself for a long time. He was mentally incompetent. I'll challenge the will."

"Challenge away. Les had his doctor sign off on his mental fitness. He knew what he was doing."

"It isn't right!" Andrea glared at her lawyer. "Say something, Trevor."

"I'll file an appeal if that's what you want. But Chad's right, I'll be wasting your money. Not to mention wasting our time."

Andrea's voice shrilled. "Damn you. All of you. Every last person in this godforsaken hellhole is a total loser. I want what's coming to me. I want that River Street property!" She clomped out of the room and Trevor shambled off after her with an apologetic look.

Chad smiled at Roxie. "So your group inherits the old cotton warehouse. You'll have that museum up and running in no time."

Her hand covered her heart. "I'm stunned. I never expected this. Les never hinted at his intentions. I wanted to buy the property from him. Now he's gone and done something ultra wonderful. I can't believe it."

"Believe it, hon."

"The Friends of the Museum will be over the moon about this. Now all we need is a rich sugar daddy to pay for the rehab."

"Let me know when you find one. I could use a rich sugar daddy myself."

****

When the phone rang the following Friday night, Roxie switched off the TV and lunged for the receiver. "Hello," she answered hopefully.

"Hey, Rox," her brother said. "Guess what? I've got great news."

It wasn't Sloan calling to beg her forgiveness. Not that she could forgive him for the nasty things he'd said, but it galled her that he'd turned on her so completely. Sloan she couldn't fix. Timmy, on the other hand, was a work in progress.

"Where have you been, Timmy? I've been leaving messages for you for weeks now. Are you all right?"

"Yeah, yeah. I'm fine. I didn't want to call until everything was all set."

She bolted upright. "What's going on? Are you passing your classes?"

"That's the reason I'm calling. College isn't for me. I've found something better, Rox."

Why did helping Timmy feel like herding mosquitoes? Roxie massaged her temples. "I thought we agreed you'd stay in school."

"We agreed I'd finish this semester. I'm going to

do that. I'm even going to pass my courses. Amazing isn't it?"

The excitement in his voice worried her. "But you're quitting in December?"

"I've always wanted to travel. I can't think straight in classrooms. I want to experience life in its fullest, while I'm young, while I can still appreciate it."

Chicken and dumplings congealed in her stomach. Disaster loomed. "Trips cost money, money we don't have. People might take advantage of you. Stay in school."

"Too late. Can't you be happy for me, Sis? For once I'm doing what I want, not what you want, or mom and dad want, or even what Gran wants. I have you to thank for it."

She sank down on the sofa, clutching a pillow to her middle. "What have you done, Timmy?"

"I joined the Army. The recruiter said I'd travel, see the world, and learn a skill. I can go to college later, on the Army. Isn't that perfect?"

Her pulse soared. "Perfect? People use guns in the Army. You could be deployed to a war zone. This is a bad idea. A really bad idea, Timmy."

"It's a great idea. I never would have considered it if not for Sloan. If he hadn't told me about his Army experience, I'd still be hating life."

She opened her mouth to protest, but no sound came out for a few agonizing seconds. "Sloan? Sloan is responsible?"

"He's not responsible. I am. I joined the Army. I'm of age, and I'm taking charge of my own life."

"But the Army? It's so...violent. Couldn't you wait tables for a year or two to save up travel money? Do something less life threatening?"

"The city's dangerous, too, Roxie. In the Army, I'll learn how to take care of myself. Can't you be happy for me?"

Her heart sank. Happy. How could she be happy about this? She'd failed to keep him safe. Her parents' faith in her had been misplaced. The Army. How could she possibly be happy? "When will you be coming home?" she asked woodenly.

"Thanksgiving. Now that I'm not trapped here for the next four years, I feel a lot better about college. I joined a study group."

"Are there women involved?"

He chuckled. "You know me so well."

"This isn't what any of us would have chosen for you."

"*I* chose it. I talked to the recruiter a lot before I signed up. I know what I'm doing. This is the first thing I've ever really wanted to do."

"That's great, Timmy. Just great."

"You're not mad at me?"

Her brother would be part of a war machine. And he thought it was a good idea. His choice went against everything she knew, against their parents' nonviolent teachings.

This wasn't his fault. Sloan had filled Timmy's head with this nonsense. Sloan deserved her wrath, not Timmy. "I'm not mad. You're my brother. I love you. But I'm worried."

"That's okay. I give you permission to stop being a worrywart. Worry no more. I'm taking charge of my own life."

With sinking heart, she realized the matter was out of her hands as Timmy extolled the great benefits of the Army and his plans to see Europe. To put himself in harm's way. Finally, the call was over. She stared at her reflection in the dark TV screen.

How would she break this news to her parents? A shaky breath rasped through her lungs. Her peace-loving parents would be so disappointed. Their hearts would be shattered at the thought of their only son handling weapons.

She'd messed up all right. But Timmy had been crystal clear on one point. This disaster stemmed from one source.

Sloan Harding.

Chapter 12

Roxie pulled two loaves of raisin bread from the oven and glanced at the clock on her cell phone. She had just enough time to let these cool before she dropped them off at the historic society for their bake sale tonight.

The cinnamon aroma filled her house, making it seem like everything was right. If she counted her blessings, she should be happy. Her Friends of the Museum owned the property they'd identified for the museum. Her brother was charting his own future. Her sales for the month were decent.

These were good things.

She pocketed her cell phone and squeezed her eyes shut momentarily against the negative things. The Sloan things. Everyone had warned her about him, but she'd ignored their advice. She'd thought she knew what she was doing, but he'd turned her world on end.

No. She wasn't wasting more time mooning over what might have been. Taking a deep breath, she marched outside, turning on the hose and staring defiantly at the shadows dappling her yard.

The now familiar twinge of dread whispered across her spine. She whipped her head around, scanning for trouble, cataloguing the images. Miss Daisy parked in the drive. Her browning lawn. The overgrown lot next door. Four flickering fireflies. An empty Prospect Street.

No one.

No guns either.

Damn.

She was losing her mind. Adults weren't scared of the dark. She had too much living to do to be governed by fear.

A dog would help. A dog could warn her of danger. A dog like Mac. Images of Mac and Sloan filled her head. Coldly, she banished them.

She narrowed the spray nozzle to reach the distant camellia bushes.

"Bitch! You ruined everything!" a woman screamed.

Heart thudding, Roxie whirled. Andrea Albert was running straight at her. She carried a rifle. Acting on instinct, Roxie aimed the hose at her, the bullet-like spray striking Andrea in the face.

Andrea screamed and sputtered. She shook her head in fury.

Roxie kept the hose trained on the angry woman. She couldn't shoot straight if she couldn't see. "Get off my property."

"Die, bitch." The rifle pointed in her direction.

Roxie dropped the hose and dove forward on the ground. The gun roared over her head, shattering the clothesline post. She grabbed Andrea's ankles and yanked hard. The woman hit the ground hard, the rifle falling beside her.

With a longer reach, Roxie shoved the gun away and sat on the squirming woman. Water from the hose sprayed over them.

"You can't have my life!" Andrea raged. "My dad loves me. He promised to take care of me. You brainwashed him, turned him against me."

"Andrea! Calm down! I don't want your life."

"You made my dad sick. You stole my inheritance. They're mine. I snuck into his lockbox before he died and saw what you'd done. You made him change his will. Now you have to pay for stealing what belongs to me."

"I didn't steal anything! Stop this crazy talk,

Andrea!"

Andrea bucked underneath her. "You and your damn real estate company. You flooded the market with too many sellers and chased the buyers away. You took my dad. You stole my inheritance. You ruined everything."

Roxie grunted with the effort of keeping Andrea pinned to the ground. Time to call Laurie Ann. She fished her wet cell phone out of her pocket, relayed the request for assistance to Jocelyn at Dispatch, and hung up. "I'm sorry your father is dead," she said to Andrea, still squirming beneath her. "I miss him, too."

Andrea started flailing at Roxie again. "You can't fool me. You're a greedy opportunist. You exploit innocent people like my dad. You make people do things against their will. You conned my dad. You conned this town. You've been all over the world conning people. I know what you did. You caused global warming. You have to die."

Global warming? Oh, dear. Roxie realized part of Andrea's problem and moved to secure Andrea's thin wrists. "Don't make me hurt you."

"You can't hurt me. You're nothing. A nobody who consorts with street trash. I saw you kiss that vampire Harding boy right after he had that mattress delivered to his house. I hope he bleeds you dry."

Sirens wailed in the distance as dusk descended. Roxie just had to hang on a bit longer. "Help is on the way, Andrea," she said between grunts of exertion as she struggled to hold onto Andrea. Was this what cops had to deal with when holding down criminals? Roxie was just grateful the woman wasn't one of those people who gained superhuman strength during a psychotic episode. "It will be all right."

Andrea seemed to soften beneath her. "Don't you

understand? Nothing is all right. The trees have eyes. They see everything. They're watching us now. Don't you feel it?"

Roxie shuddered. The dusk was thickening like fog on the marsh. "Help is on the way," she repeated, needing to hear it as much as Andrea.

A car pulled in her drive, blue lights flashing. Another followed. Headlights illuminated Roxie and Andrea, soaking wet and tussling on the ground.

Laurie Ann raced over. "What happened?"

Roxie released Andrea's wrists. "She charged me with the rifle over there."

"Andrea?" Laurie Ann shined her light in the thin woman's face.

"The trees have eyes. The trees have eyes," Andrea sang.

Officer Rusty Trumple retrieved the rifle. Officer Joe Dandy lifted Roxie off Andrea. "We got this," he said.

Andrea scrambled onto all fours and scurried toward the road. Joe picked her up in his arms. "You're safe now, hon. The trees can't get you."

Roxie shivered against the night air. "She's crazy. She said I made her dad sick, that I turned him against her. She blames me for the crappy economy and global warming."

"We'll get her to the hospital for a psych evaluation." Laurie Ann wrote down the sequence of events for her report.

"Test the rifle," Roxie said. "I believe she shot at us in the rice canal."

"She admitted that?"

"No. But she does think Sloan is a vampire."

"Gracious. We'll get her sorted out. With any luck we can stop the extra patrols down Prospect with her in custody." Laurie Ann nodded toward the house. "Grab a few things. You're coming home with me."

"I don't need kid glove treatment."

"Yeah. You do. You just got shot at, Roxie, and subdued your shooter. Shut up and do as I say or I'll call your Mama."

"Yes, ma'am."

****

A week later Sloan sauntered through the rooms of his Mossy Bog house, his dog padding softly at his side. The dark wooden floors gleamed with glossy polyurethane, and the entire house looked brand new. Custard yellow paint brightened the walls.

Roxie's favorite color.

Mac waited at the base of the attic stairs, while Sloan checked the underside of his new roof. The last three days of constant rainfall had flooded low lying areas of the coast, but his attic was bone dry. He shone his flashlight around the unfinished space, pleased to see his granddad's old trunk in its former resting place under the eaves.

As he strode to the kitchen, he noticed how fresh and clean the house smelled, how every room felt warm and inviting. This cozy place seemed like a different house entirely, a place for raising a family.

The thought put a sour taste in his mouth.

Hardings weren't family men. Neither his father nor grandfather had stayed married for more than a year. He'd never considered marriage. There'd never been a woman he wanted to spend the rest of his life with. But coming back to Mossy Bog had changed him. The thought of marriage no longer repulsed him. It would be worth the risk with the right woman, a woman like Roxie.

Roxie Whitaker.

She probably couldn't stand the sight of him. He'd hoped to see her at the office, but her associate said Roxie was out of the office. It had been fifteen days and three hours since he'd spoken to her. Two soul-searching weeks of him staring at the phone and wishing he'd said things better.

He'd replayed their last conversation in his head, analyzing the content. He wanted to find his inheritance. He'd made no secret of that. Matt Bolen's journal proved her grandfather's involvement. That damned fact had messed everything up. Roxie had yelled at him and hung up on him.

But she hadn't broken their contract. So there was hope. Even though he'd left her three messages that she hadn't responded to, she'd gotten the work on his house done.

He still dreamed of her.

Night and day.

He couldn't stop thinking how right she felt in his arms.

God, he was whipped.

Worse, her cold shoulder wasn't unexpected. In truth, this relationship had followed an all too familiar pattern. It had been only a matter of time before the Harding stink bomb went off and she left him for good. Women didn't stick to Hardings.

He was screwed, no matter how he looked at it.

The plumber's cell phone warbled, slicing through the stillness of the mostly unfurnished house. Sloan drifted toward the downstairs half-bath where Chuck Beard was installing the new pedestal sink.

"Our girl's in trouble." Chuck clipped his phone to his drooping tool belt.

The plumber packed up his gear. Sloan glanced at his watch. Three in the afternoon. He'd trained for the wrong career. Contractors made their own hours. But Roxie had taught him not to be confrontational with them. At least in Mossy Bog. "You leaving?"

Chuck nodded, lines etched into his grizzled face. "Emergency call at three oh eight Prospect Street."

Roxie's address.

Sloan's heart stalled. "What kind of trouble?"

"City water main broke. I gotta get over there and pump out Miss Roxie's house." The plumber frowned. "For years, I tried to get Lavinia to do something about that ground level foundation but she insisted there was no need. Now her granddaughter's paying for her stubbornness."

Roxie was in trouble.

Adrenaline sluiced through Sloan's veins. Even if she didn't want him, he had to help her. He'd never forgive himself if he didn't.

He locked his house, then he and Mac jogged down the backyard path to Roxie's. Smelly water covered his shoes as he splashed along the wooded path. Sirens shrilled through the damp afternoon. An ambulance? Was Roxie hurt?

He shot a rusty prayer up to heaven. *"Please, let her be okay."*

The knee-deep water slowed his momentum. Beside him, Mac leapt like a galloping pony through the shallow pond of Roxie's yard. Sloan pushed forward one leg at a time. Flashing blue lights flickered beside her house. Heart in his throat, he scanned the scene. Where was she?

"Roxie!" he yelled.

****

Who was hollering for her now?

Lord. Didn't she have enough trouble without someone else melting down? Roxie had no compassion to spare. Not one drop of sympathy or patience for a single soul. Worse, she was so damned tired.

She sloshed through the knee-deep water, dodging floating chairs, the sheriff, and the fire chief to get to the front door. After spending a sleepless few nights at Laurie Ann Dinterman's she might have been safe, but she wasn't comfortable. Still, she wished Laurie Ann hadn't driven her mom to the doctor in Jacksonville today. At least Laurie Ann wouldn't look at her like she'd caused this mess. Sloan appeared, his broad shoulders blocking the thin sunlight from the room.

Breath stalled in her lungs. Her internal engine revved, causing a surge in energy. "Sloan."

He looked thinner, more gaunt. She made herself breathe. With effort, she found her voice and good sense. "Didn't Megan give you the invoice? I can't go over it right now. Could we meet later if you need to discuss it?"

His Adam's apple wobbled. "The invoice is fine. I heard you had trouble over here."

She nodded and drew in a shallow breath. "The city water main broke."

Mac pushed his head into Roxie's hand. "Hey, sweetie."

"I'm here to help," Sloan said. "What can I do?"

His intensity hadn't lessened in two weeks. She clutched the doorjamb for support. Sloan was here. To help her.

But he'd called Pop Pop a thief. Pop Pop was family. Family stuck together.

No matter what.

"Mr. Beard will pump out the house," she said evenly. "There's nothing else to do at this point."

A city crew circled the gushing fire hydrant by the street. The fire chief and the sheriff trooped out of her house, water lapping at their knees. "Get the water pumped out. We've shut off your electrical current," the fire chief said.

A white panel truck pulled up, and Roxie heaved a sigh of relief. "No problem. Here comes my plumber now."

Sloan followed Mr. Beard into the flooded house. Since when did Sloan become a plumber's assistant? She snorted at the very idea. Out in the yard, metal clanked against metal. The sound of rushing water ceased. There was a beat of silence, then a cheer went up from the city crew.

Finally.

No more gallons of water per minute were pouring into her house. With the leak capped, the water level would only drop.

Why had her granddad built this house on the lowest part of the property? For a smart guy, he'd made a pretty big mistake when he sited the house.

"Sheriff?" The city crew chief waved Sheriff Gator Parnell over.

Curious, Roxie followed. As she listened to the conversation and studied the fire hydrant, an icy sensation chilled her heart. She turned to the sheriff. "Someone did this on purpose?"

"Jonesy is certain the thing didn't blow," Gator said. "The bolt threads are intact. Someone tampered with the hydrant."

"Why? Why would someone do that?"

"Don't rightly know. First the break in, now this. Anybody got it in for you? Any real estate deals gone sour?"

"No, of course not. Except for Andrea Albert who tried to shoot me a few days ago, but she's locked up in a psych unit somewhere."

"The guys at the American Legion told me about Andrea's meltdown. She always was a few dimes short of a dollar." Gator jerked a thumb toward her flooded house. "You got any valuables in there?"

Roxie heard someone sloshing over to them. Sloan's unmistakable scent reached her. She ignored him. "My belongings are valuable for sentimental reasons. I don't own expensive things. I don't understand this at all."

"Did you hear anyone outside before the water rose?" Gator asked.

"I was cooking in the kitchen. The first hint I

had of anything wrong was seeing the water on the floor. It seeped under the front door and flowed down the hall to the kitchen. I glanced out the window, saw the gushing fire hydrant, and called for help."

"Damn." Gator scratched his head. "I was afraid of that."

"What do you mean?"

"I mean we'll be running extra patrols down Prospect again until we figure this out."

"Again?"

Out of the corner of her eye, she saw Sloan nod his approval. Ice shot through her veins. Had he heard about the shooting? "Am I in danger?"

"Could be. Best to be aware of that possibility. But my gut says this vandalism isn't a personal threat. Just in case, you got a place you can stay tonight?"

"I thought I'd stay here. My upstairs is fine."

"You might feel more comfortable staying with a friend. Even if Beard gets this place pumped out, it needs to dry out before you turn the power back on."

Roxie was done staying with friends. She needed some sleep. "I don't want to leave. This is my home."

"I'll keep an eye on her, sheriff," Sloan said.

Roxie's face heated. "That's not necessary."

A look of understanding passed between the men. Gator studied Sloan. "You got this?"

Sloan nodded and sloshed off to help Mr. Beard with another hose. Irritation simmered in Roxie's blood. "I don't need a babysitter. For goodness sake."

Gator pocketed his notebook. "Keep your cell phone handy and lock your doors. Call me if you have even a hint of trouble."

She nodded, in defeat, hugging her arms to her middle.

Numb.

She felt so numb. When was this nightmare going to end? First the breaking and entering, then the identity theft, Andrea shooting at her not once, but twice, and now this. Someone had done this on purpose. Someone had done *all* of it on purpose.

Why?

She'd never hurt anyone.

The city crew, fire chief, and the sheriff departed. Mr. Beard, Sloan, and Sloan's dog splashed out to Mr. Beard's truck. A generator roared, and pump hoses inflated. With nothing to do, she sloshed back to the porch and sat on the wide rail.

She was tempted to ask Sloan when he'd gone to work for Beard Plumbing but the less contact she had with him the better. With his lousy attitude toward her family, they were not friends.

A horrible thought occurred to her. Was Sloan in there scoping out her house for hidden wealth on the pretext of helping?

Not good. But she was grasping at straws. If she didn't stop thinking about Sloan, she would end up with an ulcer. He was a former client now. Nothing more.

As the level of water in her yard dropped, her thoughts turned to cleaning up. Would she have to bleach her entire first floor? What would bleach do to the finish on her floor?

She wrinkled her nose at the pervasive stench. It smelled like a cross between rotting seaweed and skunk. Pungent and strong, penetrating in a noxious way. She didn't own enough air freshener or candles to counter the magnitude of the stink.

It would be a long night.

Mr. Beard came out and stood beside her. "That's all I can do, Sweet Pea. The generator will power the pumps until they run dry, then everything will automatically shut down. You don't have to worry about them. Once we get past this emergency, you need to regrade this yard and install a drainage system."

At least with business picking up, she could afford to fix *this* problem. She smiled at Mr. Beard. "Thanks, I'll do that."

Mr. Beard nodded and left. Sloan and Mac stayed put on her porch.

Awkward.

She fell back on good manners, hoping he wouldn't remember that chat he'd had with the sheriff. "Thank you for your help."

His lips quirked at the corners. She tensed. Was he laughing at her?

"I'm not finished helping yet," Sloan said. "Pack a bag. You'll stay at my place tonight."

Stay with him? Out of the question. "I'll be fine here. My second floor is bone dry. Thanks for the offer."

He prowled closer. "Let me put it this way. If you don't pack your own bag, Mac and I will go upstairs and pack for you. You're coming home with us."

His woodsy scent wafted up her nostrils, catching her off guard. She blinked in confusion, gripping her hands tightly on the railing. How was it possible to be spitting mad at Sloan and yearning to touch him at the same time? "If I choose to spend the night elsewhere, I'll call a friend."

He barred his arms across his chest. "I'm not leaving here without you."

She quickly squashed her natural tendency to soothe his upset. *Stay focused, Roxie.* "Why are you doing this?"

"I'm a concerned neighbor."

Bossy was more like it. Stubborn. Authoritative. Dictatorial, even. "I don't need your charity."

"You don't?" he growled, edging closer. "How do you think I felt knowing you and Lavinia took care of my yard for thirteen years? I didn't want *your* charity, but I got it anyway. You can't stay here. My place is clean as a whistle, thanks to you."

Heat steamed off her face. Her act of service had hurt him? She'd never considered that kindness could backfire.

Huh.

She tried to think of another plan but came up empty. Even Laurie Ann's lumpy old rollaway was preferable to this, but Laurie Ann was out of town. Dave and Megan were visiting his brother's family in Statesboro. She chewed her lip. If it were anyone but Sloan, she wouldn't hesitate.

But Sloan was complicated.

"All right." The words slipped out before she knew it.

The coiled tension in his frame eased. His dark eyes warmed and she blurted, "But I'm not sleeping with you."

He propelled her toward her front door. "Message received. I'm the last person on earth that you want to see, but I'm taking care of you tonight. I owe you, Roxie, for all you've done for me. Let me help you."

Her nervous system spiked when he touched her. A toxic brew of hormones rocketed through her body. Tempestuous winds roared, stirring the muddy waters of her emotions.

This was a very bad idea.

She ground her back teeth together. No diplomatic escape presented itself.

Camping out alone wasn't her style. And someone *had* caused this flood on purpose. If she stayed here, she'd jump at shadows all night.

He opened the front door for her, and she stepped into the small foyer. Her house reeked of sewage. Filth covered her beautiful hardwood floors. Tears sprung up in her eyes.

Her home. Her private sanctuary.

She couldn't face this disaster right now.

Going with Sloan would keep her mind off her terror. He *had* tried to contact her after that awful conversation, but she'd refused to return his calls.

She shivered and pulled herself together. "Okay. Pack up the contents of my refrigerator in those coolers on the counter while I throw some clothes in a suitcase. No sense in all that food going to waste and we'll need dinner. We can take them over in Miss Daisy."

For once, Sloan let her take the lead.

Chapter 13

The mouth-watering aroma of pot roast filled Sloan's house. He'd wanted to order carry-out but Roxie had insisted on cooking. Said something about it settled her, cooking. Sloan had to admit there was something to it. Outside on Main Street, cars whizzed past, but inside these four walls, the pace was just right. For the first time in going on twenty years, his house felt like a home. An utterly foreign and totally addicting sensation for Sloan.

Longing swept through him.

What would it be like coming home to Roxie each day? The idea hammered at him, pounding away at his good Samaritan intentions. This was what other guys got, this was why they went home on time, why they quit hanging out at bars when they got hitched.

They were the lucky ones.

He sat at the kitchen table, allegedly working on his laptop. In truth, he was drinking his fill of the woman slicing apples into a pie crust. "Sure I can't help with anything?" he asked.

"Nope. I'm good."

She didn't sound pissed off. That was an improvement. He added a few more line items to the Reicker security proposal, but sirens and motion sensors didn't hold his attention this evening. He felt like a kid with his nose pressed against the glass of a candy store.

Sure he wanted to sleep with Roxie, but his yearning went deeper than that. He wanted her. And only her. Perversely, she wanted nothing to do with him. She'd been crystal clear about that.

Mac lounged at his feet, his gaze on Roxie. Smart dog. She was the best thing that had happened to either of them. Sloan wished he knew how to make it right between them.

"Do you take lemon in your tea?" she asked.

He smiled at the domestic question. This was the first time a woman had ever brewed iced tea for him. "Sure. But I can get it."

"Stay put."

"If you won't let me help, then I'll clean up."

"Works for me."

Not scintillating conversation by any means, but she was talking to him, which was a start. He savored his iced tea, filling his lungs with the rich elixir of simmering meat and potatoes. Other women had cooked for him, but it had never felt like this. The longing returned.

Why couldn't he have this life with this woman?

He'd give anything for tonight to be about them. Not this house. Not her house. Not the missing money or their relatives. Just the two of them.

Not a mudcat's chance in hell.

That damned inheritance.

It had turned his life upside down time after time. He wished his grandfather hadn't hidden a single penny. But, like his father, he was determined to find it. If the money wasn't in this house, and it certainly didn't appear to be here, then Roxie's family was the logical place to start looking.

Worse, it was the only lead he had.

The thought depressed him further. He went back to his sensors and alarms. During dinner, he broached a neutral conversation topic. "What do you hear from Tim?"

Roxie stiffened. She put her fork down and took a breath before answering. "Don't you think you've done enough damage there?"

At her harsh tone, the delicious food in his mouth turned into a lump of coal. He washed it down with iced tea. "What?"

Her brilliant eyes flashed with barely repressed tropical fury. "You know what I'm talking about. Timmy did exactly what you told him to do."

He'd talked to Tim about a variety of topics. "He's staying in school?"

"Don't toy with me. You know that's not the case."

"I don't have any idea what you're talking about."

"You don't remember telling my brother to join the Army? How he could see the world and get an education?"

"That's nothing more than they say in their recruitment ads."

"They play with real bullets in the Army. They go to dangerous places where the rules are different. Timmy's not ready for combat. He's only nineteen."

Sloan leaned back in his chair, carefully considering his words. "Tim asked me how I came to own my business. I told him about the skills I learned in the Army."

"Did you tell him about the countries you visited?"

"He asked questions about my tours of duty. I answered. I don't see the problem."

"You couldn't have hooked him with a more potent lure if you tried. Timmy wants to see the world. He thinks joining the Army is the same as a Eurorail pass. He's not thinking about the bullets zinging past his head."

He shrugged. "What's the big deal? He'll be trained to shoot back. He'll get to travel like he wants, and he'll get the education you want him to have."

Her jaw dropped. "He wouldn't get shot at if he

stayed in college."

"You're living proof you can get shot at right here in Mossy Bog. Why didn't you call me about Andrea? I wouldn't have known about the attack and her arrest if Laurie Ann hadn't phoned me."

"There was no reason to call you. Not when you made it clear you thought my grandfather was a thief."

He winced. Damn his inheritance. "About that, I'm sorry for hurting your feelings. I care about what happens to you. I'm glad that psycho is no longer a threat."

"You and me both. If I die, then it's up to Timmy to carry on the family line. And he's putting himself in danger in the Army."

"Tim isn't happy in college. Why is it so important to you that he serve time in college?"

She glared at him. "I'm responsible for him, don't you see? My parents trusted me to guide his education."

It was easy to see why her parents trusted Roxie. She was reliable, hardworking, honest, and she genuinely cared for her brother. But from what little he knew about her brother, the boy had been adventuresome his whole life.

The Army was the perfect place for the boy to mature.

It had done wonders for him, hadn't it?

Cautiously, he tried to work his way out of this new mud bog. "I haven't known Tim for very long, but from all accounts, he's been a square peg in a round hole his entire life. Am I correct?"

She stared at him, blinking rapidly. "Yes."

"Your parents knew this too, right?"

"Yes." Her voice was whisper soft.

"Then they won't be upset by this news. You didn't fail them. You looked out for your brother as best you could. Tim's of age now. He's finding his way in the world. Step back. Let him take responsibility for his choices."

"It doesn't feel right."

"You've been shouldering his mistakes. Give him a chance to make this work."

She chewed on her lower lip. "It can't be undone, can it?"

"It would hurt Tim more than you know to interfere now." Sloan gentled his tone. "He made this decision. Let him face the consequences."

"But it's so dangerous."

Fear etched deep lines on her glum face. He wanted to hold her and keep her safe, but she didn't want that from him. All he had to comfort her with were words.

"Danger lurks in every zip code, even in Mossy Bog," he said gently, letting that subject go for now. "Give Tim this space to grow."

She shivered. "Timmy's my little brother."

"Tim's a man. Let him discover who he is."

"That doesn't sound like the Army dogma." She eyed him suspiciously.

"That's a page from the book of Lavinia." He grinned. "She was a big one for facing the consequences of your actions. Tim can't grow up until he does that."

"Did Gran give you lots of advice?"

He nodded. "Every chance she got."

Her face tugged into a frown. "I thought it was just me she lectured."

"She was hard on me, but I respected her for it. If not for Lavinia, I would have ended up in prison with Lester and Dean."

Sloan groaned inwardly as soon as the words left his lips. Why bring up his past? Why give her more reasons to distrust him?

"Gran was a great one for handing out advice," she said finally, letting him off the hook in more ways than one.

Lavinia was a link they shared, a common thread in their youth. Lavinia had fussed because she cared. Roxie was fussing at him tonight about her brother because she cared.

Could she care about him in the same way?

The possibility cheered him.

****

Roxie edged her third pawn forward. Chess wasn't her forte, but she knew which way to move the pieces. "Did you play a lot with your grandfather?"

"Some." Sloan studied the board, then moved his black knight up two spaces and over one.

She tried to see which pieces were in jeopardy. She had no offensive plan, for the game or the man. Cautiously she mirrored his move on the other side of the board.

His pawn took her white knight, and it was her turn again. She moved her bishop diagonally one space.

He apparently didn't want to talk about his chess skills. What else could they talk about? Despite the high level of tension in the house, their relationship was off limits as a conversation topic. She cast about for another subject. "Are you happy with how the house turned out?"

Over steepled fingers, he studied the board, then advanced his castle behind his pawn. His puzzled gaze drifted up to her. "You say something?"

"I asked how you liked the house. Are you satisfied with the remodeling?" She pushed her bishop across the board diagonally and picked off one of his pawns.

Her bishop fell in his next move. Yikes. How embarrassing. This would be over in a heartbeat at this rate. She reached up and twirled a strand of hair.

"The house looks great," he said.

She nodded encouragingly. "Are you ready to put it on the market? I have a persistent buyer who loves this house and this location. You could name your asking price."

"My plans aren't finalized at this time."

"You might keep the house and live here?" She hated that her voice sounded too thin. Living next door to Sloan would be hard. It was easier to ignore her feelings when he stayed put in Atlanta. She clasped her hands together and hoped he'd missed her distress.

He studied the chessboard. "I came down here to debunk the rumors of my granddad's alleged fortune. Instead, I found evidence of missing money. As long as I hang onto the house, I have a chance of finding the truth."

"My grandfather didn't take the money," Roxie interjected, her breath catching in her throat. "Pop Pop was an honorable man."

Sloan looked apologetic. "He was involved. I've got cancelled checks upstairs with his name on them."

"I don't care if you have his fingerprints on the money. Pop Pop was excruciatingly fair. If there was a candy bar to split, I'd cut it in half and Timmy chose which piece he wanted. I'm telling you, Pop Pop didn't take your money."

"You've made your position clear." He sighed. "In my line of work, we follow the evidence."

"Those checks don't mean anything. Pop Pop could have cashed the checks and given the money back."

"That's one possible explanation. But is it plausible?"

"Absolutely."

"I'm not convinced."

"Damn you. Ask anyone in town. Pop Pop was a

pillar of the community. He didn't have a mean bone in his body. His reputation is sterling."

"I've seen good people do bad things. Do you think this is easy for me?"

"You aren't having any trouble smearing my grandfather's reputation. But every time you poke holes in his honor, you're hurting my family. Hurting me."

"You think the sins of the father are visited on the son, is that it?"

"Of course."

"Huh."

Heavy silence descended for the next flurry of chess moves. Mac wiggled closer to her, resting his head on her shoes. She leaned down to stroke his head. He was the dearest dog, so affectionate and attentive. No back talk either. Maybe she needed to get herself a dog and forget about a husband and a family. A dog would be devoted to her.

A dog would never accuse her grandfather of being a crook.

"Checkmate."

She glanced down at the game board. Sure enough three of his pieces had captured her king. Her queen was in the far corner dancing with his castle and knight. "Dang. You're good at this."

"Want to play again?"

"What's the point? I'm no match for you." She picked up the black knight and studied it. "What kind of wood did your grandfather use to make these pieces? They sure are heavy."

"American walnut. Granddad made them man-sized. No wimpy chess pieces in his house. He wanted something to fit his large hands."

"He got that." She admired the finely arched neck of the knight. Delicate. Proud. Strong. "He was quite good at carving. Did he create other pieces?"

He nodded. "He carved decoys for hunters. My

father sold them all. He wanted to sell the chess set too, but that was mine. Granddad gave it to me. My father and I fought over it. Lavinia helped me hide it from him. She stored it at your place, in the hall closet during my teenage years. Otherwise, my father would have pawned it."

"That must have been rough."

Sloan didn't answer.

Why had she mentioned his father? He'd made it clear his father was taboo. She was not doing well in the small talk department. Even though it was early, she'd be better off going to bed. At least then she couldn't continue putting her foot in her mouth.

She stretched in her chair, yawning big. "I'm ready to turn in. Are you sure about the sleeping arrangements? I could sleep on the sofa in here."

"Absolutely not. You're my guest."

His steady gaze disturbed her, accelerated her pulse. "Well, if you're sure."

"I'm sure. Why don't you take the bathroom first? The downstairs fixtures were being connected when Mr. Beard got your call, so we'll be sharing the upstairs bathroom. I hope you don't mind."

The call.

Memories of her ruined house tumbled into her thoughts. For most of the evening, she'd been so distracted by Sloan's proximity she'd forgotten about her flooded house. What was a ruined house compared to sharing the evening with a brooding pirate of a man?

"It's not a problem," she said. "Thanks again for your hospitality."

Her feet weighed a ton as she climbed the stairs. She hadn't forgotten how his kisses stirred her senses, and his intense scrutiny this evening hadn't erased the memory of how magical his touch was.

It wasn't fair.

He must be immune to women falling for him.

He'd probably never had to find a date for an event with no idea who to ask. He probably didn't understand her stalwart defense of her grandfather either.

But she hadn't sacrificed her honor for lust. In spite of Sloan being a gentleman all evening, the sexual tension had been thick enough to slice. He wanted to sleep with her. He broadcasted it in his every move, the hesitation before he spoke, the sensual way his eyes gleamed when he looked at her.

Tonight she'd sleep under his roof, in his king-sized bed.

Would his pillow have his woodsy scent? If so, she was looking at a long, sleepless night. She'd have been better off checking into a motel.

But once Sloan had offered, she'd wanted to come over here more than anything. She'd seen an intellectual side of him tonight that she'd never seen before. He was indeed a man of many talents.

Staying here was a calculated risk. She'd played it safe her entire life and what had it gained her?

A lot of lonely nights.

Chapter 14

Roxie was upstairs. Sleeping in his bed. That part was right. But he was down here on the sofa. That part wasn't right. Not by a long shot.

Sloan blamed himself for the sleeping arrangements. The facts of his investigation pointed to her ancestor. Roxie's loyalty to her family was absolute.

He'd never had that kind of loyalty.

What would it be like to have a woman believe in you so much that they would stand up for you years after you were dead? Besides his own granddad, Lavinia was the only person who'd ever stood up for him, but she wouldn't side with him on this. She would stand with Roxie.

Women.

They complicated a man's life to no end.

He silently prowled the dark living room. Mac stirred by the sofa but didn't get up. Why hadn't he found a way to patch things up with Roxie? He could go to her now and tell her that he couldn't stop thinking about her. That was a fact.

She stayed on his mind.

She filled his dreams.

But such an admission would put him at a disadvantage. He'd expose a weakness to a person with the potential to hurt him. He'd be too vulnerable. That went against his street smarts and his Army training.

He needed another way to approach the situation.

She'd trusted him enough to stay here. That was

positive. She'd cooked for him, talked with him, even argued with him this evening. All good.

But easy companionship hadn't been enough to change her mind about sleeping with him. No matter how nice a polish he put on the situation, he was still a Harding. She was still Matt Bolen's granddaughter.

What good was a second chance when it was no chance at all? He raked his fingers through his hair, considering and rejecting ideas. None of them put him in her bed.

What the hell was he going to do?

Overhead, a door snicked open. Terrible hope flared white hot. Was she coming to him? His blood raced in silent expectation. Best not to greet her in his boxers. He shrugged into his jeans and waited in the darkness.

Moments later she padded softly down the stairs. Even with the home improvements that fifth step still creaked. Mac raised his head, alert. "Stay," Sloan whispered. His dog protested with a soft sound in his throat.

Light from the kitchen spilled down the hallway, brightening the living room where Sloan stood in the shadows. She hadn't come to him, but she was awake. He was awake too. Very awake. He'd be a fool not to take advantage of this opening. Like a chess gambit, he'd happily sacrifice a principle or two to corner the white queen.

He followed her to the kitchen and halted at the threshold.

As his eyes adjusted to the strong light, he studied her. Dark hair tumbled down around her shoulders, mussed from tossing and turning. Her robe cloaked her in respectability, but he knew what treasures were hidden under that soft flannel. His jeans tightened.

Her sweet fragrance met his lungs. He inhaled

deeply, savoring her scent as if it were the rarest elixir in the universe. What he wouldn't give to walk across this room and sweep her into his arms.

Instead, he cleared his throat softly. "Couldn't sleep?" he asked.

"Oh!" Roxie dropped a plastic cup. Water splashed along the counter and floor. Her hand covered her heart. "Sloan. You startled me. Did I wake you?"

"I wasn't asleep."

"I came down for a glass of water. There were no cups upstairs." She grabbed a sponge and mopped up the spilt water.

"I'll notify my property manager about the deficiency," he teased.

The sponge shot out of her hand and flew across the room.

Wild hope raged inside of Sloan. He crossed the floor and reached for the sponge. Her hand touched his unexpectedly. Electricity arced between them, incinerating his caution. Instinctively, he rolled his wrist, capturing her slender fingers in his grasp.

His callused thumb stroked the delicate skin of her captive hand. Recklessly, he pressed his advantage. "I know of a sure-fire cure for insomnia." His voice came out gravelly and rough.

She stilled. "Don't be ridiculous. Sex won't solve anything."

She hadn't tugged her hand free. He felt the jump of her pulse under his fingers. "All I want is a kiss, Roxie."

"A kiss." Her eyebrows rose. "You think I'm dumb enough to fall for that line, Harding? Kissing leads to other stuff."

He stroked her hand again, and she shivered in response. He edged closer. "Do you want to kiss me, Roxie?"

"It's a bad idea."

"Just one kiss. How can one kiss be a bad idea?"

His bare feet caged hers. He wanted to hold her so much he trembled with need. Wanting her had become second nature to him. "Please," he added.

The air thinned as he hovered on the delicate brink of rejection. In that breathless moment, he realized his future hinged on her decision. On this woman. She held him enthralled.

With each micro-second he waited, hope flickered like a neon light with a short. Silently he implored her to believe in him, to trust him, Sloan Harding. He drew in a ragged breath edged with despair.

She smiled in invitation. It was the most beautiful sight in the world. He leaned in, daring to trust in his good fortune. Her arms entwined around his shoulders, and her lips met his. He thrilled to the passion pouring through her and deepened the kiss.

She stroked his bare back, and he exhaled roughly in sensual delight. Her breasts pressed through her flannel robe, broadcasting her arousal. He ached with the need to caress her soft skin, but he didn't trust himself to move slowly.

He couldn't take much more of this torment, of being touched and not responding to her as he liked. He gathered her hands in front of her and broke off the kiss. It nearly killed him. "Roxie?"

He could have drowned in the tropical warmth in her sea-goddess eyes. Heat and something else, something much more primitive, shimmered around them.

"Yes?"

"You were doing more than kissing." He stroked his thumb over her hands again. She shivered, her hip snugged up to his. If they didn't make love, he would spend the whole night praying he didn't go mad.

"Ummm." A womanly sigh eased out of her and

tugged at his heart.

He leaned back against the counter, holding her close. He didn't ever want to let her go. "Are you sure this is what you want?"

"What I want," she said deliberately, her hands sliding slowly down his midline to the button over his fly, "Is a good night's sleep. That's what you promised, right?"

He nearly whooped for joy. He wanted her so bad he could taste it. She'd finally given him a green light.

Hot damn.

He scooped her up and bounded up the stairs. Roxie laughed wildly. "What's the rush? Afraid I'll change my mind?"

The floorboards creaked beneath his bare feet. "You wouldn't be so cruel, would ya? Not with insomnia running rampant in this house."

"Right you are. We're joining forces to thwart evil insomnia."

He placed her on the bed, taking pleasure in the tangled sheets, knowing she wanted him. He gazed at her wondrously.

Starlight poured through his unadorned bedroom window. Roxie looked perfect on his bed, her dark hair fanned out on the white pillow case. Desire radiated from her enchanting eyes in unrelenting waves. He didn't fight the strong breakers. He dropped his jeans on the floor and joined her.

He made short work of her clothes. His hands skimmed her curves, cupping her intimately.

"That feels so good," she said.

He smiled against her skin. "The best is yet to come."

Her fingers tightened around him. A sultry laugh emitted from her throat. "I'm counting on it."

He lowered his lips to hers. "Me too."

Kissing her. Touching her. They were all that mattered. His head fogged with her sensuality as his hips covered hers, fitting himself to her responsive body. Her name tripped through his thoughts, exulting his senses.

She wiggled impatiently under him.

His inner fire flared red hot. "In a hurry, are you?"

"I can't wait. Please. Now."

"Please. I love that in a woman." He rolled with her, reversing their positions. "You drive this time."

Her fast pace caught him by surprise. She was close to the edge. He could do fast. His hips matched her rhythm. His hands cupped her breasts.

Inside, a whirlwind of desire spun out of control. He rode the storm, thrilling to the heady sensation, soaking up all she had to give and more as passion ruled.

Together they found release.

Together they drifted in a moment of pure starlight.

Boneless.

Weightless.

United.

As drowsy sensation returned, he fought it, trying to hold fast to the bliss he'd found in Roxie's arms. It had never been like this before. Never. His arms tightened around her.

Nestling his face in her soft hair, he breathed deeply of her essence. He'd never forget this scent, this woman. He drew her to his chest, content.

****

The next morning Roxie sat quietly in the kitchen nursing a cup of coffee. Sloan had rolled out of bed without a word and hit the shower before she was fully awake. His absence from the huge bed this morning spoke volumes.

When she had given in to her longing for him

and kissed her way into his arms last night, she'd envisioned a perfect future. One with gleaming picket fences and happily ever after written all over it. She'd been sure her peace offering would lead to a true reconciliation where he apologized for calling her grandfather a thief.

In the cold light of day, she realized her folly. She'd invited him to sleep with her. Last night they'd made love. She had no right to expect more than that from him. Worse, she was sure a sophisticated city woman would know how to deal with the awkwardness of the morning after. The easiest thing to do would be to dash off a note on the counter and fade into the sunrise.

Not her style.

Damned if she would slink off without getting answers. "About last night," she began when Sloan appeared clad in jeans, a black T-shirt, and bare feet.

He leaned in the doorway, his dark eyes drilling into her. "What about it?"

"I'm not sorry last night happened, but we went into this with our eyes open. Last night two consenting adults enjoyed each other's company after a very stressful evening."

She risked a direct glance at his glittering eyes. His needle sharp intensity would send a weaker woman running for cover. "Do you agree?" she asked.

"What if I don't?"

She rose. "Then, I'd say we have a problem here."

"There's no problem, unless you make one." He straightened, the coiled tension in him visible from across the room.

"Nothing has changed. You're here to find your inheritance, but it is well hidden. Your life and career are in Atlanta. I've got my real estate business to run in Mossy Bog. And you believe my

221

grandfather's a crook."

"I don't want it to end this way." His voice roughened. "I want to spend time with you. I want to be a part of your life."

She shivered. "Will you apologize for what you said about my grandfather?"

"Hell no. He was involved. The cancelled checks prove it."

"My grandfather didn't steal your money."

"My inheritance is missing. Your grandfather was one of the last persons to have seen it."

"You're wrong." Roxie couldn't stay in this house another minute. She skirted around Mac and hurried to the living room to collect her things. Doing so, she had to brush past Sloan in the doorway.

Waves of anger emanated from him, big shore-eating breakers. Too bad. He could be angry all he wanted. She was plenty angry herself. He had the power to fix this. He was tearing them apart.

Her overnight bag sat next to the door. Fortunately, she'd had the presence of mind to bring it downstairs with her earlier. All she had to do was to walk out the front door. She'd never have to see him again, never have to listen to his hurtful accusations about her family.

She snatched up her purse. "I hope you find your money and spend the rest of your days counting it like King Midas."

"Damn it, Roxie." Sloan reached for her. She jumped to the side and tripped over the dog. Mac yelped and bolted past the small occasional table with the chess set. Several chess pieces clattered against the wooden floor. One chess piece caught the direct sweep of Mac's tail, flew across the room, and bashed into the wall.

"Don't curse at me." Her hands clutched the shiny new brass door knob. "You have no right to malign a good man's reputation."

"Wait."

"For what? So you can insult my grandmother? Or maybe you want to sling mud on me too. Will you say I slept with you for a cheap thrill?"

He didn't answer.

Just as well, she thought, and sailed out the door.

Chapter 15

Sloan's heart slammed into his ribs as she drove away. He staggered over to the brown plaid sofa, Mac at his heels. Grown men didn't cry, but damned if his eyes weren't watery. She'd said nothing had changed between them, but she was wrong. They were good for each other.

Why couldn't she see it?

Her curt dismissal of the paradise they'd found stung. More than that, she'd filleted him to the bone by her actions. What they had meant something. He knew it as well as he knew his name.

His name.

That was part of the problem. She saw him as a Harding first and a man second.

Once he'd noticed her bag at the front door, he'd known he was in trouble. He'd known he was nothing more than a greasy spot in her rear view mirror.

His limbs felt like a hundred pounds of dead weight.

A lonely wind howled through his gut.

He'd been a fool.

He'd believed she was different from other women, but she had followed the classic female pattern of love 'em and leave 'em, almost as if she were reading the directions from a secret handbook.

He picked up her white queen from the chess board and rolled the carved wooden piece absently in his hand. Better that she'd walked out now, before he got in any deeper in the hole he'd dug for himself.

What if he'd married her, fallen in love with her,

and she'd left him?

He wouldn't be able to breathe.

He was barely able to draw in a full breath now.

He'd been dumped before. He knew the drill. Other women would come along. They always did. There seemed to be an endless supply of women who wanted nothing more than sex from him.

His spirits sunk further.

Mac nuzzled Sloan's leg and stared at him. "She's gone, Mac."

His dog stared unblinkingly at him, as if beaming a "go get her" message at Sloan.

He rubbed Mac's ears. "She said no, buddy. I have to respect that. She's wrong about us. I know she cares for me, but it isn't enough to make her forget all the baggage that comes with my being a Harding."

She'd shivered in his arms. Together they'd surfed the crest of passion, soaring and gliding as one. She'd opened the door to a world of new sensations, dazzling him with hope. For a bit, he'd seen a different future, one with the promise of a loving family.

He'd laid himself on the line for her but she'd wanted more. He pinched the bridge of his nose. Stupid. He knew better than to hope. Lone wolves didn't attract marrying types. They prowled the edges of civilization and survived by staying out of sight.

She'd drawn him out of cover with her smiles and cooking, lulled him into a sense of false security, even slept with him to beat insomnia. The sacrificial gambit had cost him dearly. He'd never seen the checkmate coming. While he'd been gathering his forces to keep her close, she'd countered with an exit strategy.

Game over.

It was bitter and final, no matter that he wanted

otherwise.

He stalked to the window. He wanted to protect her, to make sure whoever flooded her house was brought to justice. Her cop friend would do that.

Roxie didn't need him.

Worse, she didn't want him.

Pride warred with frustration and lost.

He didn't belong in this house. And he didn't belong in Mossy Bog. He'd chased the ghost of his inheritance long enough. He'd reached for a dream and come up empty handed.

Time to face the facts.

His inheritance was long gone.

As he should be.

Mossy Bog had brought him nothing but pain. Time to return to his impersonal life in the big city. Time to sell this place and never look back.

He blinked the moisture from his eyes and shoved the chess piece into his pocket.

****

Roxie dashed the tears from her cheek and emptied her pajama drawer in a suitcase. Men were thick-headed. Sloan had the thickest head of all.

Why couldn't he let the past go?

A frisson of awareness rippled across her nerves, as if someone were watching her again. Sloan? Cautiously, she edged forward and studied the trees bordering her sunny yard. Nothing.

She sagged against her bed.

Wasn't it enough that her heart was broken?

Did she have to be going crazy too?

These feelings of being watched weren't going away. Either someone was out there or she'd completely lost it. Either way, she couldn't stay here alone. Thank God Megan and Dave were back from visiting his Statesboro relatives. She could bunk on their sofa.

She glanced around her bedroom, feeling out of

place. This house, her business—those things were her life. It was about time she focused on what she had, not on what she didn't have.

With a heavy heart, she zipped the soft suitcases and trudged down the stairs and picked her way through the slippery mud in the hallway. What a mess.

She carried the suitcases straight to her trunk so they didn't get muddy. The hairs on the nape of her neck ruffled. There it was again. That sensation of being watched.

"Who's there?"

She glanced toward the treeline.

No answer.

Not that she expected one. Her instincts clamored for her to flee to safety. But her instincts had been wrong about Sloan. Why should she trust them now?

She folded her arms and leaned against Miss Daisy, the picture of nonchalance. Her heart raced. She scanned her field of vision, looking for a slight movement, a glint of sunlight on metal.

Fear sprouted wings and insisted that she run.

A familiar sound manifested in her hyper vigilant world. A car on Prospect Street. She heaved a sigh of relief as a cruiser turned into her drive.

Not all of her senses were shot. Her hearing still worked.

Hat in hand, Laurie Ann strode over to Roxie's car and leaned against Miss Daisy. "I heard about yesterday. I'm sorry I was out of town. You doing all right?"

"Sure." She wasn't all right, but she couldn't talk about it either.

"I've been following up on the fire hydrant angle this morning. Turns out yours was one of eight that were incorrectly capped. The one on Bayside Drive was leaking too, albeit at a slower rate."

"Wait. The city is to blame for my flood?"

"Looks that way. You can send them a bill for the cleanup."

She blinked, struggling to take in the words. "It was an accident? Someone wasn't trying to ruin my house?"

"Afraid not. I wanted to make sure you knew, so you wouldn't worry."

"I understand."

"If you have concerns, you can call me anytime."

"Sure."

Laurie Ann studied her. "I'm worried about you."

Roxie choked out a harsh laugh. "Me, too."

"What's wrong?"

She shook her head. "You'll think I'm crazy. Hell, I think I'm crazy."

"Try me."

Tears welled. Roxie squeezed them back. A breeze swept across her heated face. She stared at her muddy sneakers. "Sometimes I have the sense Andrea is still out there, watching me."

"Oh honey. You should've said something sooner. First, let me reassure you that Andrea Albert is locked up. She can't hurt you anymore. Second, your reaction is perfectly normal after a traumatic event."

"It is?"

"You've got Post Traumatic Stress Disorder. Like soldiers get after a war."

"God, I am crazy. I've got PTSD."

"Your mind keeps reliving those stressful moments. It will fade in time, but you should talk to a professional. I know a counselor who's a whiz at this."

Talking about her troubles with a stranger unsettled her. "I'm not ready to see a shrink. I'm headed to Megan's. She'll help me sort this out."

"Megan's? Gator told me you were staying with Sloan."

"I spent the night over there. He insisted. It was a mistake. A big mistake."

"You want to talk about that?"

"He's a jerk. I don't want anything to do with anyone named Harding ever again."

"Want me to arrest him?"

Pain socked her in the heart. "I want you to squash him like a bug, but then he'd think I cared."

****

"I showed the Harding place today to a young couple from Savannah," Megan said matter-of-factly as she snapped pieces of romaine lettuce for a salad. "They loved the location. Her parents are coming back with them tomorrow. I expect a contract from them soon."

Roxie pulled the fleece blanket around her neck and sank into the soft cushions. She'd been living on Megan and Dave's sofa for almost a week now and overseeing the clean-up at her house. It had been pumped dry, cleaned, and then re-cleaned. Huge fans were blowing through her house to disperse the disinfectant smell.

She could go home tomorrow.

Meanwhile, Megan had kept the business going. Megan had fielded Sloan's calls. Not once had he asked for Roxie. Not once had he called her cell to talk to her directly.

Her wounded pride was a lousy companion.

Would he have continued sleeping with her if she hadn't demanded that apology? Didn't he understand that trust was a two way street? Making love with her when he didn't believe in her was meaningless sex.

She'd been foolish to allow her hormones free reign. Those tempestuous winds had blown through her heart with gale force speed, ripping at her foundations. She'd had a wild ride, but she'd never expected to end up so fractured.

Her emotions wouldn't settle, no matter how busy her hands were. Even when she'd driven herself to the point of exhaustion, her broken heart throbbed.

She'd fallen in love with Sloan.

She loved him for carving out a life for himself. For surviving a childhood of neglect and terror. For earning her grandmother's admiration. She could almost hear Gran saying Sloan had "spine." Elusive praise, that.

"Come with me when I show them the property tomorrow," her friend said. "I'm sure we can close the deal."

What was Megan talking about?

Oh yeah. Selling Sloan's house.

No need to return to the scene of that disaster. "Sounds like you have everything under control. You don't need me tagging along."

Her friend stopped working on the salad and sat down in the navy wingback chair across from Roxie. "Maybe, but this is your listing too. I've never known you to be so hands-off about a real estate deal. Should I call a doctor?"

"I'm not sick."

"There are all kinds of sick. I haven't pushed because I know you value your privacy, but I'm concerned about you. This affair with Sloan hurt you, and it tears me up to see you so sad."

She blinked back the hot tears that lurked in her eyes these days. "I'm sorry to be such a downer." She exhaled shakily. "You're right about my mood. I don't know what to do with myself. I alternate between wanting to sleep all day and cry."

"That's understandable. Break-ups are like that."

"Shouldn't I be feeling better by now? Shouldn't I want to say horrible things about him or at the very least wish him bad luck?"

"I'm no expert on love, but I had several boyfriends before Dave. After those breakups, I felt better in a few days. Maybe it takes you longer to rebound. Your grieving and healing process seems to have stalled out. That might be an answer in itself."

"What do you mean?"

"Your feelings for Sloan run deep. Is it possible your relationship can be salvaged?"

Roxie shook her head. "Not a chance. The reason we broke up hasn't changed. We have two very different perspectives. He sees the bad in people; I see the good."

"That sounds like a challenge all right, but not a deal breaker. Dave and I don't agree on everything. Instead, we agree to disagree. Oftentimes, I have to start the peace-making process. Have you thought of that? You could call him."

Tears blurred Roxie's vision. She blinked them away. "If only it were so easy. We're talking basic trust here. I took the first step the night my house flooded. That misstep made everything worse."

"He'll come around. And if he doesn't, he doesn't deserve you." Megan rose. "Why don't you join Dave and me at the movies tonight?"

Just what she wanted, to spend the evening with two people who couldn't keep their hands off each other. "I've intruded enough. You and Dave need time alone without me hanging around your necks like a rusty barge. Thanks for the heart-to-heart."

"Any time."

****

Roxie was in the middle of a Law and Order marathon later that evening when her cell phone rang. She snatched it up without checking caller ID.

Expectation caused her voice to catch in her throat. "Hello."

"Hey, Sis. How are ya?"

Timmy. She sighed out her foolish hopes and muted the television. "Okay. And you?"

"Super. And great news. I aced my history midterm."

"You did?" She sat up straight. "That's wonderful."

"I should have called sooner, but I didn't want to get hassled about the Army. This is something I really want to do. I spent a lot of time talking to the Army recruiter before I signed up. I even wrote a letter to Mom and Dad telling them why I did it."

Tears spilled down her cheeks. Timmy was growing up. "I can't help worrying. You're my little brother. I want the best for you."

"This is what I want. For the first time, I'm excited about my future. There are so many different opportunities in the Army. I can be anything I want to be, go places I've never been. I can be me."

She sucked in a quick breath. Had her vision of his future seemed so horrible to him? The last thing she wanted to do was paint him in a corner. "Be happy, Timmy. If this is what you want, I'm glad for you, truly I am."

"Is Sloan there? I wanted to tell him the good news."

Sloan. Timmy wanted to talk to Sloan. She grimaced and swallowed thickly. "He's not here. I'm not in contact with him any longer."

"You're not? But I thought—" Timmy trailed off, keeping his thoughts to himself.

She cleared her throat, anxious to change the subject. She couldn't talk about Sloan without feeling raw inside. "The important thing is your happiness. I'm proud you did well on that history test."

"We'll have to celebrate when I come home for Thanksgiving break."

"Sure thing."

After Roxie hung up, she stared at the muted TV screen for awhile. Timmy had grown up, almost overnight. She didn't have to worry about him any longer, and she had Sloan to thank for that.

How had that happened?

How did Sloan reach Timmy?

He'd done what no one else in her family could do—he'd communicated with Timmy and her brother had listened.

She had known Sloan for such a short time, and he'd had a profound impact on her life. Was that why she couldn't forget him?

****

Roxie pulled body and soul together for the Friends of the Museum meeting. Willie Mac hobbled in on his walker, a wide smile on his skeletal face. Olivia Erwin twirled around the room, energetic enough for a woman half her age. Bea Laramore carried a bouquet of flowers from her yard to grace the table. Reverend Junior Cullens brought a cup of coffee over to the table and sat.

"We're all here. Let's get started," Roxie began. "First, in case anyone's been living in a bog hole for the past two weeks, Les Green donated his waterfront property to our group."

Olivia rushed over and gave Roxie a hug. "You are such a gem. I can't believe you got that property for us. But I'm stunned at the danger you were in. I'm so happy nothing happened to you."

"Not as happy as I am. Thank goodness Andrea Albert is a lousy shot. I feel sorry for her, if you want to know the truth."

"That girl was always a bit off," Junior said. "Takes after her grandmother, she does. Les should've known better than to marry a crazy

233

woman's daughter."

Bea frowned. "Watch your mouth. Annie Robin was my fourth cousin, twice removed. My family is proud of our crazy people, old man."

Junior's jaw dropped. "You think Andrea should've shot Roxie?"

"I never said that. Andrea got what she deserved. Roxie is the driving force behind our museum, and we're lucky to have her. And the museum property."

Finally they were back on track. Roxie breathed a sigh of relief. "Les gets the credit for his generosity."

Junior raised his coffee cup. "Hear, hear. May he rest in peace."

"What about Andrea?" Willie Mac asked.

"She's in a psych ward," Roxie said. "She threatened to challenge the will but our attorney said we were good."

"Hot damn!" Bea pumped a fist in the air. "Oops, sorry Reverend."

"No apology necessary." Smiles wreathed Junior's plump face. "This is indeed a great moment for our committee."

"I agree," Roxie said. "Our goal for the year was to buy the property. Now that we own it free and clear, I say we should start the rehab of the structure."

"I don't know about that," Willie Mac said. "If we can't get everything under roof and sealed in, we could sustain weather or termite damage to the new start. My vote is to collect that much money before we do anything."

"You old sourpuss, you!" Olivia scooted around the room to Willie Mac's chair, smacking two envelopes against his thin shoulder. "I've got just the tonic for you."

"Easy, Olivia," Roxie warned.

"What's that?" Willie Mac asked.

"I got these this week and have been sitting on the news so hard I thought I'd split open like a roasted oyster. We were approved for two grants. With this money plus what we already have in the bank and a little sweat equity, we're gonna have us a bang up museum."

The approval letters made the rounds of the table. Roxie read them, did some mental math and came up short. No matter how they cut it, they still needed a big donation.

"This is great news. Every little bit helps," Roxie said. "But we can't let up now on our fundraising. We have to continue to be very visible in the community. Bea, do you have folks scheduled for our weekend bake sales out at the mall in December?"

"Still working on it."

"We're counting on that income. And any other ideas folks can think of to raise funds for the museum."

"I'm going to talk to Stewart on the County Commissioners," Junior said. "With the property acquisition and the grants, our financial status has changed. They should see their way clear to adding us to their budget."

"I'll take on the city," Olivia crowed. "It was nice of you to tackle Noreen before, but it's my turn, Roxie."

Roxie sighed out her relief. "Great. Bea, you want to talk to your cousin over at the newspaper? Maybe a press release would help us find a rich sugar daddy."

Bea beamed. "I can do that."

The meeting broke up, and everyone drifted out. Bea handed Roxie the floral arrangement. "I want you to have these."

Their cloying scent made her head reel. She set them down on the table beside her purse and dug for her keys to Miss Daisy. "Thanks."

"Is something wrong, dear?"

"I'm fine."

"Now, now. I know you better than that. You're not fine. Tell me what's the matter."

She'd be lucky to get out of here by tomorrow if she didn't give Bea something. "It's personal."

"Personal, you say?" Bea looked thoughtful. "It's that Harding boy, isn't it?"

Heat flooded Roxie's face. Did everyone in town know about her short-lived affair? "As I said, it's personal."

"Did he break your heart? Give me his phone number, and I'll set him straight. Noreen told me he'd been sniffing around you. Nothing good ever came of those Hardings."

Anger stiffened Roxie's spine. "Sloan isn't like his father. He works hard, and he's made a name for himself out in the world. Noreen is wrong about him."

"I see."

"We had a disagreement, that's all. Good grief."

****

She hadn't been at the office all week.

Sloan had called there four times on the pretext of talking about his listing when all he'd wanted was to hear her voice. Instead he'd spoken with her coworker, Megan, who had been actively showing his house.

Roxie's cell phone number cycled through his head again, but he wouldn't beg for another chance. Plus she was probably screening her calls.

He stared at the contract Megan had faxed to him. Once he signed this paperwork, he'd never have to set foot in Mossy Bog again.

He should be relieved.

He wasn't.

"Sloan, you there?" Megan's voice shot through

the phone connection, slamming into his thoughts. Her perkiness aggravated the sinking feeling in his gut.

He could end this misery today.

All he had to do was sign his name.

Panic flared.

He tamped it down.

The offering price was an insult. Roxie's South Carolina buyer must have changed his mind. Megan hadn't done him any favors with this contract. With that thought, he tossed the papers in the trash. "No deal."

"This offer is below your asking price," Megan said. "Counter with a higher price. That's the real estate game."

"Don't want to counter," he muttered.

"You should. These buyers will go higher."

"I'm not countering. If I don't get another offer, then it's my own damn fault."

He ended the call and reached for his beer. He tipped the bottle up, but there wasn't a drop of liquid left. Empty.

Just like him.

Hell.

Time for another beer run.

He rubbed his hand over his new beard. He'd worked from home this week, putting Bates in charge of daily operations. He wasn't ready to face the guys yet. Bates was too perceptive for his own good, and Reg would rib him mercilessly.

Bottom line: his heart ached. He'd fallen hard and gotten slammed.

Booze dulled the pain.

Like father, like son.

But did he want to be the town drunk?

No.

He wanted Roxie.

He missed her.

His dog missed her.

Mac came over and licked his hand. Sloan remembered how Roxie had hugged Mac. He wrapped his arms around his dog and held on tight.

Chapter 16

"He refused the contract?" Roxie paced around the island in her cozy blue kitchen. She'd been unable to calm her nerves after learning Sloan had received the lowball offer on his place. "Did he counter?"

"Nope." Megan sat down at the rectangular kitchen table.

Roxie stopped before the bay window. The grove of trees between her house and Sloan's stood illuminated against the pewter sky. The stark branches reached into nothingness. Her life in a nutshell.

Despite the light sweater she wore, she shivered at the chill in her bones. "Doesn't he know how this works?"

"I couldn't say."

Another idea occurred to her, and with it came a surge of anger. "Does he think we're incompetent?"

"I don't think that's the problem."

Megan's responses bordered on cryptic. She whirled to face her friend. "What? What aren't you saying? Is he hurt? Did something happen to him?"

"Not that I know of."

"But?"

Megan exhaled slowly, as if the subject were painful. "Look, I don't want to tell you your business, especially since I know how upset you've been after breaking up with the guy, but he sounded pitiful."

"Pitiful?" Her heart surged and stalled. "How so?"

"You know, rough. Like he hadn't slept or eaten

right."

Her stomach wobbled. She searched her friend's face. "Is he sick?"

"Not in a strict medical sense, but he sounds defeated. Tired, even. Depressed."

He wasn't ill.

He was miserable.

Just as she was.

Megan leaned forward. "The guy is whipped. You broke him."

White noise filled her ears. Had she heard correctly? A tendril of hope snaked up from her depths. "What?"

Her friend's palm smacked the counter. "Wake up! You love the guy. He loves you. Find a way to work this out before you both die of broken hearts."

"It's complicated."

"You said that before. I didn't buy it then, and I'm not buying it now. Reconcile your differences, or you'll regret it for the rest of your life." With that, Megan left.

Roxie slumped in a wooden chair. Her life had stalled the day she'd parted ways with Sloan. She'd spent so much time inside moping around that she felt vulnerable outside, as if someone still watched her.

But Laurie Ann had explained that she was reliving the stress of being shot at and attacked by Andrea, that she was suffering from PTSD.

Roxie fought her fear with facts.

Nuts had been loosened on the fire hydrants. She wasn't anyone's target, merely the victim of cosmic bad luck.

Whatever the reason, she was tired of feeling lousy.

She loved Sloan with all her heart. She was miserable without him. He wasn't doing well without her. Why wouldn't he call her and tell her?

Her stomach clenched in memory. He'd called last time they had trouble, and she didn't return his calls. It was too much to expect him to step into the breach this time. If they had a mudball's chance in the ocean, she had to make the first move.

Outside the window, downed leaves whipped around in a circle in her backyard, eddying, rising, and falling to the ground. Her emotions were likewise caught in a dizzying swirl, unable to break free of the forces that held them. How could she work this out?

Was it possible he'd had an epiphany in the past week? That he no longer believed her grandfather was a thief?

Not likely.

If he'd changed his mind on that, he'd have turned up on her doorstep.

If they reconciled, what would people think? People in Mossy Bog thought Hardings weren't good people. Roxie knew better. Sloan was a good man. He'd helped her, and he'd reached out to Timmy.

The best way to prove her granddad wasn't a thief was to help Sloan find the missing money. Could she convince him to give them another try? He'd been hurt by women in the past. His grandmother had abandoned his family; his mother had done the same.

He might not want to open those painful wounds, but she'd never know if she didn't try. With his family history of female abandonment, he might not know how to make amends. She had to do something big. Something that would get his attention and let him know she still cared.

What could she do?

His roofline glinted through the bare trees, his new shingles dark and snug. Everything had started with that roof. In his leaking attic had been treasures from his past.

Treasures.

That gave her an idea.

The more she thought about it, the more convinced she was that her plan was brilliant. If it didn't work, she could have her license suspended for trespassing.

Risky.

She'd be putting her career on the line for love.

Fair enough.

This was a risk she needed to take.

****

Sloan yanked off his tie. Under pressure from his employees, he'd attended the charity luncheon, but it had been a big mistake. He didn't want to be social.

A pushy redhead latched onto him, and he'd had to be outright rude to get rid of her. Afterward he'd felt remorse over his crass behavior and had come home to regroup. His entire life was in the toilet because the woman he wanted didn't want him.

A crisp rap on his door startled him. Glancing through the peephole, he saw the uniformed doorman holding a package. He opened the door. "Yes?"

"I tried to catch you in the lobby, Mr. Harding. You must have been deep in thought. This delivery came for you earlier today."

He thanked the doorman for the overnight package and closed the door. The return address was from Mossy Bog. Roxie's address.

His heart thudded wildly in his chest.

He sliced the tape sealing the carton with a knife. The box was flat enough to hold a pizza, but twice as deep. Inside, he discovered a gift covered in old-fashioned floral paper. A blood red silk rose adorned the top of the box.

He tore through the wrapping like a kid on Christmas morning.

Dark oak framed a glass shadowbox of black velvet and his granddad's war medals. Attached to the lower corner in the back was a small white card with the handwritten words, "Love, Roxie."

His breath caught in his throat.

They were the most beautiful words he'd ever seen. He walked the present over to his fake mantel and set it there. Mac barked his approval.

Roxie wanted him back.

The tightness in his chest eased. His fingers closed around the white queen he still carried in his pocket. Possibilities sprang to his mind, but one thing was certain. This was a golden opportunity.

Without wasting another second, he flipped open his phone and called her. At the sound of her voice, he felt alive again. He pressed the phone tight against his ear so he wouldn't miss so much as a single sigh. "Your package arrived. Thank you for the present."

"You like it?"

He'd heard that breath she let out slowly before answering. This was hard for her too. "I like it. A lot."

"I'm so relieved."

"You and me both." *Please let me say the right thing*, he implored silently. "Roxie?"

"Yes?"

"I've missed you."

"Oh, Sloan." Longing colored her voice, fueling his wild hopes.

"I want to see you again. Tonight. Will you have dinner with me?"

The line went quiet. Too quiet. He couldn't breathe. He could barely think. He heard a small snuffling sound.

His heart lurched. Words tumbled off his tongue. "Roxie? Don't cry. Please. I'm an idiot. Please. Give me another chance. Give us another chance."

"Yes," she whispered.

Relief sighed out of him. He wished she was in his arms right now. "I'm leaving Atlanta right now. I'll be there by dinnertime."

He tore through the condo, grabbing clothes, dog food, and his laptop. Mac barked excitedly. With a last glance at his place, Sloan caught sight of the framed medals. Those belonged in Mossy Bog, with him and Roxie. He tucked the gift carefully under his arm and hurried out to his Jeep.

The miles between Atlanta and Mossy Bog ticked by one at a time. Plans spun through his head. He didn't want to go through anything like this past week ever again. He wanted Roxie by his side, permanently. He would convince her of the logic. He'd sold riskier schemes in tricky international situations.

He could manage to sweet talk a woman in coastal Georgia into his bed on a permanent basis. Or if he lost his nerve, he'd tell her that was how it was going to be.

His phone rang between Macon and Savannah. He whipped it open. "Harding."

"Hope I didn't disturb you, boss," Bates drawled. "You enjoying the redhead I got you?"

"Hell, no." That explained why the woman was so persistent. "I can get my own dates."

"Think of it as an early birthday present from me and the guys."

Sloan eased around a blue Mustang. "You wasted your money."

"I dunno. Sounds like you finally snapped out of the funk you've been in all week. That was money well spent."

It wasn't the redhead who'd bolstered his mood. It was the brunette. His brunette. The lady with the eyes like flashing seas.

"Your point?" he said.

"My point is to let you know we've got the office covered. Take some R&R."

"You read my mind. I'm headed back down to Mossy Bog for a few days. If all goes well, you'll be in charge of Team Six for awhile."

Bates whistled long and low. "It's the brunette, right?"

"Yep."

"I'll be damned. She must be downright special to draw you away from work. Want us to run her background?"

"Do that and you're a dead man."

"Good one, boss." Bates barked out a belly laugh. "Wait. Hold up a sec. Reg just sent me a text. Looks like there's activity on Gilmore's credit card. He gassed up an hour ago in Richmond Hill, wherever that is."

"It's between Savannah and Mossy Bog. Where is Reg?"

"Uh. Um." His second-in-command cleared his throat. "Reg is in Charleston."

"We don't have any clients in Charleston right now."

"It's a personal matter, boss."

"Shit. He's fallen for another girl."

"He's whipped, boss. Just like you. What's this agency coming to with all these skirts horning in?"

"The agency is what we make of it. That was the deal from day one."

"Right."

Silence hummed through the line. Sloan thought back on what Bates had said. "What else we got on Gilmore?"

"He's shifted most of his assets into accounts under the name of Sonny Gifford. Don't worry, boss, we've got the money flagged. He isn't going anywhere without his stake."

Cons like Jared Gilmore didn't disappear without a score. They'd been tracking the man for weeks now.

"How many times has he been to Mossy Bog?"

"Can't be absolutely certain. He's made purchases there on three different dates at the seafood place, the gas station, the diner, and the hotel by the interstate. Those charges were all in the last six weeks."

Six weeks. That paralleled the time frame Sloan had been traveling back to Mossy Bog. He didn't believe in coincidences. That only left one logical conclusion.

The bastard was still after his inheritance.

"Thanks for the intel. Gotta run." Spots danced in front of his eyes. He shook them away and ended the call.

The Harding fortune. The bane of his teens, the downfall of his father. If two generations of Hardings couldn't find it, there was no way Gilmore would locate it.

The only treasure in Mossy Bog worth finding was Roxie. Gilmore couldn't have her. Roxie was exactly what his grandfather had meant when he'd said the real treasure was in a man's heart. Roxie was in his heart. She was his treasure, not some missing money.

About time he realized that.

He turned off I-16 onto I-95 southbound, navigating through a clot of Savannah traffic. Better let Roxie know his arrival time. She didn't answer her phone. He left a message and tried her office. No answer there either. He thumbed through the business cards in his cup holder until he located Megan's number.

"She's with a client," Megan assured him when he reached her. "Roxie's South Carolina buyer is back in town and insisted on her showing him a property. She'll be free by the time you get here. This guy is all hot air."

Sloan got a bad feeling in the pit of his stomach. "He wouldn't be from Charleston, would he?

"Yes, I believe Mr. Gifford is from Charleston. How'd you know?"

"Shit." Sloan sped up.

"Is something wrong?"

"I'll handle it." Gilmore had Roxie. Sloan pulled his Glock out of the glove box and tucked it under his waistband. He couldn't take a chance on the cops spooking Gilmore.

He crushed the accelerator pedal to the floorboard.

****

Sonny had gone crazy. Nothing else explained him tying her to a kitchen chair and trashing her house. He'd secured her ankles to chair legs and bound her wrists behind her back, and he'd done it with her old cotton clothesline.

He strode back in the kitchen and waved a handgun at her. He held it sideways like gangsters on TV shows. "Where's the money?"

The large barrel of the weapon riveted her attention. Roxie's heart raced. "There's thirty dollars in my purse. Take it."

"Tell me where the money is, or I'll bury you in that new drainage trench in your front yard."

Her wrists burned where he'd tied them. But she had sensation in her fingers, which was good because she would free herself or die trying. Dusk was falling. Sloan would be here soon. She had to keep Sonny talking until Sloan arrived.

But Sonny had a gun.

So did Sloan.

No, what was she thinking?

Guns were bad. Someone would start shooting and people would get hurt. Killed maybe. She curled her fingers up and picked at the knot.

"I don't have any money," she said. "Both my house and my office are heavily mortgaged. I borrowed four grand on Miss Daisy, but you can have my car if you want."

He jammed the gun to her temple. "Cut the crap. The Harding fortune. Where is it?"

"I don't have the money! I never had the money." Her veins iced. The man was insane.

"Sure you do. It isn't in that damned house, and it isn't here either. I've searched both places."

"No one knows what happened to the money. It's gone."

"A convenient lie." He set the gun on the counter and slapped her face. "Tell me where the money is, or I'll shoot you dead right here in your kitchen."

Her cheek stung. Roxie trembled uncontrollably. Her breath came in short pants. "I don't know where it is."

"Tell me everything that was in that house before you fixed it up."

"I don't know! I can't think." He pulled his hand back to slap her again. "Wait... maybe a plaid sofa. An end table. A chrome dining set. Broken appliances. A few lamps. A twin bed. And the Army trunk in the attic. That's it. I swear."

"The bed's gone."

"Sloan replaced it."

"I'll bet he did. I saw the screwing palace he installed. He nailed you yet?"

Fear knotted her insides.

Fear for what this man might do to her.

What he might do to Sloan.

She tugged her wrists, straining the rope. "Please. Just leave. I can't help you. I won't press charges if you go away and never come back."

He picked up the gun again. "Forget it. You're my bargaining chip. Sloan's got a thing for you. He'll tell me where the money is to get you back."

"He doesn't know where the money is. It's long gone. Why don't you understand?"

"What I understand is that I need this score. I'm not leaving town without it. I've wasted six weeks watching you and trying to find it. I have too much invested in this to walk away now."

Understanding dawned, dark and ugly. "You never wanted the Harding place—not to buy it anyway. You wanted to get in there and search for the money."

"That's the only reason I'd ever come to a cesspool like Mossy Bog. Someone should have put this backwater town out of it's misery a hundred years ago."

"This town is my home." Did that knot slip a little? She continued to wiggle her fingers, trying to free her hands. "You don't care about anything but money."

"Exactly. And if you don't shut up, I'm gonna duct tape your mouth."

When Sloan couldn't produce the money, Sonny would kill them both. She couldn't let that happen.

****

Sloan parked behind his dark house and drew his Glock. Exiting the Jeep, he and Mac loped through the woods in the thin twilight, leaves rustling under their feet. From the base of the hill, he saw there was a light on in Roxie's kitchen. It sent cold chills down his spine.

The light shifted and Sloan edged into the shadows. A person stood at the window. The silhouette was taller than Roxie, the hair shorter. Gilmore was in there.

Ice crystallized in his bones.

Gilmore had Roxie.

Sloan pulled his phone out of his pocket, called nine-one-one for backup, then inched forward, gun drawn.

Mac whined softly. The fur on his hackles rose. "We'll save her, Mac. I can't lose the best thing that ever happened to me." Sloan motioned the dog to sit and stay.

With stealth, Sloan approached the side of the house. Was there anyone else inside with Gilmore? Where was he holding Roxie? If Gilmore touched so much as a hair on her head, he'd pay for it.

Sloan stepped over the hose lying in the flower bed, angling toward the kitchen window.

His heart thundered in his ears.

Focus, Harding.

Do your job. Search and rescue. Just like in the military. *That others may live.* He'd give his life for Roxie's any day.

He gained the side of the house and peered in the window. A lanky blond man paced around the island, a revolver in his hand. Gilmore. He'd tied Roxie to a kitchen chair, her back to the window.

Her head moved, as if she were tracking her captor. Her hands tugged at the cord binding her.

She was alive.

Sloan weighed his options. If he could get in the front door undetected, he could sneak up on Gilmore. But if the bastard heard him coming, Gilmore could use Roxie as a shield. His best bet was a quick surgical strike through the back door.

In and out.

He'd done it a hundred times.

But never with such personal stakes.

It was so dark he could barely see his gun hand. Suddenly the back yard flooded with light. Startled, he backpedaled, tripping over the hose. A small azalea bush crumbled beneath him.

He scrambled for cover, but he was too late.

Too damned late.

Chapter 17

"Get up slowly or I'll shoot your woman, Harding. Lose the gun," Gilmore called from the kitchen.

Seeing the gun barrel pointed at Roxie's head, Sloan obeyed.

"Get in here where I can see you. Hands up. No tricks," Gilmore said.

As he crossed the threshold, hands held high, Sloan's gaze flicked over to Roxie. Her chalky face spoke volumes. So did the red handprint on her face. "You must be Jared Gilmore."

Gilmore smirked. "Good guess. Know why I'm here?"

Sloan stopped near the center island. "Leave Roxie out of this. She's done nothing to you."

The gun waggled. "No can do. She's my leverage point. You got any more weapons on you? Hand 'em over."

"Do what he says, Sloan," Roxie stated flatly.

He couldn't risk Roxie getting hurt. "Take it easy. We can work this out."

Gilmore jabbed the gun into Roxie's temple. "I know your type. You gung ho grunts swear by weapons. Empty your pockets."

"No problem." Sloan laid a pocketknife on the center island next to his billfold and keys. The white queen he palmed. "Now what?"

"Step back." When Sloan complied, Gilmore stepped forward and moved the knife out of reach. "Give me my money, so I can get the hell out of this dump."

"What money is that?"

"The Harding fortune. I know you've been searching for it. I had someone watching Roxie. Give it to me, or you'll both get a bullet in the gut. Painful way to die, I've been told."

Fury howled through Sloan. "The Harding fortune is a myth, Gilmore. A drunken dream my father chased his entire life. It doesn't exist."

"It better exist. I've got a lot riding on this score. Give me that money."

"I can't. The money isn't there. My father filled your dad's head with nonsense. There is no Harding fortune."

"Stop right there. Don't come any closer."

Ignoring the warning, he continued to edge around the center island, with the intent of herding Gilmore toward the back porch door. "Or what? You'll shoot me? Put the gun down and fight me like a man."

Gilmore retreated as Sloan approached, giving Sloan room to step in front of Roxie. If Gilmore wanted to shoot her, he'd have to pump the bullet through Sloan. Roxie's chair squeaked behind him. The noise reminded Sloan that Gilmore had tied her up. He growled deep in his throat and assumed a boxing stance.

"Give me the money, Harding." He pointed the gun at Sloan. "Or she gets it."

"There is no money," Roxie yelled from behind Sloan.

Gilmore moved right to see his prisoner, taking his eye off Sloan. Just the opening Sloan wanted. He kicked out at the gun. It roared into the ceiling. He charged Gilmore, slipped the white queen from its hiding spot in his palm, and hammered the man's temple with the chess piece. Gilmore went down hard, and the wooden queen shattered.

Sloan dropped the chess piece, secured Gilmore's

gun, and checked him for additional weapons. Nothing. The man was an idiot. When he turned back to Roxie, he was amazed to see her untying her feet.

"You're okay?" He knelt beside the chair and untied her left ankle.

She beamed. "I was gonna save us, but you beat me to it. Nice kick, by the way."

He swept her into his arms and allowed himself the luxury of a full breath. "I've never been so scared in my life. You sure you're okay?"

"I'm sure. But I can't breathe with you holding me so tight."

Reluctantly, he released her and examined her wrists and face. "I'm sorry. I never intended for my past to harm you."

"Sonny wasn't your past. He was a slimy opportunist. And you clocked him good."

"Speaking of Gilmore, I called for backup on the way in. The cops should be here soon to take out the trash."

From the doorway there was a sick cackle. "I'm rich!"

Gilmore. The man's head must be thick as a trawler's ice hold. Sloan glanced over at the man crumpled on the floor. A sea of glittering stones surrounded him. Diamonds by the looks of them.

Diamonds?

Gilmore swept up a handful, pocketed them, leapt to his feet and scrambled out the door.

"He's getting away," Roxie cried.

Sloan whistled twice. A loud scream rent the air. Sloan smiled and gathered up the discarded clothesline. "Got 'em."

"What? How?" she sputtered.

Sloan stashed the gun in his waistband and nodded toward the yard. "My best man is outside. You watch for the cops and direct them to the backyard, okay?"

"What about the diamonds?"

"They aren't going anywhere. Unless I miss my guess, there are more where those came from."

He kissed her, then with a smile that reached to his toes, sauntered out and took care of business.

****

Three hours later, Sloan's hands still shook. There'd been more diamonds in other chess pieces. And more in the heart-shaped Army medal. After his grandfather had converted his fortune into diamonds, he'd hidden them in plain sight. Not much of an investment strategy. And the only clue he'd left Sloan had been that remark about treasure being in your heart.

"You could have been killed," he said for the third time and snugged Roxie close to him on the sofa. Mac lay at their feet. Soft guitar music played in the background. Candles flickered on the coffee table. The scent of vanilla wafted through the air.

"I'm alive, and so are you," she answered contentedly. "But I was surprised Sonny looked so banged up when Laurie Ann got here."

Sloan allowed a wry smile to reach his lips. "He had trouble with his balance in the backyard."

She shot him a sharp glance. "Laurie Ann said Sonny won't get out on bail. That he'll go to jail for a very long time for attempted murder. Sonny also admitted to ransacking my kitchen and opening the fire hydrant so my house would flood. He tampered with the other hydrants to deflect the blame."

Fierce protectiveness surged through his bloodstream. "He won't come near you again."

"While we waited for you to arrive, he told me he stole my identity and sent the boat to mess with my head. He saw my kayak picture in my desk when he searched the place during the burglary." She rubbed her temples. "What messes with my head is the

Harding fortune is real. You're rich, Sloan."

"That money nearly got you killed," Sloan growled. "I ought to throw it away."

Her jaw dropped. "That's your inheritance. You can't throw it away. That would dishonor your grandfather."

He smiled and stroked the side of her face, savoring the welcome slide of her soft skin against his fingertips. "Wouldn't want to do that."

"I'm serious, Sloan. Your grandfather wanted you to have that money. That's why he made sure your dad couldn't find it."

And his granddad's secretiveness had nearly cost Sloan his heart. "I almost didn't find it either."

"How did you happen to have the chess piece in your hand?"

How did he explain his need for her without sounding like a dope? He took a deep breath and shoved his pride aside. "It reminded me of you. I've kept the white queen in my pocket ever since we parted ways."

"Oh, Sloan. That's the nicest thing anyone has ever said to me. Thank you."

She pulled him into her arms for a drugging kiss, wrapped her arms around his neck, holding him, loving him.

He was home.

****

The next morning, they strolled through the woods over to his house to get more food for the dog. With Sloan's hand tucked in hers, all was right in Roxie's world. And now that she knew she *hadn't* been imagining things, shadows no longer held dominion over her.

"We should put those diamonds in the bank," she said. "Someone else might be tempted to steal them."

"You got more thieves around here that I should

know about?"

"None that I know of, but why tempt fate? That's a lot of diamonds."

"Mmm," Sloan said. He stopped to kiss her again.

She sighed delightedly. She could spend the rest of her life in his arms. Easy. He seemed to feel the same way about her. But he hadn't said the words yet. *I love you.* That's what she wanted to hear.

"Rox, I've been thinking," he said. "We're not doing this again."

Her heart stopped. "Doing what?"

"This together and apart dance. It's tearing me apart."

"What do you suggest we do about it?

His dark brown eyes gleamed. "You're marrying me."

"Oh?" She retreated from his embrace, leaves crunching underfoot. If he wanted to marry her, that was fine by her, but by God he better do it right. "You're not seriously calling that a proposal. A woman likes to be asked and not told she's getting married."

His mouth dipped into a deep frown. "You're not going to make this easy on me, are you?

Two months ago, any proposal would have sounded wonderful. But now that she'd tasted love, she wouldn't marry a man who didn't have the courage to tell her he loved her. "Call me a stickler for tradition. Gran always said it paid to do things right the first time. If you want me, you have to risk asking me."

Sloan went very still. Roxie's heart stalled as her senses muted. The light thinned. The chirping of birds quieted. The rich smell of decaying leaves faded. So this was what it felt like to lay it all on the line. She wondered who was more terrified, herself or Sloan.

"I'm waiting."

Pressure built within her chest. Please, she silently wavered, please see how important this is to me. Please understand that I'm your future and that you don't have to live in the past anymore.

He reached over and cradled her hands in his. Heat shot from his dark eyes as he dropped to one knee. "Roxie, I love you with my whole heart, and I want you to be my wife. Will you marry me?"

The tightness in her chest eased. He loved her. A heady sense of power rushed through her. "What if people say I married you for your money?"

"We know that's not true. Who cares what people think anyway? I only care about what you think."

"What if something terrible happens to me, and I'm paralyzed for life? Would you take care of me or run off with a trophy wife?"

"You're the one I want, now and forever. We're going to be a family, you and me."

"What if I want to have children right away?"

"You're killing me, Roxie. Answer my question. Will you marry me?"

Her grin stretched from ear to ear. "Of course I'll marry you, Sloan Harding. I'm crazy about you."

"When?"

"My parents are coming home for Christmas. That soon enough for you?"

He nodded. "What about my past? I wasn't a model citizen. Being married to me might hurt your real estate career. If you still want to work, that is. You don't have to because we're filthy rich."

She blinked in confusion. This was what she'd wanted, but this couldn't be what was best for him. "You want us to live here?"

"I want to live where you are."

"But your security business—"

"I'll work something out with my team. Now

that I've got a fortune to invest, I was thinking of buying property. Luckily, I've got the best real estate agent in the country in my pocket."

"You do?"

He grinned. "Sure." He whipped out her business card from his pocket and kissed where she'd written "Love, Roxie."

Laughter bubbled out of her. Her wish had come true. When she'd first seen him she'd wanted him to be the real estate speculator of her dreams.

"I also plan to make a large donation to the Friends of the Museum."

"You do? I mean, you will? You don't have to do this, Sloan. That money is yours."

"It's about time Hardings gave back to Mossy Bog. Donating money to rehab the building will help atone for the damage my father did to this town." He studied her. "Do you worry that I'm like him?"

"You're nothing like him."

"I was afraid to love until you came along, Roxie. You opened my eyes and my heart."

"And you're the only man for me."

The sexy glint returned to his dark brown eyes. He scooped her in his arms and headed for his back door. "Then what do you say we get started on those children you mentioned?"

Her laughter filled the air as joy flooded her heart, mind, and soul. "By all means."

A word about the author...

Georgia native Maggie Toussaint has an advanced degree in muddy waters. She earned that high distinction by bogging through the salt marshes of coastal Georgia, rowing to the crabbing hole, and diving off the floating dock.

Her first published book, HOUSE OF LIES, won a National Readers' Choice Award for Best Romantic Suspense. NO SECOND CHANCE, another release from The Wild Rose Press, won two cover awards and benefited a horse rescue organization.

In addition to her romantic suspenses, Maggie is also a published mystery author. She's active in writers' organizations, freelances for a weekly newspaper, and leads a yoga class.

Visit her at
maggietoussaint.com

Thank you for purchasing
this Wild Rose Press publication.
For other wonderful stories of romance,
please visit our on-line bookstore at
www.thewildrosepress.com

For questions or more information,
contact us at
info@thewildrosepress.com

The Wild Rose Press
www.TheWildRosePress.com

CPSIA information can be obtained at www.ICGtesting.com
Printed in the USA
LVOW01s1009090913

351597LV00001B/3/P

9 781601 548276